MISA SUGIURA

AUTHOR OF *IT'S NOT LI...*

THIS

TIME

WILL

BE

DIFFERENT

ALSO BY MISA SUGIURA

———————— ❧ ————————

Praise for *This Time Will Be Different*

"Fresh, vibrant, affecting, and powerful." —*The New York Times Book Review*

"One of the most authentic, steadfastly real teen characters I've read in recent memory. Highly, highly recommend." —Sandhya Menon, *New York Times* bestselling author of *When Dimple Met Rishi*

"Essential." —*Kirkus Reviews* (starred review)

"Insightful. Intricate. Honest. Misa Sugiura reminds us that the past is always present, but that we hold the power to shape our future, if we're brave enough to face it." —Samira Ahmed, *New York Times* bestselling author of *Love, Hate & Other Filters*

"A gripping, emotionally charged story that presents a window into a uniquely Japanese American experience." —*SLJ* (starred review)

"At turns delightfully humorous and wonderfully insightful. I can't wait to read what Sugiura writes next." —Renée Ahdieh, *New York Times* bestselling author of *The Wrath and the Dawn*

"A timely, smart novel that readers of contemporary teen fiction will likely devour." —*Shelf Awareness* (starred review)

"A beautiful, exquisitely crafted story about finding your voice. *This Time Will Be Different* boasts complex characters with deep-rooted histories, and the exploration of what it means to be a good ally is both timely and necessary." —Akemi Dawn Bowman, author of *Starfish* and *Summer Bird Blue*

"CJ will break your heart, reassemble it, and put it in a gorgeous flower arrangement that'll make your heart soar. A lovely and complicated story of figuring out who you want to be in the world." —Sara Farizan, award-winning author of *If You Could Be Mine*

"CJ is one of my favorite characters to hit the page in a long time. This smart and thought-provoking tale will have you cheering in your seats." —Stacey Lee, award-winning author of *Outrun the Moon* and *The Secret of a Heart Note*

"Smart, funny, and huge-hearted." —Kim Culbertson, author of *Catch a Falling Star* and *The Possibility of Now*

"Strikes that perfect balance of light-hearted humor and emotional depth. A truly fun and thoughtful read." —Maurene Goo, author of *I Believe in a Thing Called Love*

———————— ❧ ————————

Also by Misa Sugiura

It's Not Like It's a Secret

THIS
TIME
WILL
BE
DIFFERENT

MISA SUGIURA

HARPER TEEN
An Imprint of HarperCollins Publishers

In loving memory of

My uncle,
Teruchi Mackenzie Ebata
Tashme Internment Camp, British Columbia, Canada

Yutaka and Haruko Kanemoto,
grandparents of my heart
Tule Lake Internment Camp, California
Minidoka Internment Camp, Idaho

Seiichi Robert Kanemoto
November 4, 1937–May 3, 1944
Minidoka Internment Camp, Idaho

HarperTeen is an imprint of HarperCollins Publishers.

This Time Will Be Different
Copyright © 2019 by Misa Sugiura

Library of Congress Control Number: 2018964875
ISBN 978-0-06-247345-5

Typography by Torborg Davern
20 21 22 23 24 PC/LSCH 10 9 8 7 6 5 4 3 2 1
❖
First paperback edition, 2020

1

HANNAH CALLS IT "A STATE OF BECOMING," BUT most people would probably call it chaos. The floor and work spaces are littered with leaves, stems, and thorns that haven't made it into the giant wastebins by the tables. Flowers and greenery explode out of buckets on every flat surface that isn't covered in piles of more greens and more flowers, all stripped of their lower leaves and thorns. The room is a riot of scarlet, green, ivory, and dusty pink.

In front of me sit twenty-five empty vases, their open mouths crisscrossed with grids of thin tape. When we're finished, the empty grids will be transformed into a lush carpet of red and cream-colored roses and white and gold Chinese lilies, accented with clusters of pink pepper berries, eucalyptus leaves, and ivy—perfect for tomorrow's mid-December wedding. Perfect for the beginning of somebody's happily ever after.

That is, if you believe in that kind of thing.

As I trim the thorns off a rose stem, Hannah quizzes me.

"Fate," my aunt says.

"Flax," I reply, and she nods.

"Self-worth," she says.

"White roses." Another nod.

"Reconciliation."

"Um . . . star-of-Bethlehem?"

"Nice!" Hannah beams at me. "Great job, CJ!"

Most kids get quizzed on stuff like state capitals, or French vocabulary words, or the elements on the periodic table. I get quizzed on the language of flowers. Hannah claims that by using it in the arrangements she makes for her clients, she can help fulfill their hearts' desires. I have serious doubts about the scientific validity of her claim, but she says that if I want to be her apprentice at the shop, I have to know my flowers, so here we are.

By *here* I mean the workroom of Heart's Desire, the flower shop that we've had in our family since the 1930s. This guy named Robert McAllister pressured my great-grandfather into selling it for almost nothing when the government threw Japanese Americans into internment camps during World War II, but after years of struggle and hardship, my grandfather eventually bought it back because, as Mom and Hannah both like to say, Katsuyamas never quit.

Katsuyamas Never Quit. It's practically our family motto.

The McAllisters have never quit, either. In fact, they've never quit so much that the family are now billionaires. My high school bears their name, as does the hospital I was born in and the library where I borrow books. It's not exactly Capulets and Montagues or anything, but I can't say that I don't feel kind of resentful and weird about the whole situation. Mom is a partner at McAllister Venture Capital, so that tells you how much she cares about the family sort-of feud (not at all). Hannah, on the other hand, despises the McAllisters. Her second choice for the Katsuyama family motto would probably be We Hate the McAllisters. But I'll come back to all that later. As Hannah and Mom also like to say, we need to be *here, now*.

Now, the phone rings, and even though we've just closed up for the night, Hannah answers it. You never know what a difference that last-minute bouquet might make in a person's life, she always says. It might be just the thing that a grieving widow needs to brighten her evening. Or it might lead to a romantic reconciliation and then a baby. Or, if you want to be pragmatic about it, it could lead to another sale and possibly even a regular customer—something we could definitely use these days.

Turns out it's one guy who wants one thing: a boutonniere. He says he's right around the corner and he'll be here in a couple of minutes. Doesn't sound like a life-altering possibility to me, but I'm not running the store.

Ten minutes after closing time, I let him in the front door.

He's not young, maybe forties or fifties, wearing rimless glasses, khakis, a blue button-down shirt, a blazer, and a bow tie—kind of an unusual look in Silicon Valley. Especially the bow tie. Or maybe not—Silicon Valley is full of quirky people. "It'll only take a minute. I just need a little flower to put in my lapel, here," he says, and glances down at his blazer.

I happen to know that this will take about twenty minutes, not just one, but I smile and say, "Special occasion?"

Blazer Guy blushes a little. "First date. Thought I'd do a little something special, you know? Make a good impression."

Before I can respond, Hannah comes bustling in from the back. "Oh, how sweet! What a lucky . . . woman?"

"Uh, yes. Woman," Blazer Guy confirms with a nervous laugh.

"And it's been a while since you've dated, perhaps?" Hannah continues.

He turns bright red and says, "Oh . . . is it that obvious? How could you tell?"

Because, you funny little man, I think, *you're wearing a freaking boutonniere on a first date.*

"Oh, I just have a feel for these things," says Hannah with an airy wave of her hand and a dirty look at me, as if she's reading my mind. "Did you tell her that you'd be wearing a flower? Did you specify what kind?"

Blazer Guy shakes his head. "I just figured something like this . . . ?" He points to a yellow carnation. "Something bright, you know? Friendly."

"Oh no! No, no, no. CJ, come on over." Hannah beckons to me. "CJ's my apprentice," she informs Blazer Guy. "CJ, tell— I'm sorry, what's your name?"

"Richard."

"Tell Richard about yellow carnations."

For the record, I never actually asked to be Hannah's apprentice. I've more or less grown up at Heart's Desire, but I never really did anything beyond take the occasional phone order until this fall, when Hannah's assistant found a better-paying job and left. Not long after that, Hannah asked me if I wanted to learn the art of floral design, and it turns out I kind of love it. I love the colors, the textures, the shapes, and the scents. I love how each flower has its own personality, and I love figuring out how to put everything together in ways that mean something.

"Yellow carnations say no. Like literally, that's what they mean. *N-O*," I say obediently, and Hannah nods her approval as Blazer Guy winces.

"Oh. I don't want that."

"I mean, they certainly have their uses," says Hannah sweetly. "But I can tell you're more thoughtful than that. You must be a bit of a romantic at heart."

Blazer Guy scratches his head and smiles bashfully.

"You deserve better than carnations, and so does your date. Let us personalize it and make it perfect for you."

Hannah proceeds to pepper Richard with silly questions: favorite color, favorite animal, favorite vacation spot. Then she gets personal: What's his defining quality? What are his hopes for this particular date?

"I guess I hope she likes me enough for a second date?" he says uncertainly. "And I hope I like her."

Hannah turns to me and asks, "Well? What do you recommend?" To Richard, she stage-whispers, "Prepare to be impressed. She's really gifted."

Right. No pressure or anything. "Hmm . . . First date, first date . . ." I drum my fingers on my chin, stalling for time. "It's the wrong season for lilacs . . . pink rosebuds for new love?"

Even before Hannah frowns, I know I've failed. Pink rosebuds? Could I have picked anything more clichéd? He could have gone to Safeway for that advice.

"Mmm . . . Pink rosebuds . . ." Hannah's nodding as if deep in thought, but it's just for show. "Those are nice, but maybe a tad conventional, don't you think? And a little presumptuous. We can do better." She smiles at me kindly. "Try again."

I feel my cheeks flush with embarrassment. I wonder if Hannah's wishing she hadn't talked me up so much. But she's still smiling at me, so I try again. Think. Flowers that convey what Richard wants . . . what was it? He wants to like his date and he wants her to like him. So. "Asters for reciprocity? Or purple pansies and white violets? Think of me; take a chance on love?"

"Bingo!" Hannah claps her hands once, and I practically melt with relief. "I love it! Unique, unassuming, but still makes a statement. Pansies and violets are tricky to use in boutonnieres, but I think I can manage to make them last a couple of hours for you. CJ, get the materials ready. I'll get the flowers. What do you think, Richard?"

"Sounds great," says Richard. But I mean really, what's he going to say? When the Hannah train is rolling, you either jump on or jump out of the way.

Hannah goes upstairs, where she grows some of the unusual flowers and potted varieties that she likes to use but are harder to get from wholesalers. I prep the materials as ordered—sponge, wire, tape, ribbon, pin—and lay them neatly on the countertop for Hannah before heading back into the workroom.

"So do you think that guy's gonna have a good first date?" I ask when Richard has gone and Hannah returns to the back.

"I have no idea. But with those flowers, something good has to happen. He looked really hopeful, and that's half the battle. Perfect choice, CJ."

It's just one tiny thing I've done well. Against the boundless field of bad decisions and disappointing performances that have been my life, it hardly even counts. But something unfurls inside me, fragile and tender as a new green leaf, and I can't help smiling as I place a bunch of freshly declawed roses in a bucket of water.

"You have all the tools, and tons of talent. You have a natural feel for structure and color. I think you could be great," says Hannah.

That should make me feel even better, but instead, my

wobbly new confidence buckles under the weight of her praise and the looming expectation of greatness. I sweep a pile of leaves into a wastebin and say, "I don't know. My arrangements kind of suck." It's true. Everything I do is like the zitty, sloppy, thirteen-year-old boy cousin of Hannah's creations.

Hannah stops her own work and regards me for a moment. Her eyes are full of affection and her voice is serious when she says, "It's not expert work yet, but Katsuyamas never quit. I know you'll get there, sweet pea. The only thing that concerns me is your reluctance to open yourself to the magic of romance."

At this, I forget my new leaf feeling altogether and roll my eyes. I love what we sell, and I love making people happy with it. But let's not kid ourselves—it's all an illusion.

"Don't you roll your eyes at the magic of romance, CJ, or you'll end up like your mom."

"Hannah."

"Oh, you know what I mean."

I do. It's not like Mom is some lonely, bitter old hag who's dead inside. She's beautiful and smart and funny, and she could probably date whoever she wants. But, to use her words, she has better things to do with her time than root through the trash heap that is online dating—a sentiment that Hannah finds highly offensive, since she, herself, has had a lot of romantic relationships that started online. Mom would say that proves her point.

Because the thing is, Hannah isn't exactly a reliable

authority on romance. However much positive influence her so-called magic may have on the happiness of other couples, it doesn't seem to apply to her own relationships. Like, at all. Ever since I can remember, she's gone through at least one, sometimes two boyfriends a year, each time convinced that this is the One, each time soaring on an updraft of romantic optimism—and each time, plunging to a bruising, painful breakup. Her life is a rom-com on an endless loop, cutting back to the beginning before it reaches the happy ending. I don't know how or why she keeps at it. You'd think she'd know better by now.

Bottom line: Katsuyamas may never quit, but we also never succeed, at least when it comes to romance and true love. And if my own history is any indication, I may never succeed at anything else, either.

2

IT'S SIX THIRTY IN THE MORNING ON A SCHOOL-staff-development day, but instead of being warm and asleep in my bed like a normal human being, I'm awake and shivering in my vintage Cap'n Crunch T-shirt and my McAllister High School sweat pants. I would say it's cold enough to see my breath, but starlight doesn't make for great visibility.

Mom has dragged me out to her favorite trail at the open-space preserve for a predawn power walk, and I am deeply regretting my decision to let her. I huff and puff to keep up as she charges ahead of me toward a one-mile climb. I wonder if mountain lions get up this early.

It wouldn't matter, though, because Mom could probably kick a mountain lion's ass. She does Pilates, lifts weights, and runs practically every day. She has a treadmill in her office at work, and another one in her bedroom; whenever she's stressed out or upset, she goes in there and runs forever. Plus, she's just an ass-kicking kind of person—there's no other way she could have made partner at a place like McAllister Venture Capital.

She's way ahead of me on the trail when she glances over her shoulder and stops. "Come on, Ceej! You're young and strong. You should have no problem keeping up with an old lady like me." She smiles like it's joke, but I see her fingers tapping impatiently on her hips as I struggle to catch up.

"I'm even not supposed to be awake yet. Young people's circadian rhythms are different from old ladies like you," I protest.

"You'll be glad I got you up when we get to the top."

"Is there a Starbucks up there? And a magical portal back to my bed?"

"No, but there's a beautiful sunrise and a sense of accomplishment."

"Yippee. I can hardly wait."

"CJ, that attitude is exactly what's making this difficult for you."

And just like that—*ka-poof!*—I feel my actual attitude slide from reluctant-but-jokey to sulky-and-defensive.

"I think the forced march is what's making this difficult for me." It's one last stab at cracking a joke, but I have to admit that I put a little heat on it. Call me rude, but she pulled the attitude card, and I know what's next.

"I'm not kidding, CJ." Here it comes. Three, two, one . . .

"Attitude is everything. If you don't get your shit together—if you don't start developing a vision for your life—you'll never get anywhere."

According to Mom, the key to living a Happy and Fulfilling Life is having a killer attitude and a grand vision, and I swear she feels personally attacked by the fact that I have not found either one yet. As if visions were just lying around like Easter eggs and I've made it my life's work to shut my eyes and ignore them. As if all I have to do is get off my lazy ass and part the right clump of grass, peek behind the right stone, and I'll find a vision waiting for me to pick it up and run with it into a bright and shining future.

Mom grew up on the edge of poverty, and she's given me much more than she ever had: summer camps, enrichment programs, trips to places like New York City and London. But when it comes to results, well. I know I must be an incredible disappointment to her. On bad days, I wonder if she wishes I'd never been born.

"You can't just slide along the way you've been doing. You need to get out there and be proactive. You need to have a road map." Being Proactive and Having a Road Map are Mom's two favorite things after Having a Vision.

"I've been helping out at Heart's Desire. Hannah says I have talent."

Mom doesn't respond right away, and suddenly I realize why I've let her think I've been watching kitten videos in my spare time since SAT prep classes ended, instead of telling her

I've been working at Heart's Desire. I think Hannah might be right, that I might actually be good at something, for once. I don't want Mom to tell me that Hannah's wrong, that it's stupid, that it's a waste of time. Crap. Why didn't I lie just now and tell her I've been doing independent research on . . . on . . . Right. That's why.

Finally, Mom says something. "CJ. Flower arranging is a hobby. I don't know what airy-fairy delusions Hannah's been feeding you, but you *know* Heart's Desire isn't doing as well as it should, and I really don't like you being part of it. Listen, I was talking to Carlos from Alphabet the other day, and this is strictly confidential information, but . . ." She proceeds to describe Carlos's job, his credentials, and how he's planning to leave Alphabet and start a new company in some hot new space in the ecosystem of big-data enterprise architecture that she's been researching lately, and I tune out because I have only the barest inkling about any of that stuff, and even less interest, and why should I pay attention anyway, since she clearly has no interest in what I want or what I think?

"CJ! Are you even listening?"

Oops. "Um, yeah. Just . . . That last part again?"

Mom releases an exasperated puff of air and says, "I told you that he said he'd be willing to interview you for an internship position. It's unpaid, but it'll look great on your college applications, and you might be able to use it to springboard to something you could monetize later. That's the kind of thing that'll distinguish you from all the other kids—the thousands of other kids, I might add—gunning for a spot wherever you apply for college next year."

"But I don't want to be an intern."

"I'm not *asking* if you *want* to be an intern. I'm *telling* you that you *can* be an intern."

"But, Mom, seriously? A big-data start-up? I mean, hello, have we met? I'm your daughter, CJ. The only person to ever fail out of coding camp." It was a three-week day camp the summer after sixth grade; by the end of it, I couldn't write the simplest program without constantly checking the help menu. My certificate of participation read, "CJ uses her time to the best of her ability!" I think we all know what that means.

"What have I told you about that word? It's not a failure, it's a learning opportunity. Growth mind-set, kiddo. Grit. Besides, this internship is a great, real-world way to practice growth mind-set *and* get hands-on experience developing a crucial skill set."

I grit my teeth. *Ladies and gentlemen, my mother, the buzzword machine.*

"All I'm saying is that you need a purpose to drive you. I don't want you to end up like Hannah, just drifting along."

That jolts me out of my sulk. "Hannah's not drifting. She runs the shop."

"Believe me, CJ. She's drifting."

This is the problem with Mom. She spends her life going full throttle, guns blazing, after these ridiculously unattainable goals, and the rest of us look like we're standing still by comparison. She will never believe that running a lowly flower shop, putting beauty into the world a little at a time, is worthwhile.

"Hannah's happy," I say. "Maybe I just want to be happy."

"'Happy' is not going to get you into college, CJ. It's not going to get you a career. 'Happy' comes from setting yourself a challenging goal and achieving it."

"God, Mom, stop being so Asian," I say, rolling my eyes. The Asian thing is a gamble, but it's my last card. She hates being compared to the immigrant Asian community.

Mom's eyes squinch shut as she lets loose a sort of strangled half scream through clenched teeth, though this doesn't slow her down at all. "For Chrissakes, CJ! If you had any idea what my Asian colleagues are putting their kids through, you'd be thanking me for going so easy on you. Listen, kiddo. I love you. I want you to succeed. I'm concerned about your future. And *you* are not concerned enough."

I am *concerned*, I want to say. What if I *don't* find one of these all-important visions? What if I'm a failure for the rest of my life? But what comes out of my mouth is, "Okay, Mom. I got it. I'm a loser and a failure."

"That's not at all what I'm saying, CJ."

I can hear the frustration in her voice, and I know that's not what she's saying, but it hurts too much to keep exploring all the ways in which I am not measuring up. I push back one more time. "Can we just not talk about this right now?"

We barrel through Rogue Valley, past little gray rabbits

that freeze, then dart back into the brush, past a flock of wild turkeys. As the valley narrows, the trail makes a sharp left to double back and uphill for a mile. We continue walking, the only sound our breath, the *crump, crump, crump* of our feet on the dusty trail, and the blackbirds chirping in the bushes around us. We pass within a few feet of a mother deer and her adolescent fawn picking their way slowly through a thicket of manzanita bushes, under a canopy of coastal live oak trees. I pause, pull out my phone, and turn to take a picture, but Mom refuses to slow down: "We're behind schedule, hon—I have a video conference at eight o'clock. Come on, let's pick up the pace."

A Series of Screw-ups: The Chisaki Joan Katsuyama Story, Part I

I bet you think I'm exaggerating. But I'm confident that when I'm finished, you'll see things my way.

Exhibit A: My Conception
The specifics remain vague (ew, not *those* specifics), but according to the cautionary tale Mom told me when I got my first period, it may have happened in a hotel room at a conference after a night of heavy drinking.

Yep. I know.

Exhibit B: My Birth
I arrived two weeks early ("The last time CJ was ever early for anything," the joke goes). To add insult to injury, my early arrival was announced by a *pop* and a theatrical burst of amniotic fluid in the middle of an important presentation that Mom was giving at work.

Exhibit C: Ballet Lessons

It was winter of third grade, and I was the star of my ballet class's annual holiday recital performance: we danced to "Waltz of the Flowers," and I got to stand alone in the middle of a ring of my classmates, the flower amid a swirl of adoring butterflies. After the recital, Mom pulled me out of ballet, and I could not understand why she'd cut short what was surely going to be a long and illustrious career as a ballerina.

A couple of years ago, I stumbled across a video of the recital. In it, I do, indeed, stand out—but not for the reasons I had always imagined. In the parts where I dance with my class, I am happy but clueless, awkwardly copying the movements of the girl next to me, one beat late. I wasn't chosen to be the flower in the center because I was talented. I was chosen because I was terrible.

Exhibit D: Soccer, Coding Camp, Piano Lessons, etc. etc. etc.

A veritable garden of participation trophies and ~~failures~~ learning opportunities.

Exhibit E: My Last Effort

Mom was a lacrosse star at Princeton back in the day, after trying it out just for fun as a freshman. "You've got a great body for it," she told me as lacrosse season approached in ninth grade. "Give it a try. Come on, Ceej, think positive."

After two miserable weeks of preseason conditioning, I

confessed to her that I was in danger of not making the team. "Then make yourself indispensable," she responded. I volunteered to be goalie—every team needs a goalie—and made the cut.

Mom came to my first two games. In the first half of the first game, I caught her face-palming after I allowed my third easy goal. By the second half of the game, every time the ball was on our half of the field, I'd glance up and see her face set in a worried frown. She spent most of the next game bent determinedly over her phone. She stopped coming to my games after that.

It was probably a good thing. By the middle of the season, whenever the opposing team got the ball, our coach would shout, "Someone get in the goal with CJ!" and we would play a two-goalie defense. When I announced at the end of the season that I was never going to play lacrosse ever again, Mom didn't argue. I couldn't believe my good luck; I'd been expecting her to remind me that Katsuyamas never quit.

Two weeks later, Mom signed me up for a journalism class, and I realized that she hadn't let me off the hook with lacrosse as I'd thought. She'd just chalked up one more failure to perform as expected and had already begun the hunt for a new activity. At that point, I finally saw my life for what it was—an endless cycle of trying and failing, trying and failing.

I used to try harder when I was young. With every new activity, I did my best to grow into the shape that Mom was so painstakingly pruning me into. But each new defeat wore me down a little bit, and then a little bit more. After that disastrous lacrosse season, I began to give up on becoming the superstar that Mom wanted me to be. Unfortunately, I'm afraid Mom will never give up.

Then again, I'm afraid that she will.

3

AFTER MY POWER WALK WITH MOM, SHE GOES
to the office and I drop in at Sweet Emily's on my way to
Heart's Desire. People travel across town for Sweet Emily's
pastries and coffee—they're that good. The line often stretches
out the door of the café, which Emily's parents named after
her. The chocolate croissants, in particular, sell out fast, but
there's always a few set aside for me. Being best friends with
the owners' daughter has its perks.

Em's on a break, and she's joined me at our favorite table,
at the back of the dining room, where we're discussing Mom's
plan for me to become a STEM goddess.

"Me, at a big data start-up? Is she out of her mind?"

"You gotta give her credit for optimism," says Emily.

"There's optimism and there's delusional . . . ism."

"She's not delusional, Ceej. Stop buying into the girls-can't-do-math-and-science baloney. We don't need more stereotypes."

"I'm not talking about girls, I'm talking about me. And anyway, if I *am* good at math, I'm an Asian stereotype," I remind her.

"Yeah . . . but, for real, though." Emily taps her cranberry-walnut scone on her plate. "You do kind of brick your way through stuff. It's like you don't care about it, or, like, I dunno, like maybe you're afraid to succeed, or afraid to fail, or . . ." She waves the scone vaguely, as if to conjure up a reason why I might not be Trying My Hardest at Life.

"Thanks for the insight, Dr. Baxter." I flick a crumb at her, and she flicks it back. Em is a bit of a paradox. She's genuinely the sweetest person I know: she doesn't swear; she isn't petty. But she's ruthless about calling me out. Which is kind of cool. But it's also kind of annoying. "Anyway, what the fuck, Em? I do not half-ass my way through stuff."

"Uh, yeah, you do," she says.

"Name one thing."

"Okay, how about school? Like, every class?" says Emily. "You could totally be in AP English if you tried. You should have applied with me last year."

"Hey, you dropped out of Korean school."

"That's not the same thing because I didn't have time for Korean school. And don't change the subject. Just admit you don't want to try."

"That has nothing to do with not wanting to try. I just don't like playing impress-the-teacher with a bunch of brown-nosers."

"Oh, thanks."

"Not you, duh. Just the others."

Em frowns. "Why do you have to be so judgmental?"

"Oh, now that you're in AP, you're best friends with all of them?"

"No. But why can't you just give people a chance?"

I sigh. "I just hate how everyone's all about *excelling* in those classes. Straight A's. Starting lineup. Class officer. We can't all be Brynn for President." I can't hold back a tiny sneer when I bring her up. I don't actively dislike many people, but Brynn Foer-Preston, current vice president of the Associated Student Body and future leader of the free world, is one of them. The thing is, Emily used to have a huge crush on her, and it did not end well. For Emily. At all. (Full disclosure: I might also kind-of-sort-of hate Brynn just a tiny bit for being appallingly talented at everything she's ever done, which maybe isn't exactly fair of me. But mostly I don't like her because I don't trust her. She's got a candy coating of sweetness and joy over a dark core of treacherous, cutthroat ambition.)

"Speaking of Brynn," says Emily. "You'll never believe it, but she said hi to me yesterday."

"Nuh-uh."

"Yuh-huh. We walked into physics at the same time."

Hang on. "I didn't know she was in physics with you."

"She just got switched in. I guess she used to have it seventh period, but she got some internship or something where she has to leave school after sixth."

"Of course she did." I take a sip of coffee. I don't like where this conversation seems to be headed. "So did you say hi back?"

Em sighs. "Well, yeah. I mean. It was actually like a friendly hi, like the kind you say hi back to without really thinking about it."

Hm.

"What do you think it means?"

This is what I was worried about. I can hear the longing in Emily's voice, and I'm sorry, but no. I'm not letting this happen. I say, "I think it means that Brynn for President is a compulsively friendly person who says hi to everyone."

"Yeah, huh," says Em with a wry little grin. But I can tell she's hurt. I hate making her feel this way, but it's better than the potential alternative.

"I'm sorry. I just . . . You know how I feel about her. You know how she treated you in eighth grade. I don't think she's changed. You deserve so much better."

"Yeah, you're right." Em's phone starts singing. "Break's over," she says. She turns off her alarm, crams the rest of her scone into her mouth, and takes a big swig of coffee. "Text me later and tell me what you want to do tonight, 'kay?"

The History of My Beef with Brynn Foer-Preston

I've invested a fair amount of time and energy over the last few years being annoyed and snarky about Brynn for President, a.k.a. Brynn Foer-Preston—a fact I'm not proud of. But she made Emily's life a living hell in eighth grade, when Emily came out. No one harassed Em about it publicly—we were well trained and heavily monitored—but it was eighth grade, after all. Even though everyone knew that homophobia was frowned upon, it didn't mean everyone was always nice to LGBTQ+ kids. People sort of watched and waited for a leader to show them how to act.

Shortly after Emily came out of the closet, Brynn invited her over to work on a math project, and—miracle of miracles—they ended up kissing. Emily, who'd had a crush on Brynn since sixth grade, went wild. Fueled by romantic delusion (and against my strenuous objections), she made the incredibly risky decision to leave a big frosted heart cookie in a pink paper bag on Brynn's desk for Valentine's Day. It would be in a bag, she reasoned. No one else would know.

Emily woke up sick on Valentine's Day, and bombarded me with impassioned texts begging me to play Cupid or Mercury or whatever ancient Roman god would have delivered Valentine's Day cookies back in ancient Roman times. I pointed out that Valentine's Day was not an ancient Roman holiday, but Emily didn't care. Eventually, I broke down and agreed to help her out.

I arrived at school early and snuck the bag onto Brynn's desk, and I will be forever grateful that Emily wasn't there to see what happened next. Ten minutes after the secret cookie drop, I was reading at my desk when Austin Brown—who everyone knew had a crush on Brynn—sauntered over, grabbed the bag, and looked inside. He wanted to know who his competition was, probably.

"Dude, check it out!" he shouted, as he held up the cookie for all to see. "It's from Emily! Are you guys . . . ?" He made kissing sounds and waggled his eyebrows at Brynn.

There were six or seven kids in the room—Brynn's little power posse—and they all looked up. Terror flashed across Brynn's face. "Let me see that," she said. Austin put the cookie back in the bag and tossed it to her. She opened it and grimaced. "Ughhh, gross. You guuuys. Look," she said, and handed the cookie off to the others. Everyone made a show of handling it gingerly, with their fingertips, screeching and laughing as if lesbianism were a contagious, fatal, but also hilarious disease.

"CJ, are you sure you want to stay friends with her? What

if she starts liking *you?*" said Brynn. "You're not gay, are you?"

I should have looked her right in her craven, panic-stricken eyes and said, *No, but I'm pretty sure you are.* The best I could do was, "No. Jeez. Anyway, it's not a big deal. You can be friends with a gay person and not be gay, you know. It's not like they're vampires. They're not out to get people."

Someone quipped, "Yeah, but I'm not taking that risk," and Brynn laughed along with everyone else. I should have said more. I should have said, *Good, because you'd be a shitty friend, anyway.* Instead, I chickened out and went back to my book, furious with myself for not having the courage I needed to face them down. But at least I hadn't totally betrayed Emily like Brynn had.

That afternoon, Brynn texted Emily that she thought maybe they should cool it. **I don't think it's going to work out,** she wrote. **Sry** ☹

Meanwhile, Brynn texted me not to tell anyone, not even Emily, what had happened in homeroom that day. She said she'd deny it if I did and her friends would back her up. As if I could ever tell Em that on top of this mysterious breakup, Brynn had laughed at her—and encouraged others to laugh at her—behind her back. It would have broken her.

Brynn didn't speak to me or Emily for the rest of the year. Which was fine with me. I wanted her as far away from us as possible.

Then—get this—freshman year—the *very next year*—Brynn announced that she was gay, and suddenly the entire homophobia squad thought it was cool to have a queer friend, though of course no one apologized to Em. At the end of sophomore year, Brynn became president of the Queer Straight Alliance, and has yet to apologize, thereby securing her spot at the top of my shit list until the end of time.

4

EM GOES BACK TO THE KITCHEN, AND I TAKE MY time finishing my croissant and my coffee. I'm just getting up to leave when the front door of the bakery opens, and who should add himself to the back of the line but Shane Morgan.

In September, the San Jose *Mercury News* did a feature on Shane, who appeared on the front page of the sports section clad in nothing but a Speedo and a smile to make the angels sing. He was standing on a pool deck with a water polo ball in one upturned palm and a MacBook in the other, to symbolize how he was equally great at sports and school, and also he was balancing them both literally and figuratively. (Okay, maybe I should have applied for AP English.)

According to the article, not only is Shane a nationally ranked water polo player and a stellar student, but he also wants to be a veterinarian, and he helps his mom foster kittens in the summer. There was another photo of him sitting on the floor, nuzzling a pile of adorable fuzzballs curled up in his strong, capable, sexy hands.

I may have developed kind of a thing for him.

I should note that when I say I have kind of a thing for him, I mean that I have it from afar. Very afar. Kind of in the same way Hannah and Mom get all gaga when they talk about Chris Evans or Mahershala Ali; he's so profoundly unattainable that I harbor no delusions about us ever being a couple. Which is a little bit sad, but also realistic. Hannah might live her life like she's the star of her own personal rom-com, but I do not.

Anyway, thing or no thing, it doesn't matter, because his affections are currently claimed by his girlfriend, Sabrina Dang, who is the Asian version of every Mean Girl in every teen movie you've ever watched.

But here, now, undeniably, is one of those rom-com before/after moments. An opportunity to change the narrative. An opportunity to make an entrance and engage Shane in some flirtatious banter, the way it always happens in the movies. I mean, why not?

Because this is real life, that's why not.

Because in movies, the kooky but lovable girl argues with the barista, gestures too enthusiastically, and spills coffee on the uptight but devastatingly handsome guy's sweater, and they spend the next ninety minutes engaging in witty banter, fighting their attraction to each other, and finally sharing a swoony kiss in the rain and presumably living happily ever after.

But in real life, no one meets in adorably comic situations. In real life, crushes go unrequited, people have to stop kissing to spit out their gum, and the first time you feel your boyfriend's erection through his jeans, you get so self-conscious and embarrassed that you avoid making out with him for a whole week. And people don't live happily ever after.

So. In the real-life version of the Shane-CJ rom-com, I have no reason to go anywhere near Shane and spill my coffee on him, lovably or otherwise, or banter wittily with him or even look at him. At best, I would wander over to him and open my mouth and say . . . what? Nothing. We have nothing in common.

I prefer the fantasy. It's comfortable and much more satisfying. So I turn around to face the back of the bakery, slide down into my booth, and begin plotting a way to get out of here without his seeing me.

But I can't resist peeking over my shoulder to catch one more glimpse. Light blue eyes fringed with impossibly long blond eyelashes, chiseled cheekbones, aristocratic nose. Wide, generous mouth. His light brown hair has a silvery white sheen from all his time in the pool, and, combined with his facial features, it makes him look like he's walked right out of the elven council in Rivendell. Except, of course, for his tan and his body; he's quite a bit buffer than most residents of Rivendell, I suspect. He looks over and meets my eye, and I realize with a start that my little glimpse has turned into a long—and longing—gaze. I may as well be mopping up my drool with my paper napkin.

He nods, and even though we've literally never spoken to each other, he calls, "Hey, CJ!" and smiles. Because that's the kind of friendly guy he is.

"Hi, Shane," I croak. Mortified, I clear my throat.

"What's up?"

I dig frantically for something clever and rom-com-worthy to say, but all I can come up with is, "Nothing. This." I hold up my cup and plate, realize that it looks like I'm trying to make a punny joke about things literally being up, and wish I could die. "I mean. I was eating here." Duh. Last try: "You?"

"Same."

He grins again—I notice that it's slightly forced this time, and I cringe inwardly. He shifts his focus to the menu above the counter. "So, what's good today?"

Finally. A question I can answer without sounding like I landed on the planet yesterday. I go over to him and open my mouth to tell him about the chocolate croissants and the blueberry muffins, but I never get to say anything because that's the moment when Brynn Foer-Preston, aforementioned queen of my shit list, empress of hypocrites, and object of Emily's ill-fated eighth-grade crush, comes striding in. Because of course she does.

Brynn strides everywhere, as if she's wearing seven-league boots. She's one of those perpetually energized, enthusiastic, and engaged people who exhaust me just to look at. Over the last couple of years, she's dropped the bitchy eighth-grade attitude and is now friendly to everyone, but I find it hard to believe she's really changed. If she'd changed, she'd feel bad about what she did. And when forced to interact with Emily or me, she'd be awkward and quiet and smile with her mouth closed. That's what I'd do, anyway. But nope. Not Brynn for President. Upon seeing me, she exclaims in a voice made of plastic (BPA-free, of course), "CJ! Hi! How are you!" as if we were BFFs.

Reflexively, I smile and say, "I'm good, how're you?" and realize that Emily's right. It's hard to snub that kind of aggressive affability. Not only that, I find myself wanting her to like me, despite how little I like her.

Maybe it's because Brynn—and Shane, actually—is a winner. Or perhaps more accurately, a #winner. Being a #winner is different from that old Mean Popular Kid cliché, which is super rare at McAllister. #Winners are popular, but they're not shallow or mean or obsessed with clothes. They're the kids who are accomplished and good-looking and nice to everyone. They live on planes of existence so stratospherically high and rarified, they're practically divine. If you even care about them (a lot of kids don't), the only thing you can hate about them is that they make you feel like a loser. Not actively—just by comparison, by the very fact of their existence. *And* they make you want their approval, despite how little you like them, which is a hateful quality.

Brynn's friendliness is so expansive that I experience a jolt of panicky certainty that she's going to fake-hug me, but then she flings her arms around Shane and cries, "Hey, what's up?" She releases him and adds, "Dude, I just scored the sweetest parking spot! Check it—right across the street!" She points.

"Sick." Shane nods his approval, and they exchange high fives because #winning.

Brynn turns to me now and says, "Hey, CJ. You're still good friends with Emily Baxter, right? Don't her parents own this place?" The plastic in her voice is still there, but I pick up a slightly obsequious tone this time. Usually the next question that people ask when this happens is, "Could you hook me up with some free muffins?"

"Um, yeah, they're the owners." I prepare myself to tell Brynn that I can't hook her up with free anything.

"Is she here?" Brynn looks around the dining room, and out of the same old reflexive agreeableness, I almost tell Brynn that I can go get her, but something stops me. I realize with pleasure that I'm feeling possessive and protective of Emily right now, and that's giving me a backbone.

"She's working in back. She'll be too busy to talk, though. She's not even allowed to talk to *me* when she's working." Which is total BS—I often go in back and chat with Em while she's working—but Brynn doesn't need to know that. I shrug. "Sorry. Why do you need to see her?"

"Oh, no real reason. I'm actually here to ask her parents if I can put this up in the window." She presents me with a flyer.

"I figured I'd say hi to her if she was around."

Since when has Emily been on "say hi to me if you're around" terms with Brynn? I take the flyer with a little surreptitious side-eye at Brynn.

The flyer reads:

Are you a teenager?
Are you LGBTQIAP, curious,
or just looking for something fun to do
on a Saturday night?
Join the crew at the
South Bay Queer Teens' January Mixer,
sponsored by South Bay OUTlet,
for great music, great food, great people, and great fun!

At the bottom there is a map, some photos of happy teenagers, and a website URL.

"I'm on the teen advisory committee," she says. As if I'm supposed to care. "We're actually looking for allies to be on it. Do you know anyone who'd be interested?"

In case anyone's wondering, I do get how twisted it is to simultaneously not care that Brynn is on the OUTlet teen advisory committee *and* be insulted that she's not inviting me to be on it with her. I don't like either of those feelings, but there they are.

I don't have long to stew in my own pettiness, though, because Shane moves in next to me to take a look at the flyer, and my heart starts bashing itself against my rib cage like an overwrought boy-band fan: It's-SHANE! It's-SHANE! It's-SHANE! It's-SHANE!

He says, "Sabrina's brother was talking about going to this with his boyfriend. You got any extra? I can put them up at the pool for you." The mention of Sabrina quiets my pulse somewhat.

"Aw, of course! You can double-date! Here," says Brynn. She hands him a few flyers, and as he reaches out to take them from her—"Sweet! I'll put them up today"—his arm brushes mine and I'm so stunned by the physical sensation of fantasy blurring into reality that I hardly notice when Brynn asks me, "You think it would be okay to put this one up in here? I should probably talk to Mrs. Baxter or a manager or something, right?"

"Huh?"

"I was wondering who I should talk to about putting a flyer in the window. Like Mrs. Baxter? Or . . ."

"Oh. Yeah, probably."

"Okay, cool! And oh! I already got your aunt to put one up in her shop. Tell her thanks for me, okay?"

"Um, yeah. Sure."

I'm acutely aware that, faced with this barrage of jovial, civic-minded enthusiasm, practically all I've been doing is grunting and nodding. Shane is still grinning at me, probably wondering what's wrong with me, and he glances at Brynn, who grins back at him, and suddenly I get the distinct feeling that they're politely waiting for me to leave so that they can laugh at me behind my back. I try to think of something to say to convince them that I am, in fact, an actual human with actual thoughts in my head, but my thoughts feel as foggy and vague as clouds, impossible to condense into something small and neat enough for this smallest of small-talk conversations. *Come on, Ceej. Say* something. I dig deep, summon up a couple of exclamation points, and say, "Okay! Well, I should be going! Try the blueberry muffins!" And bolt out the door.

5

I BOMBED THE "JUST A FORMALITY" INTERVIEW with Mom's friend Carlos from Alphabet by informing him right away that I had no expertise or interest in data, big or otherwise. For two days after the interview, Mom didn't even mention it, and I began to worry that Carlos might actually take me on as an intern. I swung between dread (he'd said yes despite my obvious lack of talent or interest, and I'd spend every afternoon of the foreseeable future miserably wasting everyone's time) and a bizarre, hopeful fantasy (he'd seen a hidden spark of greatness, and I would finally blossom into the genius that Mom wanted me to be).

On the third day, I was washing the dishes after dinner when Mom called me down the hall to her office and told me that Carlos had said thanks, but no, thanks. "He told me that same afternoon, you know," she said. "I've been waiting to see if you'd ask me how you did, but you clearly don't even care enough to ask."

I didn't want to admit that maybe I'd bombed the interview accidentally on purpose because it would have been too humiliating to bomb it by accident for real. I didn't know how to explain that even though I didn't care about the internship, I was also terrified of hearing that I'd failed her yet again. So I shrugged and said, "Sorry." It came out sounding sullen.

"I don't understand it, CJ. What is wrong with you? I give you all these opportunities and you just throw them away like you don't even care. I don't know what to do anymore."

I couldn't bear to listen to another lecture, so I cut her off. "You could leave me alone."

She stared for a moment, too surprised to speak, I suppose. I was a little surprised myself. I hadn't meant to be quite so rude. But the only way I could think of to stop throwing away opportunities was for her to stop handing them to me. I bit my lip, waiting for the inevitable fallout.

Finally, she said, "Okay. Fine. You don't want my help, I won't bother you anymore with it," and swiveled her chair back to face her laptop.

"Good," I said, and left.

That was last week. Ever since then, Mom's been as good as her word. Dinnertime has been a little strained, and I can tell it's killing her not to ask how I've been spending my afternoons.

Maybe she really is trying to give me some space.

Actually, no. The most likely scenario is that she's quietly strategizing a new approach. Because Katsuyamas never quit.

I really hate that motto.

I'm a little stressed as I pull into the lot behind Heart's Desire, because today's rainy weather has caused accidents and made me late. But it occurs to me as I get out of the car that the upside to Mom's freeze-out is that for the time being, I can spend as much time here as I want and not have to listen to her drag me about it. Plus, winter vacation starts in two days, so I won't have to squeeze in homework after work, which has been busier than usual because of the holidays. Cheered by this thought, I sprint through the rain and burst through the back door with a theatrical sweep of my arm, shouting, "Fear not! I have arrived at last!"

I mean, based on my experience, there was probably only an 80 percent chance that Hannah was going to be back there to appreciate my grand entrance. But there was a 0 percent chance that this guy pressing his lips together to hide his smirk was going to be there to scare the shit out of me holy-shit-is-he-an-ax-murderer-did-he-kill-Hannah-is-he-going-to-kill-me-should-I-call-911?

"Hey, you okay?" he says. "You're white as a sheet."

Well, no shit, strange dude who's not supposed to be here and who might be about to chop me into little pieces, my brain says. But I'm still too freaked out to do anything but stare warily at him.

He's about my age, and obviously I don't know him, but

something about him is vaguely familiar. He's tallish and lanky-bordering-on-skinny with stiff, shaggy black hair that needs a trim. He's wearing black Vans, jeans, and a plaid flannel shirt over a black T-shirt that reads,

HISTORY BUFF
I'd find you more interesting if you were dead

Which calms me a little, because if he were a florist-murdering ax murderer, he probably wouldn't be wearing a nerdy history T-shirt.

On the other hand, if the shirt is to be believed, he'd prefer for me to be dead.

"Oh, I see you've met!" It's Hannah coming in from the front of the shop, alive and well, thank goodness. I can actually feel the relief coursing through my veins like blood.

"Not formally," says the history buff.

"Ah! Well. Owen Takasugi, this is CJ Katsuyama, my niece."

He extends his hand and says, "Nice to meet you."

"The guy from *Weekly History Minute!*" *That's* how I know him. *Weekly History Minute* comes on the midday video announcements, usually on Thursday or Friday. It's nerdy history trivia, acted out by nerdy history kids—sometimes even in costume. It always ends with a sign-off from the host: "I'm Owen Takasugi and this is *Weekly History Minute*, brought to you by . . ." He always pauses dramatically before finishing with "the History Club!" as if the entire school is waiting breathlessly every week, wondering to themselves, *Who brings us* Weekly History Minute?

I shake Owen's hand, still a little bewildered, but bewildered is better than terrified. I can't believe I thought this guy was going to kill me. "You scared me half to death," I tell him.

"Yeah, I could tell. Sorry about that." The corner of his mouth twitches upward, and I suddenly remember seeing a flash of that suppressed grin just after I made my (oh my god) unbelievably dorky grand entrance a minute ago. I've done something that Owen Takasugi of *Weekly History Minute* is trying not to laugh at. I have officially bottomed out.

Hannah, oblivious, explains, "Owen's dad owns Takasugi Nursery, and he was telling me about how he wanted Owen to broaden his experience in the industry, so I offered to let Owen be an apprentice! It's perfect timing, because we could really use the extra help right now."

"I am your humble servant," says Owen, and he bows slightly and does a fancy little flourish with his hand, and I can tell right away that Hannah finds this incredibly charming.

I can't decide whether I find it charming or dorky, though I'm leaning toward dorky. Kind of like *Weekly History Minute*, actually, which—to be totally, brutally honest—is über geeky and hardly anyone watches, but which is also often cooler than actual history class. Like this week, they did a thing about how Italian pasta actually came from Arab traders who passed through Sicily and not from China via Marco Polo's expedition.

That was cool. In a geeky sort of way.

"Well, anyway. I'm glad to have you with us. And you should know that CJ loves history," says Hannah, and she's not lying, but oh my god. "I bet she'd love to go out for coffee or something and chat about it with you. Right, sweet pea?"

"Hannah." I can't even look at Owen, so I don't know whether he thinks this is funny or weird or horrifying or what.

"Oh, I'm just kidding, love. I'm sure Owen has a girlfriend anyway, he's so handsome and sweet. Or do you have a boyfriend?" She nods at me and winks, and I want to die.

But Owen seems to be taking it all in stride. "Neither, at the moment. Thanks for the compliment, though."

"Of course!" Hannah winks at me *again*, and now I want her to die, too.

At that point, thank God, the front-door alert beeps, and Hannah says, "Well, enough chitchat. CJ, why don't you take Owen out there and the two of you can get to know each other while you show him the ropes."

6

I LEAD OWEN OUT TO THE FRONT AND MUMBLE, "Sorry about Hannah," just in time to see Sabrina Dang, captain of the award-winning McAllister drill team, perpetual officer of the Social Service Club, and girlfriend of Shane, strolling toward the counter. She doesn't stroll so much as sashay, hips swinging like she thinks she's some kind of fashion model, with her fancy bag tucked under her arm.

Sabrina's dazzling smile is plastered on the McAllister High homepage—she is literally the face of McAllister High. "Don't hate me because I'm beautiful," she likes to say with a toss of her head. She says it like she's joking, but it's pretty clear that she really does think she's beautiful. To be fair, everyone else thinks so, too. And I do have to give her credit for overcoming the way people tease her about her name and say, "Sabrina, *dang!*" every time she does or says something noteworthy, which is often. She must hate it. But she turned it around and used it as her campaign slogan for ASB secretary. I've heard she's probably going to be valedictorian.

"Hey, Sabrina!" Owen calls, and maybe it's unfair of me, but I'm surprised he knows her well enough to be on speaking terms. "I'm Owen. We're in English and trig together." Okay, so he doesn't know her that well. A frisson of irritation sweeps over me—why do guys have to lunge after every pretty girl who crosses their path?

"Oh, right, hi!" She smiles sweetly.

Enough of this. "Can I help you with anything?" I ask Sabrina.

"Well, actually . . ." She hesitates, and I know right away that she wants to get flowers for Shane. "I wanted to get flowers for my boyfriend? Shane Morgan?" Her voice rises up to the question mark like maybe she thinks we might not have heard of him, but really she knows we have.

"Oh, yeah," says Owen. "Big dude, looks like Legolas on steroids?"

Sabrina gives him a funny look, and I can't say I blame her. "Uh-huh."

She continues, "So he's got this huge water polo tournament this weekend, right? Like the coaches for the national team are going to be there and everything. So I want to get him something special for good luck, you know? Like, kind of unusual, but not weird. Not too feminine, either. He's *such* a guy's guy." She rolls her eyes and gives me a confidential smile: *Boys, amirite?* "I want it to be, like, totally spectacular. Cost is no object when it comes to the really important stuff, right?"

I smile. Be nice. We need her. She's about to drop some serious cash.

"Anyway, my parents are helping pay for it," Sabrina continues. "They, like, *love* Shane. They'd probably be sadder than me if we ever broke up."

"Okay, let me think." I mentally scroll through a list of appropriate flowers. "Um, how about . . ." I'm about to suggest primrose lilacs for confidence, but they're totally out of season—it's nearly Christmas, for crying out loud—and super pricey, but she said she was willing to spend lots of money, right? Then Sabrina, who's been scanning the shop while I think, holds up her hand to stop me.

"No, wait! Sunflowers! They'll be perfect. Because he'll be in the spotlight, like having his face to the sun, right?" Not the best choice; apart from being summer flowers like lilacs, sunflowers denote pride and pointless adoration. Though given who's buying them, maybe they *are* the right choice.

But I'm a professional. So I ask, "Are you sure? I mean they're impressive and all, but if you're looking for symbolism, I'd recommend these." I take her to a bucket of cream-colored primrose lilacs. "They communicate confidence. And you could combine them with some white heather for good luck and add a palm leaf or some bay leaves for fame and victory. I could make it look really nice, and I guarantee you it's unique."

Sabrina wrinkles her nose. "No, I think I'll stick with these. Use all of them! I'll tell him I bought out the store. Won't that be romantic?"

I hesitate. "I guess . . . Are you sure you—"

But I'm interrupted by a low "Doooo iiiittt" from Owen.

I try to motion discreetly for Owen to shut the hell up, but it's too late. Sabrina takes Owen's encouragement and runs with it. "Okay. I will. All the sunflowers!"

Oh. Well, alrighty then. "It'll be impressive, that's for sure." I try one more time to add a flower that makes sense. "How about tiger lilies? Those stand for passion and, like, the good kind of pride." They're out of season, too, but I mean. If money is no object . . .

"Ooh, great idea—they're so bright. He really does like stuff that stands out," muses Sabrina, and maybe she only means flowers and not girls, but I still can't help feeling like a dowdy little chamomile blossom next to her in all her glorious, sophisticated calla lily beauty.

I arrange the tiger lilies and the sunflowers with some bay branches for victory and fennel fronds for strength and worthiness. When I'm finished, I wrap the arrangement up in a bright paper cone and tie a big golden bow around the whole thing. It does look impressive, an enormous armful of bright orange and yellow, and for a moment I feel better. I've done good work.

Sabrina purses her lips and tilts her head as she scrutinizes the results. "It looks a little off. Could you like . . . move this one over there? And that one . . . make it higher up?" She reaches over and points and prods as she explains exactly how she wants me to do my job.

Holding back a sigh, I rearrange the flowers and hold them up for Sabrina to see, and she nods her approval. "*So* much better."

The worst part? It *is* better.

I ring her up as Owen chats with her about some essay they have to do for English. After she pays, she fusses with the bow one more time, then holds out her arms to receive the bouquet.

"Thanks for being so patient. It's just that I'm kind of a perfectionist. It's a thing." She smiles at me: *Sorry, not sorry*, and tosses a "Thanks, byeee!" and one last smile over her shoulder as she sashays out the door. I clench my teeth on my frustration and—let's be honest—my envy and my insecurities. Smile as I wave back and swallow everything down.

"Good luck with those," I call. Then when the door closes: "Ughhhh." I can feel the ugliness churning inside me.

"Whoa. Not a Sabrina fan, I guess?" says Owen.

"No. I mean. I don't *hate* her or anything. It's just that she—" I look at Owen, who's watching me intently, and I hesitate. This is dumb. He doesn't need to know. I need to chill.

"She rearranged the bouquet," he says.

It's like he's popped open a shaken-up soda can: *sklick!* Everything comes bubbling out. "Yes! Who does that? Who walks around with that kind of attitude?" I flip my hair and sashay around the store. "I'm Sabrina Dang! I'm better at everything than everyone! Byeee!" Owen's still giving me that intense listening face, and I become uncomfortably aware of how ridiculous I'm being. I sigh. "Though I wouldn't be surprised if she had, like, a black belt in floral design or something."

"Is that how they rate floral designers? I didn't know." Owen grins at me from behind the counter.

I groan. "Forget it. I shouldn't have said anything. It was unprofessional."

"Well, for what it's worth, I liked yours better."

He looks sincere, and I'm touched. Flattered, even. Still, what does he know? "Thank you, but you have no idea what you're talking about." I make my way back toward the counter, pausing to shift buckets around to cover the space left by the now empty and absent sunflower bucket.

"Sure, I do."

"You a floral design expert?" I raise a skeptical eyebrow.

"Just accept the compliment," he says.

"I said thank you."

"True," he concedes. "But then you said I don't have any idea what I'm talking about—"

"You don't."

"—so that cancels out the value of the compliment." He crosses his arms like he thinks he's won.

I try to explain. "It's just that a compliment means different things from different people, so it's nice of you to say that you like my arrangement, but—"

"I wasn't saying it to be nice," he says. He gives me that same serious look, and I feel myself faltering.

"Okay, fine. I'm glad you liked it, but—"

"Just say thank you."

Ughhh. "Fine. Thank you."

"You're welcome."

He smiles, and it's kind of a cute smile, and I'm absurdly pleased that he thinks my arrangement is better than Sabrina's, even though it's not; and even more pleased that he wanted me to take his compliment without trashing myself, except why do I even care? So he's sincere. So he has nice eyes. And a cute smile. So what? He still has no idea what he's talking about. He's wearing a history joke on his chest.

Which reminds me: It's partly his fault that Sabrina didn't listen to me in the first place. "So actually, about those flowers. Next time? Just let me choose them, okay? Like, obviously Sabrina wasn't about to take my advice anyway, but just as a rule, don't encourage customers to choose something unless I tell you to, okay?"

"Oh, sorry about that! I thought I was doing you a favor. You know, trying to encourage her to spend more money."

"It's not about money. I mean it is, obviously. But it's more important to make sure that the flowers are the right ones." I'm about to add, *At least, that's what Hannah says*, but I find that I mean it. Huh. Look at me, being all experty.

"Okay. Got it." Owen nods and gives me a thumbs-up. "Only . . ." His voice trails off. He shifts his weight from one foot to the other and starts rubbing the back of his head.

"Only what?"

"I mean. Don't you guys, like, *need* to make money?"

"Well, duh. Of course, we do. Doesn't everyone?"

"Well, yeah. But no, I mean, like . . . *really* need to make money." When I don't reply, he coughs and kicks the floor. "Don't take this the wrong way, okay, but my dad said something about my 'apprenticeship'"—he throws a pair of air quotes up—"being like a favor to Hannah because your store is um . . . struggling."

It takes me a beat to absorb that, and when I do, I'm pissed at his presumption. "No, it's not! We're just going through a bit of a rough patch, that's all."

Owen puts his hands up in front of him and steps back. "Okay, okay. No need to get defensive. I'm just telling you what my dad said."

"I'm not defensive. And your dad's not running the store, is he, so what would he know?"

"Okay, you're right."

"We're doing just fine."

"Got it."

Owen does not look convinced, though, which bugs me. I'm not convinced, either, which bugs me even more. It was stupid to get so defensive—I know we're not doing fine—but to hear that Heart's Desire is *struggling*, from someone who's not Mom . . . I don't know. That worries me.

7

HANNAH HAS LIVED WITH ME AND MOM EVER since I was born, and she basically raised me during the early part of Mom's career when Mom was working crazy hours and traveling all the time. But she's Mom's baby sister, and Mom often treats her like she's still a kid, so in a lot of ways, Hannah's more like a big sister to me than an aunt.

Like tonight, two days into the new year—Hannah warned me things could get tense between her and Mom, and I promised her I'd have her back. She's brought home takeout from Krungthai for dinner: chicken satay, tom kha gai, veggie panang curry, pad thai, and rice. Thai is Mom's favorite, and Hannah has some serious buttering up to do. Owen may have been exaggerating when he said Heart's Desire was struggling, but he wasn't totally wrong.

"It's just for the first quarter, to tide us over till April," Hannah is saying. "It's just that we didn't get as big a bump from the December holidays as I'd hoped for. But I've got a couple of big weddings coming up, and then there's Valentine's Day, of course, so all I have to do is pick up a few extra funerals and hustle a little harder on the wedding front, and pretty soon we'll be right back on track."

Mom reaches for the sriracha and shakes an ocean of it onto her pad thai as she replies. "Hannah. You're having CJ and that boy help you out at the shop because you can't pay for an assistant. You are not going to be right back on track."

Can't pay? I thought I was helping out to save her trouble, not to save her money. "I didn't know you couldn't afford an assistant." Oops. So much for having Hannah's back. I look guiltily at her; she appears to be totally absorbed in picking lemongrass out of her soup. Then I see Mom giving her an accusatory frown, and I feel awful for having gotten her in trouble, even by accident. I try to give her an out. "That's not true, right, Hannah?"

"Only until April, sweet pea," Hannah says. "We just need to get through February, line up a few more weddings for the spring, and then we're golden." Her voice is calm and reassuring, but Mom has made me nervous. Maybe Owen's dad was right and Heart's Desire is worse off than I thought.

Mom puts down a forkful of sriracha-soaked pad thai and rolls her eyes. "Jesus Christ, Hannah, please don't tell me you seriously think that's possible. Even in the unlikely event that you'll make enough to pay all your debts by April, there's no way you'll keep making enough to pay an assistant a living wage *and* make an acceptable profit." And with that phrase, "make an acceptable profit," I relax. Heart's Desire isn't in trouble. It's just the same old thing: me and Hannah against Mom's impossibly high standards.

"Mom, come on," I say. "It's like all you ever talk about: profit, profit, profit. Heart's Desire is never going to be profitable enough for you. Just chill a little."

"Thank you, CJ," says Hannah. "Anyway, Meems, you know that Heart's Desire isn't about making money. You know it's really about honoring Jii-chan and Baa-chan's legacy, about how they kept growing flowers and creating beauty and connecting people through the internment. And CJ's really showing a lot of promise. You know Mom and Dad would have loved for her to carry on the tradition. Family first, right?"

"Katsuyamas never quit," I add, grinning at Mom.

"Actually," Mom says drily, "running a family business *is* about making money, and I'm tired of you pretending that pouring *my* money into it is actually honoring the 'family legacy,' as you so grandly put it." Then she turns to me and says gently, "CJ. I'm sorry to break this to you, kiddo, but we're not even talking about profit. Heart's Desire is *losing* money."

I look at Hannah again, openmouthed. She's never once even hinted that we were losing money. "Since when?"

"Since forever," says Mom grimly, which is not helpful.

"If it's all about profit, maybe we could ask McAllister VC

to kick in a few bucks," mutters Hannah.

Oh no. Hannah has just pressed the nuclear button. Mom's eyes widen and then narrow, and I leap in, desperate to prevent the train wreck on the horizon. "Hey, I have an idea!" I say. "What if I, um—"

Mom cuts me off. Though if I'd had an actual idea, I might have been able to keep going. "Are you really going to go there, Hannah?"

I try again. "Can you guys just let that go and focus on the real issue here? How about if we have a sale that coincides with—"

This time, Hannah steamrolls me. "I'd say McAllister owes us at least that much, considering what they've done to our family. It'd be very appropriate, really."

"Oh, Hannah, please. They owe us exactly nothing. You're acting like the internment happened yesterday."

"And you're acting like it never happened at all."

"You guys!" I plead. "Let's not talk about the McAllisters. We don't need to involve them. Let's just stay focused on how to turn the shop around. Okay? Let's just start over." God, they're like children.

Hannah clears her throat. "Okay. You're right, CJ. Let's go back to square one. Meems, you can totally afford to pitch in a little extra this quarter."

"I have been pitching in 'a little extra' for several quarters, Hannah," says Mom. "Stop acting like I'm not the only reason Heart's Desire is still in business."

"Wait, what?" I feel like I'm lurching from one revelation to the next, trying to catch up, and I'm the tiniest bit annoyed with Hannah for keeping all of this from me. There's so much I didn't know. What was I thinking, trying to control the direction of this argument?

"It's not like you don't have money to spare. Just skip a couple of spa days. Or don't buy a new dress and shoes for the next fancy fund-raiser you go to. Slum it in something you've worn once before."

"Hannah, that wasn't nice," I say desperately. "That's not what I meant by starting over."

"Yes, it is. We're starting this conversation over, and I'm asking your Mom why she can't help her family by giving up one completely unnecessary luxury."

"Really. Maybe we could *both* save money on clothes and spa days. And girls' week getaways to Bora Bora."

"That was for *Kerri's wedding*, Mimi. My best friend. What was I supposed to do, not go?"

Their argument is whirling further and further out of my reach, and I feel like I'm grabbing at the threads whipping around its perimeter. "Stop it. You guys are supposed to be grown-ups! Can you please just stop fighting?"

"We're not fighting," says Mom. "I'm just trying to help your aunt, who, as you have pointed out, is a *grown-up*"—she pauses dramatically and glares at Hannah, who glares back—"to get a handle on her financial situation."

"That's bullshit. You're totally fighting." I look from one to the other, willing them to stop.

Hannah crosses her arms and says to Mom, "I asked you for help. I didn't ask you to attack the way I do business."

I see Mom get ready to argue, and I brace myself for another verbal stampede. But then I hear a deep breath: in, out. And Mom says, "I'm sorry, CJ. You're right. The core issue is still important, but there's no need to hash it out in front of you."

Whoa. Stunned and hopeful, I try again. "And you didn't need to be so mean to Hannah. She's working really hard."

Mom's jaw clenches when I say this, as if it hurts her to hear it. Then it unclenches, and Mom says, "Yep. Right again, CJ." She comes over to me, gives me a quick squeeze, and kisses my forehead. "I love you, kiddo. Thanks for keeping us accountable."

I can't believe it. "You're welcome."

"What would we do without you?" Hannah adds with a fond smile. "Our own conflict-resolution expert. Right, Meems?"

"Oh, the conflict's still there," says Mom, side-eyeing Hannah.

"Mom. Seriously?"

"Okay, okay. I'll stop." Mom smiles, and it's a little forced, but I can tell she's trying. "Here's the thing, though. Back to square one, as you said." Mom looks sternly at Hannah. "I won't bug you anymore about finances. But I'm not putting any more of my personal money or energy into the business. You said you'd get it together by April, so, fine. But if it's not profitable by then—*sustainably* profitable—I shut it down." She crosses her arms and raises her eyebrows: *End of discussion.*

I look at Hannah, who has the frenzied look of a trapped cat in her eyes. "Fine," she says, and crosses her arms, too. "I'll make it work. You'll see."

"What do you think, though?" I ask Hannah later. "Really."

Hannah shakes her head slowly. "I don't know, sweet pea. But we'll figure something out."

We?

"You'll help me, right?" she says, sensing my hesitation.

I don't have the slightest idea what I could possibly do to help. But Heart's Desire is Hannah's life. And it's starting to become mine, too. If I want to continue doing the only thing I've ever been good at, there's only one answer I can give her.

"Yeah. Of course I will."

The History of the Katsuyama Family, Part I

I've heard the Katsuyama Comeback story a bunch of times; Hannah loves to tell it. This first part is a little sad, but don't worry. It gets better. Remember: Katsuyamas never quit.

1890
Mom and Hannah's great-grandfather Ippei Katsuyama immigrates to California from Sanda, Japan. He works as a field laborer, marries a picture bride, and has five children. Two of them start a tiny little company called Katsuyama Brothers Seed Company. I'll let you guess what they sold.

1938
Ippei's son Toshio (my great-grandfather) sells his share of the Katsuyama Brothers Seed Company and opens a flower shop called Heart's Desire. Toshio is a hardworking, harmonica-playing, people-loving guy with a family of his own: his wife, Mary, and their three sons: George (after George Washington),

Tom (after Thomas Jefferson), and Frank (after Franklin D. Roosevelt).

December 7, 1941
Japan bombs Pearl Harbor.

December 8, 1941
Toshio goes to work in the morning to discover that someone has painted GET OUT DIRTY JAPS on the sidewalk in front of Heart's Desire.

Frank (my granddad) punches Robbie McAllister Jr. in the nose when Robbie Jr. and his friends start chanting, "Japs, go home! Japs, go home!" at recess. Frank is suspended from school.

February 19, 1942
President Roosevelt signs Executive Order 9066. As the order goes into effect over the following months, Japanese Americans on the West Coast have to figure out what to do with their homes, their businesses, and all their worldly possessions before they are banished to who knows where, for who knows how long.

March 1942
Robert McAllister Sr. (as in McAllister High School and McAllister Venture Capital, lest you forget) offers to buy all of Toshio's property for one thousand dollars. It's worth at least

ten times that. But Toshio has no one to run the business in his absence. He has no renters for his soon-to-be-vacant house. What choice does he have?

One day before the family leaves town, Toshio sells his home, his business, and everything inside to McAllister for the price of a Ford station wagon.

8

IT'S BEEN KIND OF A BUMMER OF A MONDAY afternoon, what with the financial pronouncement that Mom made yesterday. Plus, my assignment today is an order for someone whose friend just had a miscarriage; florists don't only do happy occasions. Hannah suggested a potted arrangement of succulents, which stand for grief, solace, or enduring love, depending on the context. Or all of them, in this case. Of course, no one wishes grief on a friend, but I guess it makes sense to acknowledge it. I imagine the little aloe plant whispering words of solace as I place it in the pot and pat the dirt around it.

I wish that flower magic was real and we could use it to solve our money problems. Jade plants, another succulent, are supposed to help bring in money. Maybe we should order a bunch of jade in big ceramic pots. I bet Owen's dad could get us some.

Hannah's meeting with a potential wedding client in her office, and I've just made up my mind to ask her about the jade plants when the bell announces a customer, and seconds later, Emily and Aviana walk into the workroom.

"We come bearing gifts," announces Em, and she holds aloft a bag of day-old snickerdoodles, my favorite cookie. I know she's brought them because I told her about Mom's financial ultimatum at lunch today, and I smile at her gratefully. My afternoon is starting to feel better.

Aviana's presence today is a minor miracle. She used to hang with us all the time, but she's gotten so busy with swimming and martial arts that, these days, we see her only at lunch—when she's presiding over meetings as the president of the Asian Students' Coalition.

"The filter broke at the pool," she explains, "so they canceled practice."

"Cool." I pick up a blue echeveria to go next to the aloe, and as I settle it into the soil, Aviana leans over and says, "Sooo. When's Owen gonna show up?"

"I don't know. He's on a delivery." Wait a sec. "Is that why you guys are here? So you can check out Owen?"

Aviana recoils in mock shock. "Never! We're here because we love you!"

"Also my mom says that Hannah says you guys are hecka cute together." Em nibbles on a cookie and smirks at me.

"Why do you guys insist on playing in the shallow end of the pool?" I grumble. "Can we talk about something besides boys?"

"Sure. Let's talk about the History Club," says Aviana, and she and Emily high-five and collapse into giggles. Hilarious.

At least the History Club joke has died by the time Owen walks in the door, back from a delivery. He takes off his jacket to reveal another T-shirt with words on it—*If history repeats itself, I'm getting a dinosaur*—and a picture of a cartoon guy riding a cartoon T. rex. I'll admit, it makes me smile.

Spotting Emily and Aviana, he sticks out his hand. "Hey. I'm Owen."

They raise their eyebrows at each other before smiling at Owen and shaking his hand. I can tell they're already scheming.

"So do you like working here?" asks Aviana after the introductions are over.

"Sure. Spreading love and joy and beauty all around—what could be better?" He grins, and I roll my eyes. "For real, though," he says.

"But you have to be all by yourself in the car. I'd rather hang here with CJ," says Em. "She's the best. Right, Aviana?"

Aviana nods enthusiastically. "She's the best. Like *the. Best.*"

That's it. "Okay, thanks for the cookies. See you later," I say. I grab the bag of cookies out of Aviana's hand and point my so-called friends toward the door.

Em winks at me, and I try to kill her with my eyes on her way out.

"Sorry," I say to Owen once they're gone. "My friends are weird sometimes."

"No worries," he says. He comes over to the table and examines my handiwork. "Hey, this is really nice."

"Thank you." I swallow the urge to show him how the mistletoe cactus isn't at quite the right angle, and then peek to see if he noticed how graciously I've accepted his compliment. He catches me looking and smiles at me. And I blush, which, ugh. Why.

To redirect his attention, I tell him about the order and the ideas behind my arrangement. I slide a bit of juniper in. "This one means 'hope in adversity.'"

He nods.

Hope in adversity. Ha. We could use a little of that around here, I think, and then I remember my idea about the jade plant. "Hey, do you guys—I mean, the nursery—do you carry jade plants?"

"Yeah, lots of them. Hannah ordered five this morning, in fact."

I should have figured. I wonder if she told him why.

"They're supposed to bring money and good luck, right?" He gives me a smug little grin, and I know that she has.

I will not react. I will not give him the satisfaction of—

"Right?" he repeats, and I lose my resolve.

"Yes, Owen, they're supposed to bring money and good luck, and Hannah ordered them for the store because we need a lot of both. You were right, I was wrong; we're in debt and losing money, so you can just wipe that gloaty little *I told you so* look off your—"

"Hey! Hey! That's not what I meant at all!" He waves his hands in front of him. "I was— I mean, I may have been gloating, but I was just proud of myself for knowing a little plant symbolism. I swear, I wasn't making fun of you or anything."

Oh. Well. This is awkward. "Really?" I narrow my eyes at him.

"I swear." He crosses his heart and holds his hand up.

I sigh. "Fine."

"I'm sorry you guys are having trouble," he says.

"Yeah, well. So am I."

"Do you know what you're going to do?"

"Buy jade plants?" I scoff. Owen remains silent, so I keep talking. "Apparently my mom's going to pull the plug if we're not back on our feet by April. I guess I can't blame her. But this store's been in our family since like, the 1930s. How do you just throw that away?"

"I don't know," he says.

I pause to consider my own question for a moment. "I think I wouldn't be so upset if I thought she was sad about it," I say. "Or at least, like, conflicted. But I don't think she is."

"She might be, though," says Owen.

"Trust me, she isn't sad." It's Hannah, coming in from her

meeting. "I'm sure she'd be glad to see this place disappear."

Owen looks at me and shrugs. I shrug back. He's never met Mom, so how would he know, anyway?

"But guess what, guys!" Hannah continues. "That woman I was talking with out there? She does ad sales for *SV Magazine*—you know, that one for millionaire lady types? She used to do in-house marketing for Instagram, and she's marrying an early YouTube employee. If we get her wedding, do you know what that means?" She holds out one palm and brushes the other one over it, pretending she's making it rain money. "Those jade plants are working their magic already!"

I'm tempted to point out that technically we can't say they're working until we have a signed contract, but I don't want to be a buzzkill. How *can* we nail that contract, though? I rub some dirt between my fingers as I think, and slowly, the germ of an idea forms in my head.

"Hey, Hannah? What if you offer her a discount on her wedding flowers in exchange for a discount on ad space in the magazine? That way, you give her an incentive to go with us, and we could get our name in front of a lot of rich eyeballs."

Owen jumps in. "You should offer something in the ad, though, like a sale. Give people a reason to come in after they see it."

"A fiftieth anniversary sale!" says Hannah. "Fifty years since we bought Heart's Desire back from the McAllisters. It's perfect!"

"I thought you said that Grandpa bought it back from the

McAllisters in the seventies," I point out. "Wouldn't that make it forty-something?"

Hannah brushes that off. "Forty-somethingeth, fiftieth, whatever. The point is, if it works—and I'm sure it will—we are on our way back to financial solvency. You two are brilliant!"

"Three cheers for financial solvency!" Owen shouts. "Hip, hip—"

Oh my god.

"Hooray!" Hannah shouts.

"Hip, hip—" Oh, well. Why not?

"Hooray!" I join Hannah this time.

"Hip, hip—"

"Hooray!"

We cheer and wave our arms around and high-five each other, and it's all ridiculous and silly, but I don't care. It's fun. We do another cheer for Heart's Desire and another for *SV Magazine*, and Owen tries for yet another one for jade plants, which is where I draw the line because it's just too absurd.

"But you'll kill their magic," he says. "Come on, let's hear it. A little love for the jade plants! Hip, hip—"

"No."

"What—seriously? Just straight-up no?"

"I'm not cheering for magical plants, Owen."

"But they need you!"

"They'll survive."

Owen shakes his head mournfully. "That's cold, CJ. You've

got a cold, cold heart."

"Get used to it."

"Never," he says stoutly. I look away to hide a grin.

The bell announces another customer at the front of the store. "Go," I say. "Go spread your love and joy out there."

"As you wish." He bows, doing that hand-swirling thing in some bizarre imitation of a European courtier, I suppose, and exits. I can't even.

I watch him go, and as I turn back to my work, I catch Hannah smiling at me.

"What?"

"Oh, nothing," she says airily. "Nothing at all."

Right. I know what she's thinking. My aunt, the rom-com queen. Well, she can think what she wants, but she will never see it happen.

9

He is so hot I stg 🔥🔥🔥 , I text Emily during the video announcements. Shane and a couple of the other guys on the water polo team are making a needlessly—but gloriously—shirtless appeal to everyone to support the team by buying pizza at a special booth they're setting up at lunch.

CJ: 💯 getting pizza for lunch 🍕

She replies with an eye-roll emoji.

CJ: Come on. Even if you don't want to date him you can't deny he's hot

E: *Sigh* Fine whatever

CJ: And he's nice. Like truly nice

E: 😑 And you know this how?

CJ: I told you. He talked to me FOR NO REASON AT ALL last month

E: You're pathetic 😔

CJ: I know 😂

After shirtless Shane and his water polo bros shill their pizza, Brynn comes on and announces the LGBTQ+ mixer that was on that flyer she put up at Sweet Emily's. Almost instantly, I get another text from Em.

E: Hey if I went, would you go with me?

CJ: YES

CJ: Except

CJ: You know who's in charge right?

CJ: You-Know-Who's in charge lol

E: I know

CJ: You okay with that?

E: Ya it's cool

The thing is, I've been hounding Emily to go to one of these local LGBTQ+ mixer things ever since we started high school. She didn't join the McAllister QSA freshman year because she still felt weird around Brynn, and I supported her on that. But I know that her online LGBTQ+ teen community isn't enough. I love her like crazy and I try to be a good listener, but I know I'm not enough, either.

At lunch, I buy two pieces of pizza from Shane, who is no longer shirtless. We've exchanged exactly zero words since the Great Bakery Encounter, but he greets me with a big open smile and says, as if it were yesterday, "Hey, great call on the blueberry muffins!"

"Oh!" I am mortified to hear myself giggling. Giggling. *Stop. Be casual. Be low-key. Mention something you both know about.*

"So," I say casually, in a low-key manner. "Are you going to the OUTlet mixer?"

Shane's eyebrows draw together for just a second before his face softens and he says, "Ohhh, no. I've got a family thing that night. Thanks for asking, though. It sounds like it's gonna be fun."

Oh my god. "No! No, I wasn't asking you, sorry, was that—I mean, I know you're going out with Sabrina, so of course, ha ha . . . no, I was just, you know. Making conversation." Great. Very slick.

Shane smiles sadly—I can tell he doesn't believe me. But then he says, "Actually, Sabrina and I broke up over winter vacation."

Oh. "I'm sorry," I say. Maybe that's why he's sad?

"Nah, it's fine. It was for the best."

"Oh, well, that's good then, I guess," I say.

We both stand there for three hundred years and finally I say, "Well-I-should-probably-go-eat-my-pizza-now-bye," and turn to flee.

"Hey," Shane says. I turn back around. "Give me your phone number. Maybe we can hang sometime."

I literally die from shock.

But I am only metaphorically dead, of course, so after I type my number into his phone, I book it over to Emily and Aviana to tell them why. Once I've returned to the land of the living, I check in with Emily about her OUTlet mixer situation.

"So you really want to go? Even though Brynn for President's going to be there?"

"Yeah."

"She's still our mortal enemy, though, right?"

I expect Em to laugh, or at least roll her eyes and shrug. But instead she says, "I dunno. She seems different these days. Like she talks to me, like actual conversation, and not just because we're lab partners."

Whaaat. "You're *lab partners* now? How come I haven't heard about this?"

"I know. I—I just, I don't know; it slipped my mind," she stammers, and I know right away she's lying.

"The girl who broke your heart and tossed the pieces in the trash is your new lab partner and it slips your mind to tell me about it?" I turn to Aviana. "Did you know about this?"

Aviana mumbles, "I dunno, kind of, I guess?" She announces that she forgot she has to talk to someone about something she didn't understand in calculus, and disappears.

"I'm sorry," says Emily. "I— She asked me to be her partner, and I knew you'd give me shit about it, so—"

"You *agreed* to be her lab partner?" This is getting worse and worse.

"See, that's what I mean. You're doing it right now."

I sigh. "I'm not giving you shit. I just think you shouldn't have—"

"What was I going to do, Ceej? Say no, right to her face? That would have been rude. That's not who I am."

"Okay, fine." She has a point, I guess. Still. I don't like that she's keeping secrets from me about Brynn. I know it's silly, but it feels like she's defecting from Team Em & CJ to Team Em & Brynn.

We crunch on the bag of Kettle chips I brought to share while I try to process the situation and get us back on familiar ground. "Is it super awkward?"

"It was at first. Because, you know. Broken heart in the trash, and all."

I nod sympathetically. This is better.

"But it's like I said. She's, I dunno . . ." Emily's voice drifts off, and she looks out across the quad for a second. "I just think it might be time to move on, that's all. Things are different now. I think maybe she's changed."

"Doubtful."

"Changing, then."

Still doubtful. "Emily. People don't just change from bad to good like that. They are who they are."

"But she wasn't a bad *person*. She just did a bad job breaking up with me."

"And she never spoke to you again until this year," I remind her.

"Fine. But I still think you're being kind of harsh."

I consider telling her the Valentine's Day story, but how do you tell your best friend about her own humiliation?

I'm licking potato chip salt off my fingers and wondering what I'm going to say when I see Owen across the quad with Will Taylor, another *Weekly History Minute* geek, which reminds me of the most recent *Weekly History Minute* video (sponsored by . . . the History Club!).

It seems that George Washington, despite leading the colonies to freedom from the British and swearing that he would never buy any more slaves after he became president, was kind of a dick about the human beings he already owned. Washington had a slave named Hercules who cooked for him, and Washington loved Hercules's cooking so much that he brought him along to the capital to be the official presidential chef or whatever. But the capital was Philadelphia at the time, and Philadelphia had this law where any enslaved person who lived there for more than six months would automatically become free. So instead of allowing Hercules to become a free man, Washington arranged for him to go to Mount Vernon after six months and then return to Philadelphia, so he could get around the law and continue to keep Hercules enslaved.

Which, I think, serves my point about people not changing. I'm sure Washington was a stand-up guy in a lot of ways, but he said he was going to change his slave-owning ways and what did he do? He turned around and royally screwed Hercules and his family and all the rest of his slaves. Turned out he valued money and convenience more than freedom for all humans the whole time.

Okay. I know that Brynn being an unscrupulous,

girlfriend-betraying jerk is not nearly as bad as Washington being a racist douchebag slaveowner. But the underlying principle is the same. People are who they are. Once an unscrupulous girlfriend-betrayer, always an unscrupulous girlfriend-betrayer.

I'm about to tell Em about my brilliant analysis when Owen sees us and waves, and Emily nudges me so hard, it would be more accurate to call it a shove. *"He's* nice," she says, and I smack her with the Kettle chips bag. "I think you two would be cute together," she insists.

"Well, I don't," I say.

"Come on. He's hecka cute."

"Well, I mean. He's not horrifying or anything."

"No, for real. Take a good look at him sometime."

The five-minute bell rings and ends that conversation, thank God. On my way to Algebra II, I find myself going over and over it in my head. I'm worried about what's happening with Emily. It was so easy to talk about Owen and whether I should be into him. And it was so easy to tell her the other day about Heart's Desire, and I love that she knew a bag of snickerdoodles would make me feel better—how the cookies were shorthand for "I love you and I'm here for you." But I feel like the ground is shifting under my feet. First she bugs me about not trying hard enough in school—since when do friends do that?—and now all this stuff with Brynn . . . I don't know what's gotten into her. I don't know why she thinks things will be any different this time around. I wish I could figure out a way to make her see that they won't.

A Brief History of Chisaki Joan Katsuyama's Romantic Learning Opportunities, Part I

Preschool through Kindergarten: Joel Schumacher
We had several playdates together. We played firefighters, store, and fairy kingdom. We talked about getting married, and we even played wedding one time (Hannah made a little nosegay and a tiny boutonniere and took a zillion pictures), but we drifted apart in first grade.

What I learned: Your colleague at the fire station may be cute and also a great shopper, a fairy king, and even a willing groom, but he is not necessarily marriage material.

Third Grade: Hiccup from How to Train Your Dragon
This was a one-way thing, for obvious reasons.

What I learned: Animated characters will never love you back.

Sixth and Seventh Grade: Zayn Malik (yes, that Zayn Malik)

Also a one-way thing (you might even say one direction, ha ha) for nearly the same reasons.

What I learned: You don't have to be a good dancer to be sexy.

Beginning of Eighth Grade: Ryan Cardoso

I was thrilled when he asked me to be his girlfriend, and we texted constantly for about three weeks. Hannah took us to the movies on a Saturday afternoon, and there may have been some sweaty, awkward handholding toward the end. He broke up with me the day before graduation. His friends reportedly told him that as my boyfriend he was expected to buy me a present (I'd gotten him a Golden State Warriors snapback), and I guess he couldn't handle that level of commitment. I was hurt and confused and angry, plus I was now stuck with this stupid Warriors hat. To be honest, though, I was also a little bit relieved. All that texting had started to feel like a chore, and anyway, Ryan was a terrible speller.

What I learned: Keep your receipts, because many stores don't accept returns without them.

Sophomore Year: Andy Catalano (Emily's cousin's best friend)

Andy and I randomly started following each other on social media via Emily. A few likes and a lot of DMs later, Andy invited me and Em to see him perform some comedy at an open mic, where he totally killed it. Afterward, Emily went home, and I went back to Andy's house to make out—I mean, hang out. Andy was a senior, his texts were hilarious and correctly spelled, and I felt incredibly sophisticated and lucky to be his girlfriend.

Things got pretty serious pretty quickly, and with Mom and Hannah both working, it was easy for Andy and me to start having sex—my decision, by the way, after months of saying "No, not yet." Andy never pushed me to do it; I just felt like it was time. Or maybe curiosity got the best of me. Real talk, though: after all that waiting, all that buildup, the actual sex part was disappointing. On our first attempt, I cracked a joke to ease the tension and collapsed into giggles so debilitating that we had to call it off. And it never did stop feeling kind of awkward and comical to me. I mean, come on. The mechanics are completely ridiculous.

It was a little like our relationship, actually. Not that Andy was disappointing—he was great. But I kept waiting to feel like I was in love with him, and it never happened. How do you go out with someone for months, spend all that time together holding hands, laughing, making out on the couch, having sex, even talking about the future (he was going to Northwestern)—and never once feel . . . whatever it is you're supposed to feel? I didn't feel like I was finally home when I was in his arms. I didn't feel like I'd been waiting my whole life for him. I didn't feel like he could see into my soul.

Still. Having Andy as a boyfriend was fun and horizon-expanding. When I was with him, I laughed and watched movies and went to comedy clubs and had sex and never worried about anything until I missed my period.

10

OUR AD FOR THE (SORT OF) FIFTIETH-ANNIVERSARY sale will appear in the magazine in March, two months from now. In the two days since we came up with the idea, Hannah has spent every spare minute working on the details. She wants to kick off the week of the sale with a big seventies-themed party; if we have a good February, we'll be able to pay for a caterer, so this afternoon, she's out talking to caterer friends, trying to finesse a bargain.

In Hannah's absence, Owen's taking calls and dealing with customers while I work at the demonstration table putting the finishing touches on a ginormous arrangement that will be part of someone's twenty-fifth-anniversary party tomorrow. Because all the snipping and clipping generates a lot of mess, we usually work in the back. But sometimes if a piece is really impressive, like this one, we finish it up in the front to give people something to admire.

The arrangement is made up of red chrysanthemums (longevity) and incredibly expensive out-of-season red peonies (good fortune), and holly branches (enchantment) and orange branches (sweetness and generosity) nestled in sage (health, long life) and wrapped in ivy (fidelity, friendship). It's a tricky one, so Hannah did most of the framing and structural work, but she's letting me do a lot of the filling in. With some poking, clipping, and shifting, I think I'm making it work.

I've been sneaking peeks at Owen every now and then. Now that I'm paying attention, I guess I can see what Emily sees. He kind of has a K-pop/J-pop thing going for him, what with his mussed-up hair and serious brown eyes.

Owen looks up from his phone and wanders over from behind the counter. "That thing is huge," he says, gesturing at the flowers. "It must have taken forever."

"It did—don't touch!" I surprise myself by slapping his hand away as he reaches out to play with the sage leaves. I didn't know I felt so strongly about protecting my work—Hannah's work, really. But also mine.

"Sorry! I didn't know it was so fragile." He makes a show of putting his hands in his pockets and smiles. "This better?"

"No, sorry, it's okay. It's me. I—I think I'm nervous about it. It's the first really fancy one that Hannah's let me do so much work on. I guess I want it to be perfect."

"It looks great," Owen says.

I step back and walk slowly around the demo table, checking for anything out of place, and he walks with me. "I mean, Hannah did most of it."

"You're welcome."

Dammit. I grimace. "Right. Thanks."

"Twenty-fifth anniversary, huh? That's cool," he says, once we've completed the circuit.

"Nuts is more like it."

"What're you talking about? It's beautiful. Two people in love for over twenty-five years—they must be, what—fifty? I mean, isn't that what we all want? A love that lasts forever?"

Eye-roll. Of course that's what he wants. Of course he thinks that's a real possibility.

But what about when no one falls in love in the first place, like Mom? Or when someone falls in love so often that you wonder if it's really what they're feeling, like Hannah?

"First of all, no. Not everyone has to fall in love, and it's not a tragedy if they don't." I don't think Mom is aromantic, but still. It's a thing.

"I guess," he says. "But—"

"Nuh-uh! I wasn't finished."

"My apologies." He inclines his head graciously. "Do continue."

"Thank you." I clear my throat and say, "*Second* of all, I don't think being married for twenty-five years is a *bad* thing. I just don't believe that it's as great as everyone says. I bet tons of people are faking it."

"Damn. Hello, jaded."

I shrug. "Hello, person who's watched too many Disney movies." I go back to making adjustments on the arrangement, adding a bit of sage here, twisting the ivy there.

Owen laughs. "Okay, maybe. But happy endings do happen. Plenty of people stay married forever."

"How many of them are really happy, though?"

"My parents are still happily married."

What a surprise.

"I mean it hasn't been easy," he continues. "Things got really rocky at one point, actually. Like, I thought for sure they'd split up. But they pulled through. Maybe that's rare, I don't know. But it's possible. Just because some people get divorced doesn't mean that true love and romance is dead. It just means other shit got in the way."

I fiddle with a holly berry. My story would be such a great counterpoint to this true-love fantasy of his, but is it worth risking his getting all judgmental about me and Mom? I've always told myself that I'm not ashamed of how I was born. I decide to go for it and give him the SparkNotes version of my origins.

He listens carefully, running his hand through his stupid K-pop hair, and I wait for him to tell me that Mom was crazy, or irresponsible, or brave. But instead he just says, "Well, okay. Maybe true love forever isn't for everyone. But you're never going to convince me that *falling* in love is just for rom-coms and Disney movies."

This guy. "You might be the sappiest person I know," I say.

"Except for Hannah. And Emily."

"I'm the sappiest person *I* know," he says, like it's something to be proud of. "Except for Hannah. And maybe my dad." He picks up a twig that's fallen to the floor and twirls it in his hands, which are callused and strong. He catches me looking (God, why does that keep happening?) and says with a grin, "I work for my parents when I'm not working here. Manual labor. I literally sling flowers and bullshit. So, you know. Depending on what you think about my opinions."

"Huh. That explains a lot."

"Team Romance and True Love Forever, man. For life. I'm never backing down."

I just roll my eyes. Owen may be on Team True Love Forever, but Team Shane Morgan for As Long As He'll Have Me is on my horizon, and that's good enough for me.

11

SOMETHING IS UP WITH MOM.

When I went to ask her for help on my Algebra II homework, I could hear her on her phone, speaking in a low, earnest voice to whoever was on the other end. "I don't know," she was saying. "I'm not sure if she's ready to hear it. I don't want to keep it a secret from her, but—"

I knocked and opened the door, and Mom spun around, startled. She smiled and nodded at me: *I'll be with you in a moment!* and changed the tone of her voice. "Uh-huh," she said brightly, and much more loudly now. "Sounds good. Okay. I'll talk to you about it tomorrow. Okay! Bye!"

She put the phone down and asked me, a little too briskly, "What do you need, kiddo?"

"Who was that?"

"Oh, that? No one. Just work. Anne from MVC wanted to discuss an account with me, but it can wait till tomorrow. So." She gestured to the textbook in my arm. "Algebra?"

I've heard Mom talking to Anne on the phone plenty of times, and when she does, she is neither low and earnest, nor bright and cheery. And while Mom talks about a lot of stuff for work that she wants to keep from the public, this secret sounded much more like a personal secret than a work secret. And it was clearly a secret that she was keeping from me, or else why the fake voice and the quick hang-up?

As Mom reviewed the textbook and looked over my problem set, I asked to borrow her phone so I could use the calculator.

Her last phone call wasn't from Anne. It was from Trey McAllister.

"Do you think she's having an affair with him?" I whisper to Hannah, who's taking her makeup off.

The door to her bathroom is shut, as well as the door to her bedroom, and Mom's in her own room with her own door shut, but I don't want to take any chances.

"He's not married, sweet pea. It's technically not an affair," says Hannah, dabbing her right eye with a cotton ball.

"So she *is* going out with him?" I ask, incredulous.

"No, I meant if she was, it wouldn't be an affair."

"She said she didn't want to keep it a secret from someone, and that someone might not be ready to hear it. A her. She didn't want to keep it a secret from a woman."

Hannah starts on her left eye and says, "Or maybe she's getting ready to break the news to you."

"Why not 'them,' though? Wouldn't she want to tell us both? If she was dating him?"

"She's probably thinking that you'd take it harder than me."

"You're the one who hates the McAllisters," I remind her.

"Good point." Finished with her eye makeup, Hannah starts washing her face. "On the other hand," she says between splashes, "maybe if they got married, we'd be billionaires, and we could just keep Heart's Desire without having to worry about how profitable it is. I might be able to stomach a McAllister in-law if he paid for the store."

"That would be so cool. Billionaires," I sigh.

"I wouldn't count on it, though. You know your Mom."

"Yeah."

"Whatever it is, it sounds like it's done, so there's no point speculating. She'll let us know when she lets us know," Hannah says. "Anyway, we've got secrets of our own, don't we?" She smiles at me. "I can't wait to see the look on your mom's face when she sees our client list in April."

12

RAINY DAYS IN CALIFORNIA ARE THE WORST. I know, I know, we need the rain—it's what we always say, and it's true. Still. Apart from being generally depressing, it means that you can't eat in the quad, and you have to either brave the smelly cafeteria (hard pass) or eat your lunch standing up, freezing cold and huddled under the awnings of one of the school buildings.

Which is what Emily, Aviana, and I are doing as we discuss the OUTlet LGBTQ+ mixer, coming up next weekend.

Em is nervous. What if it sucks? What if she hates everyone? What if no one wants to talk to her? What if someone does talk to her and she responds by laughing inappropriately or fainting or throwing up?

As I listen to her, I dab a paper napkin at the pools of grease in the pepperoni circles on my cafeteria pizza slice. It's gross compared to Bibo's, which is what the water polo team sold last week, but greasy cafeteria pizza is better than the whole-wheat veggie sandwich that Em's got.

"Em," I tell her. "It's going to be fine. It'll be just like a school dance."

"Which you hate," she points out.

"This is true."

"You literally just said the mixer was going to be fine because it'd be like a school dance, which you then admitted you hate," Em says. "You're not making any sense, and you're not making me feel better."

"Sorry."

"You always have fun at dances," Aviana protests.

"I have fun when we're all together," I explain. "But like—It's like I *only* have fun when we're all together. I hate it when I get left alone. Like at homecoming, Em, you ended up talking forever with those people from your English class. And—I'm just being honest, here—I felt like such a loser, like people were looking at me and thinking, *She doesn't have any friends.*"

"You had me," says Aviana, a little huffily.

"I didn't. Three of them were, like, your besties from swim team."

"Well, you're not a loser," Aviana says.

"I *know*. But that doesn't stop me from feeling like one when I'm wandering around without anywhere to go or anyone to talk to. Come on. Please tell me I'm not the only one who feels that way."

"Now you get why I'm nervous about the mixer," says Em.

"But you'll have me, Em. I promise. Unless there's a cute girl you want to talk to," I say, and she smacks me on the arm.

"Ceej, you should make her one of those magic flower things," says Aviana.

"Yeah, right. Because she definitely won't look like a loser with a corsage on her chest."

"So make something else," she says. "Like a hair thing."

"A hair thing."

"I'm not wearing a flower crown," says Em firmly. "Or carrying a bouquet or wearing a corsage." But I can tell from her face that she's considering it.

"So have CJ make something *else!*" says Aviana. "She's creative."

This is ridiculous, I want to say. But I kind of like that Aviana has this much faith in my abilities.

That's all Em needs. She turns to me, her eyes hopeful. "What do you think, Ceej? Could you make something? Like, just a small thing? I'd totally pay for it."

"I don't know."

"Come on, it would be so cool. Like, let's see, what do I need . . ." Em starts ticking off on her fingers the things she thinks she needs. "Self-confidence, inner calm, talkativeness? That's not a word."

"Loquacity," says Aviana. She's a vocabulary demon. "And

charm, you should definitely ask for charm."

"*It's not real*," I say.

"But it might be," says Aviana, and Em nods her head.

"It can't hurt, right?" she says. "Please?"

"It could be really expensive," I warn her. "It could be like thirty dollars or more. Just for one little mixer."

"I'll pay for it," she insists. "Do it through Heart's Desire! I'll be part of your expanded client base!"

As if thirty dollars and one high school student would make a difference in our situation. Still, it would be something. And it would be my very own thing, and as Mom says, *Own your power.* "I'll think about it, okay?"

Satisfied, Em and Aviana move on to other topics, namely me again. And Shane, who hasn't texted so much as a "hey sup" since the Great Pizza Purchase last week.

"Have you heard from him?" asks Aviana.

"Not since you asked this morning," I say. I bite off a bigger hunk of pizza than maybe is polite, but at least this way I won't have to answer any more questions.

"Are you gonna text him? You should."

"Mmmf-mm-mff," I say, grateful for the pizza in my mouth.

The ten-minute bell rings, and Aviana and I toss out the remains of our pizza slices in their paper plates while Em shoves her Tupperware sandwich box back into her backpack. We start walking toward the center of campus.

The sad thing is, despite his deafening silence since the Great Pizza Purchase (or maybe because of it), my feelings for

Shane have evolved from Hopeless But Entertaining Crush from Afar to Hopeful (and Obviously Delusional . . . and Yet Still Hopeful) Crush from a Medium Distance. I just need to accept that guys like Shane don't reciprocate crushes from girls like me. Because reality. I need to move on. "I have moved on," I say out loud, to myself as much as to Emily and Aviana.

"I still think you need to get together with Owen," says Em. "I like him."

"Then you date him."

"It's okay to admit you have a crush, CJ," she says with a smile and a shake of her head. We've reached an intersection between buildings, and Em and Aviana turn right to go to physics. "See you after school."

"I don't have a crush on him!" I call after them.

"Have a crush on who?" says someone in my ear. Shane. I leap away and whirl around like one of those freaked-out internet cats, banging him in the elbow with my backpack in the process.

"Oh!" I squeak. I clear my throat and try again. "Sorry! No one! I don't have a crush on anyone!"

"High-strung much?" he says, rubbing his elbow and grinning. "Man, that hurt!"

"I can be lethal when I'm surprised."

He laughed and says, "Aw, you're too cute to be afraid of."

Suddenly, I realize that I've just said a flirty thing and Shane has just said a flirty thing back, so naturally the next thing I do is stand there as silent as a department store mannequin. And there's Shane, waiting for me to continue our flirty conversation.

"Be afraid," I say. Ooh, good one, Ceej.

But Shane throws his head back and lets loose a great burst of laughter. "You're funny," he says, and I'm saved from having to think of another clever response by one of Shane's bros, who half-tackles him out of nowhere and says, "C'mon, bro, hurry! I'm one tardy away from a detention!"

Shane takes off running, and I float to history because Shane Morgan just laughed at a joke I made.

I'm in my seat and pulling my history textbook and binder out of my backpack when my phone buzzes.

Hey, sorry I ran off like that

BTW, I will never be afraid of you

Cuteness factor > fear factor

How nice it must be to be Shane Morgan, who can type *Cuteness factor > fear factor* and risk nothing because there is probably not a single boy-liking person at this school who wouldn't have the exact same internal reaction to it that I'm having, which is basically a million bedazzled exclamation marks.

It's so extra of me to go all starry-eyed over one flirty text. I pull myself together, then type, *The cuteness is just a facade.* He's probably having twenty conversations like this with other girls, but I don't even care. Because when does this kind of thing happen to people like me? Never. Because reality. Until now. So take that, reality.

A Brief History of Chisaki Joan Katsuyama's Romantic Learning Opportunities, Part II

Day 33

Unlike Mom's, my periods have always been regular. After that first year of randomly spaced periods, during which I lived in terror of blood-splotched jeans (I wore a shirt tied around my waist pretty much constantly), my periods settled down like good little children to every twenty-eight to thirty days. So when I woke up on day thirty-three and saw nothing, I edged into low-grade anxiety.

Maybe it's just a fluke, I told myself. *Maybe it's nothing.*

I spent much of that day in my room, googling terms like "missed period" and "teenager period three days late."

It could be stress, one article read, or increased strenuous physical activity. No and no. It was summer vacation. Unless I was stressed about Andy leaving in the fall? *Be honest with yourself, CJ*, I told myself. *Are you?* No. I wasn't even very sad, really.

New birth control prescription was another possibility,

though not for me. Why *wasn't* I on the pill? Or any of the other things the articles listed: copper IUD, hormonal implant, shots, rings—holy ovaries, there were a shitload of birth-control devices I'd never even heard of. Why, why, *why* hadn't I thought to get myself one of them? I mean apart from the obvious problem of expense, or the nightmare of having to talk to Mom about my sex life.

Most websites also said something like, "Sometimes you'll be late for no discernible reason other than the fact that your body is still developing." Please, let my body still be developing. *I can't be pregnant*, I told myself. *I can't. I can't. I can't.*

Days 34–44
I clung to the "body still developing" explanation for the next several days, praying silently to whatever deities there might be who looked out for girls in my situation. What *was* my situation? Not pregnant. It had to be. I frantically hacked down every *but what if I am?* that dared to sprout.

But the what-ifs got stronger and wilier. They twined their way like ivy into the cracks of my denial and started pulling it apart. Because what if I *was* pregnant? (Please, God, no.) But what if I was?

Meanwhile, self-accusations buzzed like angry wasps in my head. *How could you have allowed this to happen?* they would say. *Swept away in the moment*, I told myself. *Stupid. Lazy. Careless,* buzzed the wasps. *It could have happened to anyone,* I said. *You should have known better. You should have been more careful.*

You should have been stronger. You should have been smarter. It was relentless and exhausting.

I didn't tell Andy why I was so surly and skittish because it was probably nothing. It had to be nothing.

Day 45

After two weeks, I woke up with a feeling of intense nausea when I got out of bed. The steady thrum of denial and self-abusive rage, now the soundtrack of my life, was joined by a whine of panic, like sirens in the distance, like fork tines screeching across a metal dish.

By the end of the school day, I was spent. I felt simultaneously that I would faint if I didn't have something to eat and that I would throw up if I did.

I made myself a cup of mint tea (according to Google, a good stomach settler) and gave myself a talking-to. It was time to stop pretending nothing was wrong. It was time to make a mature, responsible decision. Because if I made a mature and responsible decision, everything would be okay. Wasn't that what every grown-up, ever, always said?

So I did the mature, responsible thing. I drove three towns away, bought a pregnancy testing kit, went home, locked the bathroom door, and took the damn test.

With the threat of pregnancy looming large and gray over my shoulder, I was still praying as I watched my pee soak its way up the little testing stick. I channeled all my mental and emotional energy into not being pregnant, as if the sheer power of my dread could keep me safe from a mistake I'd made weeks ago. I felt as if taking my attention off that stick for even a second would cause me to be pregnant, the way people trip on the sidewalk or bump into things when they're distracted.

Obviously, it didn't make a bit of difference whether I watched the stick or checked my Snapchat, whether I prayed or fell asleep. But I stared and prayed and stared and prayed. And watched in horror as a blue plus sign materialized almost immediately in the little window on the stick in my hand.

13

WE WEREN'T GOING TO TELL MOM ABOUT THE
sale-slash-party because Hannah wanted the satisfaction of
a mic-drop moment when she presented Mom with a shiny
new client list and full-to-bursting calendar in April. But Mom
has connections everywhere—in this case, with Hannah's *SV
Magazine* ad lady's fiancé. So she came home from work and
demanded an explanation, and now we're all sitting around the
kitchen table as Hannah tells Mom about our plans, with Mom
still in her suit like we're having an actual business meeting.

Hannah finishes her pitch, and Mom takes a slow sip of
wine from her glass.

"Help me out here, Ceej," she says. "Tell Hannah that if
she can't afford to pay assistants, she's dipping into her personal bank account *and* mine, and she's bartering her services

for publicity, a few clients who she hustles from a money-losing sale are not going to save the day." Mom's talking to me, but she's looking at Hannah. Her voice is measured and patient—it's like she's talking to a child, and Hannah bristles: a tense reset of her shoulders, a defiant jut of her chin.

"Actually," Mom continues, "I have some news about Heart's Desire, myself." She takes another sip of wine. "I've been talking to people who might be interested in making an offer on it."

"An offer, like—to buy it?" I stare at her.

"It hasn't even been two weeks since you said I had till April! You haven't even given me a chance!" protests Hannah.

"An opportunity arose and I'm considering it," Mom says evenly. "I have to start making plans in case you don't come through. I'd say I'm doing you a favor by being transparent about it."

It's impossible to argue against making a plan. Making a plan is the smart, logical thing to do. I hate that about her.

"Well, I will come through," says Hannah. "You just stay out of it."

Mom looks skeptical, and I wish I didn't feel the same way. But now that she's dismissed it, the sale looks childish and unrealistic. "This is the offer on the table," she says. Mom drops a number: three million dollars. Cash. My jaw falls open.

We're doomed. There's no way we can make Heart's Desire successful enough—by April!—to compete with an offer like that.

Hannah swallows. Then she squares her shoulders and says, "I don't care. You can't put a price on family."

"We're not selling people, Hannah. We're selling dirt and concrete."

"*We* are not selling anything. *You* are selling history. *You're* selling our childhood. *You're* selling blood, sweat, and tears. And pride and hard work."

Mom closes her eyes and shakes her head like she can't even do this. "Your memory of that place is not the same as mine. It wasn't as great as you think it was. I'm getting sick of throwing away money for the sake of your nostalgia."

"And what about CJ? Doesn't she get a say?" Hannah turns to me.

I've been listening to this argument with growing alarm as the implications sink in. Heart's Desire connects me to the only history I have—and I know it sounds bizarre, but I feel like *myself* when I'm working on an arrangement. I feel grounded when I work there, like I've finally found my feet. The thought of that going away makes me slightly panicky.

"Who's making the offer? Who has that kind of money? Is it another florist?" I ask. *Maybe I could get a job with them*, I think desperately.

"Some corporate real estate monster, probably," grumbles Hannah.

Mom takes a sip of wine before she answers without looking at either of us. "McAllister Venture Capital."

There's a long beat of silence, filled slowly by our stunned understanding, which expands until its edges are stretched as taut and thin as the skin of a balloon about to burst. This was the secret she had with Trey. This was what we weren't ready to hear.

"What?" Hannah says finally. "Are you fucking kidding me?"

"Nope." Mom is almost defiant, popping the "p" loudly and raising her eyebrows. She peers down at her glass and swirls the wine around in lazy circles. She looks relaxed, but I can see the muscles in her jaw twitch as she clenches her teeth.

"Is that—is that even legal?" I ask. It can't be. It seems so wrong. Because (a) Mom works for MVC, and (b) it's the McAllisters. That can't be okay.

"It's perfectly legal, kiddo. People do stuff like this all the time. McAllister is looking to find a small urban space to incubate a couple of start-ups, and our property is perfect. I can sell it to them as a private citizen. What they do with it afterward is their business."

"But it still doesn't seem *right*," I say. I wish I could say it in a bigger way. Somehow, the fact that I thought this secret was something else entirely makes the truth feel like even more of a betrayal.

"That's right, CJ," says Hannah. "Mimi, we're not talking about the legality of the process, and you know it."

"Hannah." Mom sets her wineglass down, and the wine sloshes back and forth inside. "What happened in the past happened. It's over. The only person who's still upset about it is you. Move on."

"What?" She can't possibly mean that. "Don't you even care a little bit about what happened? Or about what Heart's Desire means to us?"

"Frankly, CJ, not as much as I care about three million dollars."

I gape at her. She really doesn't care at all. "How can you say that?"

"Because money is all she cares about," Hannah says, sneering. Normally I would wince at how nasty she sounds, but right now, it feels fair.

"Well, *someone* in this family has to care about money," Mom says pointedly.

Something in Hannah seems to snap, and she stands up and starts shouting, her eyes wild and chest heaving. It's hard to even look at her. "How dare you do this to us? How dare you? If Dad were alive today—"

"He'd probably want to sell it, too." Mom, on the other hand, has become icy cold and calm. She leans back in her chair and takes another sip of wine, and once again I can barely believe how she can be this cruel.

"You know he wouldn't. You've always put money ahead of family. That's what killed him, you know. When you went to work for them. You betrayed him. You betrayed all of us. And now you're going to do it again."

"I am trying to do what's best for our family," says Mom. "So you can just take a seat." *What's best for our family.* The phrase spins in my mind like a coin on a table, a blurry, unstable illusion.

Hannah looks daggers at Mom and says quietly, her voice full of righteous fury, "How dare you say that. You traitor."

At that word, "traitor," Mom leaps up, shoving her chair back so hard it almost falls over. I swear I think she's going to smack Hannah, and I brace myself, terrified, because my family is legit falling apart, but instead of lunging at each other, she and Hannah just stand there and stare at each other for a long, silent moment. A tear trickles down Hannah's cheek. She wipes it away. Her face is contorted with grief and rage, and her lower lip is trembling. She turns her back on Mom and runs down the hall, sobbing audibly.

"How dare *you*!" Mom shouts after her. A door slams, but Mom keeps yelling. "Don't you take the moral high ground with me! I loved him, too! He was my dad, too!" But there's no answer.

Mom sinks back onto her chair, her hands covering her face, elbows propped up on her knees. I can see her back and shoulders move; she's doing her stress breathing. In, out. In, out.

"Mom? You okay?"

She puts her finger up: *Don't bother me.* She takes one more big breath, gets up, paces furiously around the room a couple of times, and stalks out. The door to her room opens and closes. A few minutes later, I hear the treadmill turn on.

Someone taps on my door. Mom pokes her head in, flushed and sweaty from rage-running on the treadmill. She's still breathing hard. "Ceej," she puffs, "don't tell anyone about our conversation tonight. There's no sale yet—it's just a conversation. I'd like to keep it private for now, okay? Can I trust you?"

"I guess."

"I'm sorry you had to see me and Hannah fight like that. I should have known she'd lose her shit—she gets so emotional about that goddamn store. I shouldn't have brought it up with you there."

Something in Mom's voice, in her face, when she talks about Hannah losing her shit over "that goddamn store" gets to me. She's so dismissive of it all—of the store, of Hannah's love for it and everything it stands for. I've had my doubts about how much she really valued Heart's Desire, but it's only sinking in just now how truly worthless she thinks it is.

"It's not nothing, you know," I say.

But she misunderstands me. "Oh, don't worry, kiddo. Hannah's been mad at me before. She'll get over it."

I can't believe it. And I'm not just stunned anymore. I'm angry. She can't treat this like some sisterly spat, or like Hannah's had a silly little tantrum. She can't pretend that Heart's Desire is just some stupid thing we should all "get over."

"No," I say, letting my anger lend power to my voice. "I mean the store. It's not nothing. It's practically the symbol of our family. I mean, I know Hannah's all weird about magical connections and stuff, but, like . . . it's not nothing. It's real. Or it's important, anyway. I feel it, too."

Finally, I have her attention. Mom's eyebrows shoot up, and she blinks, twice, like she can't believe what I'm saying. *Welcome to the club*, I think. This is a big night for disbelief. Though, honestly? I kind of can't believe what I just said, either. I don't believe in flower magic. I think Hannah's full of shit about romance and love and all of that. But what I'm saying is true.

"I like being at Heart's Desire. I like the way I feel when I'm working there. I'm—I think I'm good at it, too." A sort of understanding takes root inside me and pushes itself into the light. After a lifetime of being shepherded from one "learning opportunity" to the next, I think I may finally have found something I really care about, a place where I really belong, and I don't want it to go away.

"We can't sell the store, Mom."

Silence like wood. Mom's face is unreadable. I imagine my words settling like seeds in her heart. Small and quiet, but undeniable. Full of beauty and strength. *Please, Mom*, I beg her silently. *Please.*

She closes her eyes and takes a deep, cleansing breath. When she speaks, her face is like stone, her voice tight, controlled. "CJ, life is bigger than your newfound hobby and your emotional attachment to a failing family business. You and Hannah need to get your heads out of the sand and face reality."

"But, Mom!"

"Don't 'but, Mom' me. I'm not in the mood for another argument. I just came in to apologize for fighting and to tell you not to let any of this leave the house." She withdraws and shuts the door, and I hear the treadmill start up again.

The History of the Katsuyama Family, Part II

November 1945
Toshio, Mary, and sixteen-year-old Frank (my granddad) are released from the Heart Mountain internment camp with travel fare and twenty-five dollars each because the US government is generous like that. Back in San Jose, Toshio tries to buy back the flower shop that he sold to Robert McAllister three years earlier. But McAllister is a shitty person, so he refuses to sell it back unless Toshio pays market value, which is twenty times more than what he sold it for in 1942.

June 1973
After twenty-eight years of hard work, Toshio Katsuyama and his son Frank finally scrape together enough money to buy the building back from the McAllisters. Because Katsuyamas never quit.

Spring 2000
Frank's daughter Michelle (a.k.a. Mimi, a.k.a. Mom) wins the McAllister Scholarship, which pays for her MBA at Stanford.

June 10, 2002
Mimi takes a job with McAllister Venture Capital and has a huge fight with her father (Frank) and her sister (Hannah) about whether she has betrayed the family to make money for the greedy, soulless McAllisters.

June 13, 2002
Frank Katsuyama has a heart attack and undergoes triple-bypass surgery. Hannah blames Mom.

June 24, 2002
Frank suffers a second heart attack and dies. Hannah continues to blame Mom.

July 2002–present
Hannah takes over Heart's Desire. Mom gets pregnant and has a baby (me). Mom rises through the ranks of MVC and becomes the first woman and first woman of color to make partner at one of the most successful, powerful venture capital firms in the world. CJ Katsuyama (me again) wonders how you can be proud of someone and disappointed in them at the same time.

14

HANNAH HAS BEEN UNCHARACTERISTICALLY snippy at work all afternoon. She chastised Owen for not handling the arrangements with proper care as he loaded them into the delivery truck, and now she's mad about the flowers we're preparing for tomorrow's wedding. She grumbles and mutters to herself as she wraps a pale green satin ribbon around the stems of bunches of blue hydrangeas, the savagery in her voice a bizarre contrast to the gentleness with which she handles the blooms. "Out of season, unlucky, I don't even know why I took this one on." She tucks the end of a ribbon into the bouquet she's working on and brandishes a pearl-headed pin at it, as if to stab it. "She wants larkspur in the main arrangement, CJ, in addition to the hydrangea. She insisted.

'We met in Larkspur!' she said. Like that even matters. Why would you start off your marriage with symbols of frigidity and infidelity? No wonder it's pouring rain outside."

There's no arguing with Hannah when she's like this, so I make some assenting noises and keep working.

She nods at the table arrangements I'm doing. "Could you try to be a *little* more careful, Ceej? That one's a bit sloppy, and it has to be perfect. You'll need to do better on the next ones if we want to keep getting business."

I thought I *was* being careful. "Sorry," I say, stung.

Hannah must hear something in my voice because she puts the hydrangeas down and comes over and plants a kiss on my cheek. "No, I'm sorry, sweet pea. You're doing fine work. It's just that this bride is a monster, and I'm letting her get to me. It doesn't help that she reminds me of your mom."

I'd been trying to forget about last night. That's one of the things I love about this place: I lose myself in my work. Though maybe not for much longer.

"Do you think she's going to go through with it?"

Hannah says nothing.

I try again. "I don't want Heart's Desire to go away," I say.

"Oh, sweet pea." Hannah's eyes fill with tears. "Neither do I, but you know how your mom is when she makes up her mind about something. I just don't know what to do."

My heart sinks. I realize that I wanted her to offer some encouragement, to help me scrape together the will to keep trying. But Hannah seems so hopeless. Are we just going to give up?

The bell rings. Hannah glances at the security monitor, which shows a guy shaking out his umbrella. He turns toward the camera and she brightens immediately. "It's Richard! He said he'd be dropping in around this time. Ugh, my eyeliner's running. CJ, you go out and chat with him, and I'll fix my makeup and get his order."

She hustles into the bathroom, and I go out to the front to talk to this Richard person who, I realize when I see him, is the first-date guy we made the boutonniere for. Violets and pansies. *Romantic Richard*, I think.

Evidently that date did not work out. "But I'm going to try again," he says, blushing. "Hannah and I worked out a new formula this time."

"Added a rose leaf for hope," says Hannah, sailing in with the box held aloft in her hand. "Ta-daa!" She sets the box down on the counter with a flourish and a little flip of her hair.

Richard pays, and Hannah gives him a big smile and two thumbs up as he waves goodbye at the door. Once he's gone, she rests her elbows on the counter, chin in her hands, and sighs. "What a sweet, sweet man."

"A little desperate, though, don't you think?" I say.

Hannah frowns. "He's optimistic. And resilient. I admire that. It's tough out there as a single adult, you know."

I shrug; I actually don't know since I'm not a single adult.

"I don't see why it's such a big deal. Why put all that effort into looking for a girlfriend or a boyfriend or whatever? Seems like odds are that you'll end up being unhappy and breaking up eventually, anyway."

"That's no way to talk, CJ. You have to have hope. How do you expect anyone to cultivate a happy relationship with an attitude like that?"

"I don't. That's my point."

"People should never give up on finding love, CJ."

I roll my eyes. "You know, some people actually don't need true love. Some people are happy without it."

Hannah tsks. "Yes, okay. But not this guy. Your bad attitude is going to drain the power out of your work—no wonder that first boutonniere didn't take. It's a good thing I worked with him on his second one. In fact, I should reconsider even letting you work on wedding arrangements."

"Hannah! You wouldn't."

"Your attitude is important, CJ. It flows into your work. It's part of the magic."

It occurs to me that except for the magic part, Hannah sounds just like Mom right now, and I can't suppress a grin.

"You're laughing at me, but it's true. Be like Richard, sweet pea. Resilience. Optimism."

"I'm not laughing at you. It's just that you kind of reminded me of Mom just now." I wag my finger at her. "Attitude. Resilience. Optimism."

It's Hannah's turn to roll her eyes. "Do not mention your mother to me, and do not compare us. We are not the same at all."

We walk back to our tables in the workroom, where Hannah picks up a hydrangea and scowls at it.

"Attitude, Hannah," I caution her slyly. "Don't let it ruin the wedding."

Hannah says nothing, just measures out a length of ribbon, snips it off the wheel, and starts wrapping the bouquet. She secures the ribbon with a pin (without threatening to stab it this time) and holds it out at arm's length, admiring her handiwork. "You know what, CJ? You're right. There's no use sitting here complaining about this awful bride—or your mom, for that matter." She sets her work down and turns to me. "We are not going down without a fight, CJ. This place has always been about creating beauty and magic and bringing people together, and we are not going to let the McAllisters"—she practically spits the name out of her mouth—"trash everything our family stands for. We have to figure out a plan. We can't let history repeat itself."

"It is *pouring* out there." Emily enters and shakes rain out of her hair, adding, "What plan? What history?"

Hannah and I exchange glances. Mom said not to tell anyone.

Emily pounces on our hesitation. "What is it? But actually, before you tell me, I know we were supposed to hang tonight, but apparently Juliana's in, like, active labor."

"Oh my god!" I say.

"I know!" she responds. "So my mom said I could go over."

Juliana and Ceci are Em's across-the-street neighbors, and they have one adorable little girl named Isabella, and one soon-to-be adorable little baby boy whose name they haven't told us. Em agreed long ago to babysit Isabella when Juliana went into labor so that Ceci could focus on helping her wife give birth.

"These are to make up for bailing on you." Em plunks a bag of bakery treats on the counter.

"Aw, thanks, Em. You could've just texted. It would've been totally fine."

"It's no big deal. The doula's already at the house, and I guess they're not expecting the midwife for another couple of hours. So tell me about this plan you're so fired up about, and then I'll go."

I look at Hannah again. I love this right now, me and Emily back to normal, supporting each other, sharing everything. I want it to keep going. So I tell her.

Em is appropriately shocked and offended. "I still can't believe he got away with it all. I mean, he basically stole your family's entire livelihood. I've always hated that they named our school after him."

"Racist McAsshole High School, you mean?"

Em laughs mirthlessly. "Yeah, exactly. I love-slash-hate when you call it that."

"Yeah, me too." You gotta love a perfect nickname, after all. But I shouldn't have had to make it up.

"So what's the plan? How are we gonna keep this place out of their clutches?" asks Emily.

Hannah shakes her head. "I don't know yet. The anniversary sale might be enough to help us scrape by, but I have a feeling we'll actually have to beat MVC's offer in order to keep the store."

I think about losing the store, losing my apprenticeship, and my heart constricts with a pang of . . . I don't know, premature regret, I guess, if there is such a thing. Anyway, it hurts. If we let Mom sell Heart's Desire to the McAllisters, this pain will be here in my heart forever. We have to think of something.

15

JUST AFTER EMILY LEAVES TO BABYSIT, OWEN returns from his deliveries. He's hanging up his jacket when Hannah says, "Owen, where did you put the Monterey pine cones?"

Owen stares at her. "Monterey . . . ?"

"Pine cones. The ones that were delivered earlier, with the eucalyptus branches. For the wedding reception. They're going to go on the cake table. Where did you put them?"

Owen rubs the back of his head and waits until Hannah is standing with her arms crossed, drumming her fingers on her elbows to say, "Um . . . I didn't see any pine cones."

"What? You're—you're kidding, right? Please tell me you're kidding." Here we go: flower-magic crisis alert. It feels so tiny in comparison to the real crisis at hand that I can't help feeling a needle of impatience.

Owen says, "No, I'm not kidding. Sorry. The invoice only said pine branches." Hannah and I follow him to the file cabinet, where he pulls out an invoice. He shows it to Hannah, who takes one look and groans. "But I need those pine cones! Monterey pine . . . I'm sure I said it! I specifically called it out on the order because they met when the groom was hit on the head by an unripened Monterey cone!" She wrings her hands and mutters to herself, her mouth pulled into a tragic frown. "It was going to undo the ill effects of the larkspur."

"Can't we just use some of the ones we have in stock?" I suggest. We have a big box of pine cones left over from the December events.

"CJ, you *know* we can't use substitutes. Otherwise the magic is completely lost!" She paces, and Owen kicks at the floor in silence. I feel torn. Wasn't I just marveling last night about my newfound connection to flower magic? But Hannah's dogmatic attachment to the rules of the magic is so irritating. *We don't have time for this,* I want to tell her. Just use the other pine cones. I wonder if Owen would back me up. I bet he would if he knew just how desperate things have become.

I'm about to speak up when Hannah stands still and holds out her hands: *Stop the presses!* "I've got it." She turns to me and Owen. "You two need to go and collect some. There's a few groves of Monterey pines at the Los Altos Country Club golf course. You can sneak in there and pick up what I need. You'll have to climb a little, so make sure to bring a ladder."

What.

"You're kidding, right? What if we get caught?" I say.

"It's dark. No one will see you."

"Can't we just call and ask?"

"They won't have grounds staff at this hour. And there's no way they'd let you do it yourselves. They don't want to risk getting sued."

"So we should risk getting arrested instead?" This is ludicrous.

"I'm telling you, sweet pea. You won't get caught."

"What if we do?" I ask.

Hannah sighs. "Do you remember Lewis?"

"Loathsome Lewis? The asshole with the Maserati?" That was about two boyfriends ago.

"He's on the board of the country club. If you get caught, I can promise you they won't press charges. But I'd rather not have to call in that favor ahead of time."

"What if they call the police and the police call Mom?"

"Ugh, your mom." Hannah grimaces. "Let them call. I'll defend you. I will fight her to the death if I have to." I catch Owen's eye and I can tell that (a) he wants to do this, and (b) he's going to ask me later why Hannah's so upset. I wonder if I should tell him.

"We won't get caught," says Owen. "This'll be fun." Sigh.

"See?" Hannah smiles triumphantly at me. "Now, go."

★ ★ ★

If you've never run across a golf course carrying a fifteen-foot ladder with a partner, with a pair of security guards in hot pursuit, let me take this opportunity to advise you never to try.

Operation Monterey Pine started off okay: sneak into the golf course, find the trees, put the ladder up. But the pine cones were high up in the tree, and the ladder was heavy, and every time Owen shifted his weight, the entire thing swayed dangerously. And the rain made everything slippery and unstable.

And then I saw a flicker in the distance that could only have been a flashlight.

"Owen, hurry up. I think someone's coming," I said anxiously.

"Just a couple more," he muttered from the top.

I was squinting into the darkness, trying to anticipate where I'd see the next flicker of light, when Owen cursed and I felt the ladder lurch out of my hands. I looked up to see him dangling from a branch, thank God, instead of plummeting to the earth. The ladder teetered precariously for one heart-stopping moment—and then toppled over and crashed to the ground.

Shit. I glanced over my shoulder to see not just one, but two flashlights now, side by side, like a pair of unblinking eyes. They were still too far away to catch us in their beams, but they were unmistakably heading toward us.

After several seconds of frantic struggle, I got the ladder vertical. Then I had to walk it forward, pivoting clumsily from one leg to the other. Pivot, plant; pivot, plant. I glanced up and saw the two flashlights bobbing, coming ever closer. Pivot, plant; pivot, plant.

"Jeezus, fuck! CJ, the ladder! Hurry!"

"I *am* hurrying!"

Finally, I got the ladder close enough for Owen to swing himself over to it and come scrambling down. Once Owen was back on the ground, we each grabbed an end of the ladder, threw a last backward glance toward the advancing pair of flashlights, and took off running.

And now here we are. Owen and I aren't exactly well matched in speed or strength, and—probably the biggest obstacle to a well-coordinated sprint for our lives—we don't have matching memories of the path we took to get to the Monterey pine grove in the first place. I'm sure we have to veer slightly to the left, but Owen keeps screaming (no point in trying to be stealthy anymore, as galumphing across the fairway of the fifth hole in the pouring rain with a giant ladder in your arms is not an endeavor that lends itself readily to stealth) that we need to push farther to the right. I'm starting to imagine—or maybe it's real—the voices of the security guards shouting at us: "STOP! You with the ladder!"

"There it is!" pants Owen from the back as the van finally comes into view—about a hundred yards to the right of where I'm headed. Dammit.

We execute a clumsy course correction, stagger up a steep hill to the chain link fence surrounding the property, and collapse the ladder back down to its original eight feet. Owen shimmies through the muddy gap under the fence and then turns around and drags the ladder through as well. Then it's my turn. The flashlights are coming closer, but we should have time to escape before the guards get a good look. As Owen lugs the ladder to the van and throws open the back doors, I slide under the fence.

And then I stop. My backpack, bulging with pine cones, has caught on one of the steel links, and now I'm stuck, facedown in the mud. I tug, I pull, I squirm, but I can't move backward or forward. Why, oh why didn't I think to take it off first? I try to wriggle out of the backpack, but I can't twist my body to free my shoulders of the straps.

"Owen! Help!" I'm so wet, I have to blink the water out of my eyes, but I can just see the flashlights. They'll be on us in a minute. The engine starts. I thrash like a fish in a net, one last desperate effort to free myself. Through the swirling haze of my panic, I have one clear thought: *We're going to get caught because of Hannah and her damn flower magic.*

But then a hand is unbuckling my left strap and Owen's voice is urging me to scooch out. Suddenly free to move, I push myself through the rest of the gap and leap into the passenger seat. Moments later, Owen appears in the driver's seat, tosses the backpack in my lap, and we're off. I look in the side-view mirror to check on our pursuers, but I don't see anything. We're safe.

16

A COUPLE OF BLOCKS LATER, OWEN SLOWS DOWN and backs into an unpaved alley between two properties, bound on one side by a high redwood fence and on the other by an oleander hedge, all of it sheltered by a large Monterey pine. How ironic. He cuts the engine and turns off the lights. Rain drips onto the windshield of the car. My heart is still thundering in my chest.

"Do you think they called the cops?" I ask. "Do you think they saw the van?"

"God, I hope not." He takes a deep breath. "Let's wait ten more minutes, and then we'll bring our ill-gotten gains back to the shop."

"Sounds good."

Owen looks at me and grins. "You're a mess."

I can't help grinning back. "So are you." I'm feeling a little euphoric after that narrow escape, if you want to know the truth.

"When that ladder fell, I thought for sure I was going to plunge to my death," he says.

"Oh, I know."

"No, seriously. My hands were slipping off the branch."

"Holy shit." I shudder. How awful would it have been if he'd fallen? I don't even want to think about it.

"Yeah."

"I kinda saved your life, then, huh? Doesn't that mean you have to serve me forever until you repay the debt, or something?" I smile at him, and then I wish I hadn't. I don't know if it's the close quarters, or the adrenaline, or even the rain, but this is starting to feel like flirting, and I don't want him to get the wrong idea.

"Does saving your ass when you got stuck under the fence count as repaying the debt?"

It doesn't, not if we're being literal. But I'm glad for the opportunity to kill the flirty joke about how he owes me a lifetime of service, so I say, "I suppose. I guess we're even, then."

"Even." He nods, then says, "You know, we make a good team."

"Or a terrible one."

"None of that, none of that. We make an excellent team. Put 'er there, partner." Owen extends his muddy hand, and

I shake it, despite how incredibly corny this feels, and then I have about seventeen feelings at once, among them: *Wow, he has really strong hands. But he is such a dork. But he is kind of cute, though, Emily's right. What the fuck; where is all of this coming from? Stop, it's just the adrenaline from the chase. But what if it's not? It totally is. But what if it's not?*

I'm working myself into an internal frenzy when I realize we haven't let go of each other's hands, and I look up and see Owen smiling at me—holy shit, is that a let's-be-more-than-friends kind of smile?—and then I panic and drop his hand like it's poison, which is reassuring, actually, because it's now obvious that I am *not* interested in him, so I can calm down, for God's sake.

Owen reaches into my backpack, pulls out a couple of pine cones, and regards them thoughtfully, gently tapping them together. I worry that he's going to say something more about us being partners, but thankfully, he changes the subject. "I wonder if maybe Hannah would make more money if she was more flexible on the flower-magic thing. She'd save money on supplies and she wouldn't have to pay her assistants to drive all over the peninsula for a couple of pine cones."

He doesn't mention the fact that both of us are working for free, which is nice of him. What would he say if he knew we were way past worrying about saving a few bucks on flowers here, or a few hours of work there?

"Maybe if the ad thing works out and she gets more clients,

we could mention that to her," he says. "What do you think?"

I should tell him. "Yeah, about that . . ."

"Hey, so my mom says we should have caviar pie for the anniversary sale," he says. "That was a thing in the seventies, apparently. Isn't that weird?"

"My mom said she might sell Heart's Desire to McAllister Venture Capital," I blurt. And I tell him the whole story.

"Damn," he says. "What are we gonna do about it?" We. He's put himself on our team without even thinking about it. I could hug him for that.

"I don't know. I was all fired up about it right after she told us, but . . . it just feels so big. I mean, they're the freaking *McAllisters*. Where do we even start?"

"There has to be something. You could tell someone. Or get the community involved. Or do a fund-raiser or something."

"What community? This is just between us and them. Anyway, my mom doesn't want us to tell anyone."

"Why not?"

"I dunno. Probably because it could mess up the deal . . ." Oh.

One of the many superstar things that Mom does is mentor other women. I've heard her on the phone, strategizing with them about how to negotiate a deal, how to hire and fire people, how to make themselves heard at meetings full of men: Know more than everyone else. Be careful about what you share and who you share it with. Own your power, and don't apologize for demanding respect. Control the narrative.

I think I know how we can control the narrative.

After presenting Hannah with those accursed pine cones back at Heart's Desire, we tell her about our idea.

"What if we went to the *Mercury News*, or KRON, and told them about what's happening? It would be a great story." I put my hands up to frame an imaginary headline: "Rich racist cheats local family out of property; family struggles and succeeds in buying it back; racist takes it all away again."

"That's perfect!" cries Hannah.

"Kind of long, though, don't you think?" Owen jokes. Ha ha. I make a face at him.

"But the concept is perfect," says Hannah. "It's local, it's topical, and everybody loves family drama. And it's terrible press for McAllister. And free advertising for us. CJ, you've saved the day!"

"It's all about controlling the narrative," I say sweetly.

Hannah cackles. "This is a total Mimi move. She'd be so proud of you. And here I thought you were more like me." I don't know how to feel about that. This *is* a total Mom move. Do I want to be like her? And is going to the press behind Mom's back—after she explicitly told us to keep things quiet—something to be proud of?

By the time we finish the email to Geoffrey Acosta at the *Merc*, Hannah is positively gleeful, but I'm starting to have second thoughts. As I re-read it for the last time, though, I remember that we're sending this email because of the move that Mom pulled on us in the first place. That's it. I decide to be proud of myself.

"All right," I say. "Send it."

17

MOM'S ANNOUNCEMENT OF WHAT SHE CALLS her contingency plan has made being at home super stressful. Mom and Hannah seem to have come to some kind of agreement not to fight in front of me again, but that doesn't mean they're getting along. It's like they're constantly circling the ring, ready to strike; when the opportunity arises, they lunge at each other with a few sharp, stabby, passive-aggressive comments, and then retreat to their corners once they remember I'm there.

Work hasn't been much better: Hannah made a few calls to places like the Japanese American Citizens League to see if they'd donate money to help out a historic Japanese American business, but since our problems are really more personal than civic, they declined to get involved. And since Mom poked holes in the anniversary-sale idea, Hannah has kind of dropped the whole thing. Even the fact that I'm free tonight is tempered by the fact that we don't have a wedding to prep for tomorrow. The email to the *Merc* feels like our only hope. It's been a full week since we've sent it, and with every day that passes, I feel my optimism wilt a little.

All of which is to say thank goodness I'm going to the OUTlet mixer. It'll feel nice to leave all that stress behind and focus on being Emily's wingwoman for a few hours.

Earlier this week, I hit upon the idea of a silver locket for Em to wear tonight. Inside, I've put the dried petals of all the things that feel right: a couple of tiny primrose lilac blossoms for confidence, pink rose petals for friendship (bonus: pink rosebuds stand for new love, so the petals could really go either way), purple rose petals for enchantment, and I even raided Hannah's herb cabinet for a pinch of southernwood, which is supposed to make people vivacious and—if you believe the books—sexy. Em is wearing the locket around her neck on a narrow silver satin ribbon, fiddling with it as we pull into the parking lot of Quinlan Community Center in Cupertino. As we approach the building, Emily starts fussing with her blouse, an emerald-green off-the-shoulder tie-front that I got her for her birthday last year. She pulls the shoulders up, then back down again, ties the tie, loosens it, and then starts the process over.

"Em, you look fine," I tell her. "Calm down. It's gonna be fun."

"I know." But she keeps fidgeting with her clothes.

We check in and head over to the snack table. We're surveying the chip selection and debating the relative merits of Ruffles (me) versus SunChips (Em) when a hand reaches between us and taps Em on the shoulder.

"Emily!"

We both turn toward the speaker, who is none other than Brynn, looking perky and athletic and just all around large and in charge.

"Oh—hey!" says Emily. Her cheeks flush, and her hand goes to her locket.

Oh no. I did *not* spend all my time on that thing for Brynn.

"Hey! I'm so glad you came!" Brynn looks at me with slightly less enthusiasm and adds, exclamation mark intact, "Hey, CJ!"

"Hey."

"Are you here as an ally, or . . . ?"

I want to give her a cold stare, but I don't have the guts. So I stumble my way through an answer. "Oh. No. I mean. Yes, but. Well. I'm here as her friend."

"Oh, okay. I didn't want to assume anything!" Then she peers at Emily's face and says, "Hey, you look amazing. That shirt really brings out your eyes." She sounds so sincere—she even looks a little bit shy—that I feel my animosity waver for a moment. Maybe I should give Brynn a chance. Maybe she has changed.

"Oh. Uh, thanks," says Em.

"It's not your usual look, is it?" It is, in fact, slightly dressier than her usual look. But we all know that's not what Brynn really means. I *knew* she hadn't changed.

"Uh . . ." says Emily, not sure how to respond.

"I think she looks amazing no matter what she wears," I say, emboldened by Brynn's rudeness.

Brynn's eyes open wide, as if she's just figured out what she said. Right. "Ohhh, shit! I mean—"

"It's fine," Emily mumbles.

"Oh God, I'm such an idiot." Brynn winces and squeezes her eyes shut. "I should've stopped while I was ahead, huh?" Then she opens her eyes and says, "I'm sorry, I totally fucked up. CJ's right. You do look amazing, no matter what you wear. It's just that you look especially great in that shirt." And smiles her patented dazzling smile.

I can feel Emily's defenses crumbling. Heck, mine are crumbling. Only Brynn could make a backhanded compliment like that, laugh it off, and still come out ahead. She should teach classes.

A grown-up materializes out of nowhere and says, "Excuse me, ladies, I need to borrow Brynn for a moment."

"Right, right!" She nods at him, then turns back to us. "Hey, I'm so glad you guys came! I'll talk to you later, 'kay?"

She waves, and we watch her as she strides off, nodding vigorously at whatever the chaperone is saying. She's full of vigor.

I say, "Holy shit, Em."

"Yeah."

I add a drop of bitch to my voice and mimic Brynn: "'That's not your usual look, is it?'"

Emily shrugs and looks at Brynn, who's still nodding vigorously. "I don't think she meant it that way."

"Emily."

"She apologized, didn't she? And said that thing about . . ."

"You looking amazing?"

Em nods.

"I don't know. She seems pretty much like the same old Brynn for President to me."

"Yeah, maybe." She plays absently with a lock of hair, her gaze still focused on Brynn across the room. "But, CJ . . ."

"Em. What's going on?"

Em groans and covers her face. "I don't know. I thought I was over her."

"Please don't tell me she's the reason we're here."

"No. Maybe. I don't know," says Em through her hands. "I was just . . . I can't help it if I feel that way about her." She drops her hands and faces me. "Is it really that big of a deal? Why do you care so much?"

"Because I'm your friend, and because she's toxic." I don't know why she can't see that. "And because there are so many girls here who'd be better for you than her," I add, to try to get her to smile.

"I'm not here just to find a girlfriend," she says irritably.

"No. You're right. You're here to meet new people. So let's not talk about Brynn. Let's find someone new and interesting."

The adults take over and separate us into groups for a few rounds of icebreakers, after which we're released for a snack break. I've ended up in a corner on the opposite side of the room from Emily, talking to this really fun girl named Fiona with tight dark curls and thick lashes and a tiny rosebud mouth who talks a mile a minute and loves fantasy novels. She'd be perfect for Emily. I bring her over to introduce her. "Hey, Em, this is Fiona. You know what? I'm starving. You guys stay here and I'll get some food for all of us."

I go to the snack table and take my time loading up on chips and veggies. I bloop some ranch dressing next to a pile of baby carrots and a mountain of chips, and I'm just turning to go when I see Owen walk in the door with Will Taylor from *Weekly History Minute*. *Oh, right,* I think. *He has the night off, too.*

But mostly I'm thinking, *Well, well, well.*

What did Owen say about having a boyfriend or girlfriend when Hannah asked him that first time we met? *Neither, at the moment.* Interesting. I take a bite of a chip and watch them for clues. Are they boyfriends? Friends? Not that I even care whether he's dating right now.

I check out Emily and Fiona; Em's laughing hysterically at a story that Fiona's telling. Brynn is on the other side of the room, deep in conversation with a gorgeous Latinx girl whose aura of self-confidence and general awesomeness indicate that she's probably a #winner at whatever school she goes to. Brynn glances over at Emily and Fiona twice but doesn't move. Good.

I'm deciding what to do next when Owen sees me. His face

breaks into a big smile, and he waves. I raise my plate-o'-chips-'n'-carrots in greeting and walk over.

Owen gestures at Will and says, "Hey, this is Will."

Okay. That was unhelpful. Is Owen single or is he taken? NOT THAT I CARE, BECAUSE I DON'T. As I'm wrestling with this, we're joined by a guy with dark brown skin, close-cropped hair, and a body like a barrel, who introduces himself as Will's boyfriend, Sam.

"Look at those guys over there." Sam nods in the direction of some certifiably hot boys. "Whaddaya say, O?"

"Nah, he's good," Will says with a half grin and a sideways glance at Owen. "There's this girl he's kinda into these days."

These days?

"Oooh! Pray, tell me more!" says Sam, articulating my exact thoughts.

"Nothing to tell at the moment," says Owen, reddening. He scowls at Will, and his hand strays to the back of his neck.

Will's grin becomes a smirk, and he elbows Owen in the ribs. "C'mon, O. You can tell us. This is a safe space."

"Whatever, punk." Owen shoves Will, who shoves him back, and when Owen shoves Will back again, Will stumbles into Sam, who shoves Will back into Owen, who shoves Sam, who shoves him, and then, as if in response to some kind of secret signal that only they can hear, they all stop shoving each other and start straightening out their shirts. I swear. I really don't get guys sometimes.

Will turns to me and asks, "So what the hell is wrong with

you, CJ? What are you doing with Ruffles on your plate when there are perfectly good SunChips on the table?"

"I like Ruffles," I say.

"You can't like Ruffles," says Sam. "It's not allowed. Not if you want to be friends with us."

"Hmm," I say, crunching a delicious chip. "Ruffles"—I hold one up and contemplate it—"or you guys. This could be tough."

"I recommend the Ruffles," Owen stage-whispers near my ear, putting his hand on my shoulder. "Those bozos are not a wise choice."

"You're a Ruffles person?" I ask.

"What, you're surprised? Aren't all decent people Ruffles people?"

"My friend Emily is Team SunChips," I tell Will and Sam. "She's just as deluded as you guys. See her?" I turn to face the spot where I left Emily and Fiona. "She's that girl with the brown hair, talking with that cute curly-haired girl over—"

Wait. That's not how I left them.

There's Emily playing with her hair and smiling politely. There's Fiona, also smiling politely. Neither of them are talking, though, because there's a third person there who's doing all the talking. A tall, athletic girl with long auburn hair.

Brynn. The Latinx girl she was talking to earlier is now holding hands with an Asian girl on the couch, totally forgotten.

God. I turn my back for one minute.

"Hang on a sec. I'll just get her and bring her over."

I put my plate down and hurry over to Emily. "Hey, Em!" I call. "Fiona!" All three of them look over at me, and I could swear that Brynn tenses up.

I take Emily's hand and motion for Fiona to follow us.

"I just need Em and Fiona for a sec. Very important chip-related business." I smile and give Brynn what I hope looks like a casual nod.

Okay, I know it's disrespectful and rude. But she deserves to be on the receiving end of a little disrespect every once in a while. It's good for her.

In the car on the way home, Emily and I do a postmortem of the evening.

"So. You did it, Em! Total success."

"Yeah, right? Your flower magic worked!"

"It wasn't the flowers. It was you being you. Did you get Fiona's number? You'd make a great couple."

"Oh my god, Ceej," she groans.

"What? I'm sorry, who's always all, 'I'm sick of being single'?"

"Whatever. Jeez."

"Did you get her number, though?"

"Maybe."

"*Yes.*" I hold up my palm for a high five and she slaps it, blushing. This is great.

"But mostly it was nice to hang with other queer kids, like, in real life."

I nod. Again—so great.

Em yawns, then smiles at me. "Thanks for having my back, Ceej. You're the best, friend."

"So are you, friend." I could not be happier for her. She's got a new community, a new (potential) girlfriend—everything we could have hoped for.

Em's staying over tonight, and we drive the rest of the way home in comfortable, dreamy silence. As we pull into the driveway, though, I have to make sure about one thing. "Hey, I'm sorry I left you stranded with Brynn. Why didn't you text me or something? I would have rescued you a lot earlier."

I meant it as a joke, but Emily takes me seriously. She looks out the window and says, "God, Ceej, it's not like she's going to ask me out. I don't think she likes me that way. I mean . . . What do you think?"

Oh, Emily. "I don't know, and I don't care. For the millionth time, there are way better girls out there for you."

"Yeah."

"Fiona, for one." I know it's pushy. But seriously. How hard has Emily been pushing me and Owen? In fact, I'm surprised she hasn't mentioned him.

"Yeah." Em smiles just a little, like she can't help it. A thrill of vicarious excitement zings through me, and I smile, too. She deserves a good girlfriend.

Emily falls asleep almost immediately on the air mattress next to my bed, and I'm just about to do the same, when a question we haven't addressed floats through my head: Who is the girl Owen is into, though?

What if it's me?

I don't know what I'll do if it's me.

I hope it's not.

Right? Because I don't like him that way.

No, really. I really don't.

18

E: Guess who's going to Golfland with someone she met at

OUTlet

THIS GIRL

CJ: Yesssssssss, I knew it 🙌

Em and Fiona

Sitting in a tree

K

I

S

S

I

N

G

💋 💋 💋 💋

Now if only my life would follow suit. Shane and I finally started texting, but there's been no invitation to do anything or go anywhere in person. Though in some ways, online is more my speed. I have time to think of funny things to say, I can send memes and emojis when I can't think of funny things to say, I don't have to worry if my breath stinks or if my hair looks weird or if he's grossed out by the giant zit on my chin.

So instead of going out with Shane, I'm at Pizza My Heart sharing a Figgy Piggy pizza (bacon, figs, sage, and feta—it's an acquired taste but once you've acquired it, it's addictive) with Emily and Owen after work, talking about Emily's burgeoning love life.

"It was the flower magic, Ceej."

"It was most definitely not."

"Coulda been, though," says Owen.

"I've been wearing the locket every day, and I'm telling you, I am so much more confident and funny with it on. You have to make me another one for Golfland." She gasps. "You should make them for everyone! Like a business, like on Etsy."

"I dunno. Do you think people would buy that stuff?"

"I'm buying it, aren't I?"

"You're my friend. And you're desperate." Em throws a fig at me and I add, "Okay, sorry, that wasn't nice."

"Brynn sells her photography through Etsy," says Em. "I could, you know, I could text her about it and see if she could give you some advice."

I don't know whether I'm more shocked that Brynn has an Etsy business (is there *anything* that girl doesn't do?) or that Em has Brynn's number. I look at her. She blushes and says, "She gave me her number at the mixer."

I give her a hard stare. "Really?"

Em shrugs. "It's nothing."

I can sense Owen watching our exchange with interest, but he remains silent, thank goodness. I may have told him a little more than was advisable at the mixer—okay, I told him everything—about how little patience I have for Brynn.

Well, whatever; Em's been giddy with excitement about Fiona, so maybe the Brynn thing really is Brynn-initiated nothingness. Anyway, Emily and Owen are all fired up about the Etsy-style flower-magic business venture, and the more we talk, the more I feel like maybe they're right. Maybe this could be my thing. "I could do custom bouquets for Valentine's Day, or do lucky flowers for promposals, or prom, even," I say. "I could have my own, like, student line of flower magic."

"Look who believes," says Em, patting my shoulder.

"If it'll make money, I'll believe in it," I say. And then I wish I hadn't, because I'm thinking about making money for myself, not for Heart's Desire. Not that it would be nearly enough to make a difference, let alone save the store, but still. Saving Heart's Desire should be my first priority.

"You should make a flower-magic locket for yourself and go talk to Shane at lunch someday," says Em, which stops me for a second. All she ever talks about is how I should go out with Owen.

"Ha ha, right. I think not."

"Shane Morgan?" asks Owen, and I think I might die of embarrassment from the look of incredulity on his face. Like he's thinking, *CJ? With Shane? What reality does she live in that makes her think that's even possible?*

"They've been texting like crazy," says Emily. "With the occasional Snapchat and Instagram. They have a seven-day streak going." I kick her under the table and she kicks me right back.

"Seven days," says Owen with a grin. "Impressive."

"Shut up. We only just started texting, anyway. You don't have to be a jerk about it," I say, annoyed at . . . Owen? Emily? Myself? Because I'm . . . embarrassed? I realize that I kind of didn't want Owen to know about Shane; except why, why, why do I even care what he thinks?

"I'm not being a jerk," he protests.

"You are."

I turn to Em to back me up, but she excuses herself to go to the bathroom, saying, "I'll let you two work things out." It's becoming clear to me why she brought up Shane. Some friend.

"I'm just surprised that you'd be into him, that's all," Owen says. "He doesn't seem like your type."

"And what do you know about my type?"

Owen shrugs. "Not much, apparently."

"Anyway, there's nothing wrong with Shane."

"No, I know. He's cool, I guess."

"You think I could never get a guy like that."

Owen looks offended. "I totally think you could 'get a guy like that.'" There's a sarcastic undertone to his voice to go with the air quotes, and I'm even more annoyed. "You're smart; you're talented; you're interesting . . ." He trails off. "So, yeah. You're a catch."

"I notice you didn't say 'pretty.'"

What. Even. What the hell is wrong with me? I'm about to tell Owen that I'm kidding, I don't care if anyone thinks I'm pretty, I'm not that shallow, but before I can, he says, "Seriously? Okay, you're pretty."

"I was just kidding."

"No, you weren't."

"Yes, I was."

Owen taps a piece of crust on his plate and says, "Look. Shane Morgan's a nice guy, but he's . . . Well, let's just say that if he's interested in you, it's because he thinks you're pretty. So now you know."

To be 100 percent embarrassingly honest, I actually think I am kind of pretty. I like my face: my eyes are so dark, they're almost black; I have deep dimples on both cheeks, I have a cute nose. Is that conceited? I mean, I don't think I'm gorgeous like Sabrina or Brynn. I'm not fishing for compliments to make myself feel good. I literally don't think looks should matter at all. Only. I guess they do. I *do* want Shane to think I'm pretty. And hearing Owen say I'm pretty enough for Shane is making me happier than I want it to. Which makes me mad at Owen, which isn't fair, but there it is. Asshole. He thinks Shane is shallow. Worse, he thinks *I'm* shallow, and I'm not. There's nothing wrong with being attracted to a person's looks. And just because I'm not looking for my happily-ever-after soul mate doesn't mean that I don't care about what's underneath.

"I don't think Shane's that shallow."

Owen shrugs. "Suit yourself."

"I'm not shallow, either."

"I never said you were."

"You're thinking it, though."

Owen smiles infuriatingly. "You care about what I think?"

"No." God.

"Well, for what it's worth, I don't think you're shallow. I do think you could do better than Shane, but whatever. I could be wrong."

"Hmph."

"And while I'm giving unsolicited advice, I think maybe you could give Brynn a second chance."

"Or you could stop giving me unsolicited advice."

"I just think maybe you're being a little . . . judgmental." Which—I mean, coming from him, that doesn't carry a lot of weight.

"Actions speak louder than words," I say.

"Brynn is president of the QSA. How much louder of an action do you want?"

Did I not tell him everything at the mixer? Was he not listening? "All that means is that she decided it was time to come out. It doesn't erase how she treated Emily, and it doesn't mean that she wouldn't break Em's heart again. I'm sorry if it makes me sound judgmental, but I'm not going to pretend the past didn't happen. She doesn't get to leave her baggage behind."

"Maybe." He looks unconvinced, and it upsets me, because I don't want him to think I'm some kind of thoughtlessly vengeful monster. I have good reasons for how I feel.

"You think I'm being unfair."

He tilts his head, looks at his hands. "I just think life is complicated. And so are people. Especially when you feel like you have to hide who you are. I mean, I've been there. I know."

"And I think you can't go around letting everyone off the hook because 'life is complicated.' I get that she was afraid. But she shouldn't have used Emily to protect herself. And she should have done something to make up for it instead of just pretending nothing ever happened."

I don't know why it's so hard to understand. If you drag someone for being gay, you're a homophobe. If you do it even though you, yourself, are gay—especially when you could just keep your mouth shut—you're a hypocrite. It's that simple. And, while we're talking about defining actions, if you take unfair advantage of someone of a different race and cheat them out of everything they own, you're a racist and a crook. Oh, but she feels bad about it. Oh, but he's a nice guy. Oh, life is complicated.

Nope. I'm sorry, but none of that gets a pass.

19

LIFE *IS* COMPLICATED THOUGH. FOR EXAMPLE, there's the Heart's Desire mess. I get that the smart thing to do would be to sell the property. But it's clear that the ethical, kind, and loving thing to do would be to choose family over money and help Hannah figure out a way for Heart's Desire to succeed. The problem is that Mom only cares about what's smart, and she hates that Hannah only wants what she calls "emotional gratification." I wish there was some middle ground, but that has never been the way we operate.

I've been working in the back of the store most of the afternoon, ruminating on complications and family and what's smart versus what's emotionally gratifying, and I'm ready for a break. I poke my head into the front to see if Owen wants anything from Icicles when the bell rings, and in walks a little boy. He looks about six years old. I bet he's hapa, or what Avi-ana used to call half-and-half when we were little; his face looks Asian, but his hair is light brown, almost blond, and his eyes are hazel. He has a cleft chin, which is something I always notice because I've got a cleft chin, and they're unusual. A white woman appears behind him—his mother, probably. She's model-thin and wearing jeans and high heels and the kind of pure white sweater that I would never trust myself to wear. She looks like a mom version of Taylor Swift.

"Look, Blake! Oh, these are just gorgeous!" she exclaims, click-clacking in her heels around the shop and caressing the blooms with a perfectly manicured hand. When she does, her sleeves fall back a little, and I can see what looks like a diamond bracelet sparkling on her wrist.

She's here to pick up a custom birthday arrangement, which I fetch from the back. She asks for a card, and when she's done filling it out, she hands it to her son, who opens the card and reads, "'To Tom, the love of my life. Happy birthday from your Delia and Blake.'" He looks up and smiles, and two deep dimples appear in his cheeks. Next to me, Owen breathes in sharply and starts coughing. "It's for Dad!" exclaims Blake.

"He's so cute," Owen tells the mom. "Those dimples."

"Oh, how sweet of you to say that. He is pretty cute, isn't he?" She looks fondly down at Blake. "He gets the dimples from his father. He's a carbon copy, really. I mean, right to the core, except for the hair, obviously."

Owen rings her up, and we help her put the arrangement

in the back of her Range Rover. She buckles Blake into his booster seat, and Owen hands him a rose, which Blake accepts with another (dimpled) smile.

"Oh, you're so sweet! Say thank you, Blakey!"

"Thank you," says Blake.

"You're welcome. And happy birthday to your husband, Mrs. . . ."

"Ohara. It's Japanese. Sometimes we pretend it's Irish, though. Ohara, O'Hara, get it? Our nickname for our daughter Aubrey is Scarlett." She laughs: *Aren't we clever!* "Ah, well. Anyway, the flowers are gorgeous. Thanks, guys." She climbs into the driver's seat and waves as she shuts the door.

Wow. Mrs. Ohara was so glamorous and so swimming-in-money wealthy. Maybe she's someone famous. Maybe she's a tech billionaire. Maybe she's book-group friends with Sheryl Sandberg and Susan Wojcicki. If we could start building a clientele base of people like her, maybe Mom would give us a little more time. Dammit. We should have asked her to refer us, or at least review us—she was so plainly taken in by Owen's charms. Such as they are.

On our way inside, Owen steps a little too close to me and bumps me slightly, which feels more like a deliberate gesture than an accident. I sneak a quick look at him, and he catches my eye and immediately looks away.

Once inside the shop, Owen hovers next to me, clearly anxious to say something, so I get a broom and start sweeping to get away from him. After a while, I can't take it anymore.

"What?"

He bites his bottom lip, as if reconsidering telling me anything, like he's trying to trap in his mouth whatever was on the tip of his tongue.

"*What?*"

"Oh. Uh." He clears his throat and rubs the back of his neck. "I was just wondering how you're doing. You okay?"

"Uh . . . yeah? Why are you asking me? Why would I not be okay?"

"Well. I mean. Did you get a good look at that kid? At his chin? And his dimples?"

I recall that gasp I heard when Blake smiled, and suddenly I know what's bothering him. "What, because that's unusual? Because I have dimples and he has dimples? Because his chin looks like mine?"

"Well, yeah. . . ." Owen begins giving the back of his head a scalp massage.

"Oh no."

"He looked just like you, CJ. Like, so much it's kind of freaking me out. Are you telling me you didn't see the resemblance?"

I used to do the same thing to myself all the time. I would gaze at my reflection in the mirror with a childhood picture of Mom in my hand, parsing out which of my features were hers, which might be my father's. I'd examine the face of anyone I saw who had those same non-Mom features: Was this girl my half sibling? Was that old lady my grandmother? Might these random people lead me to my father?

"Lots of people look alike, Owen. You've seen those 'separated at birth' celebrity things online, right? It doesn't mean anything."

"But it might."

I've only told a few people that I don't know who my dad is, and sooner or later, the questions always come: Are you sure? Have you checked this database? Did you know about that test? I'd started to think Owen was different. But he's the same as everyone else. "It doesn't, okay? Hannah gave me a genetic ancestry test for my sixteenth birthday and the only thing we learned is that my dad is 'broadly Western Asian'—and don't tell me I don't *look* mixed, because I'm tired of hearing that. So this Ohara dude is most definitely not my dad."

"Oh. Right. Okay. But what if he's half Western Asian?"

"Owen. I don't think *you're* related to everyone who has, um . . . brown eyes and, and"—I search his face for something I can use—"and a square jaw."

"A square jaw?" He grins a little and checks out his image in his phone, running his finger along his jawline. "You really think so? That's supposed to be a good thing, right?"

"Oh. Uh . . ." Shit. He doesn't think I think he's cute, does he?

Owen looks at me, still grinning. "I was afraid you were going to say 'big ears.'"

I take a closer look, and maybe it's because I'm freaking out about my weird comment about his jaw, but I don't say what I should, which is, "Oh, they're not so big." What I say instead is, "Holy shit, you *do* have big ears. They're like, like—sails!" And then—look, not my proudest moment—the idea of his ears as sails suddenly strikes me as hilarious, and I break into a fit of nervous giggles. "Sorry! I'm sorry!"

"Nice. Thanks, CJ. I make myself vulnerable, and the first thing you do is attack." I think he's smiling, though . . . ? Please let him not be really hurt.

"Sorry," I repeat.

"No, you're not."

"No, I am, really." I can't help it. I stifle another giggle, and Owen sighs and shakes his head.

"Remind me never to open up to you about anything I'm sensitive about, ever again."

"Okay, okay, I'm sorry. I'm sorry. I won't make fun of your ears anymore." I put my hand on his arm. "I promise."

"Thank you."

"They're not so bad, actually. For real. I mean, for ears, they're pretty nice." They are kind of nice, though. For ears. I give his left ear a tiny little pat, to show that I mean it.

"Okay, that was the weirdest compliment ever. But thanks, I think." He's blushing. Which is cute, but oh, crap. I've over-corrected.

To steer us out of Awkward Compliment Land and back to reality, I hand him a dustpan and motion for him to hold it while I finish sweeping. "Anyway," I say, "I only brought it up because if I saw a kid with a jaw like yours, and eyes—"

"Or good-looking ears?" Owen preens, his humor apparently restored. "Like mine?"

I roll my eyes and finish my sentence. "I wouldn't assume you were related. I'm just tired about people guessing my origins, I guess. I get it enough as it is, being biracial. Like why do people want to know? Why does it matter? I don't want to put myself into a cubbyhole with a label on it: Japanese. Indian. Scottish. Ghanaian. I'm not coffee or tea or chocolate. It shouldn't matter where I was sourced."

"Yeah, okay. I get it. That was messed up. I'm sorry."

"It's all right."

"I just—it's that whole happy-ending thing, I guess. I want them for everyone."

I wish "happy ending" didn't have such a narrow gateway: True love. Changed hearts. Reunited families. I doubt that kind of happy ending exists for everyone. But I do know one thing. "I don't need to have a dad to have a happy ending. I mean like, what—what if I found the guy? What then? He's hardly gonna be all, *Oh, yay, I have a teenage daughter I never knew about! I'm going to be the father she never had!* And what does that even mean? The father I never had—that's bullshit. I have my mom, and I have Hannah, too. Plus, plenty of kids have terrible fathers. That's way worse than not having one."

"Fair enough."

Owen stands and empties the dustpan into the garbage, and I put the broom away. A couple wanders in to buy a premade bouquet and Owen takes care of them while I go back to the workroom.

It's true. I'm not ashamed of where I'm from or how I came to be. But I'll admit that it's a painful thing, not knowing who your dad is. I sometimes think Mom blames a lot of my failures on him: my crooked teeth, my complete inability to handle math, my lack of ambition, my aversion to spicy food; because where else could they have come from?

I trusted Mom when she told me that she knew what she was doing when she decided to have me on her own; I still trust her about that. The only thing I'm not sure about anymore is whether Mom thinks she made the right decision.

I guess that's complicated.

The Complicated History of Chisaki Joan Katsuyama's Imaginary Relationship with Her Nonexistent Dad

Before I Was Even Born
Granddad had just died; Mom had just started at McAllister. Mom went out with some B-school classmates and got shit-faced, and a few months later, she learned she was pregnant. Though you know that already.

Five Years Old
Emily's parents got pregnant with her little brother, Tanner, when we were five. She whispered the news to me at my fifth birthday party, as soon as she arrived. When the party was over and Mom and Mrs. Baxter were gossiping at the kitchen table with coffee and two pieces of leftover cake, Emily told me the rest. After breaking the news about her pregnancy, Mrs. Baxter

had sat Emily down and told her all about how the baby had gotten in there, and read her a book about it, complete with illustrations. I still remember the key sentence about "how it happens": "When two people love each other very much, they lie down together in a special way." When Em told me what that special way was, I thought she was lying.

"Is she telling the truth? Is that how I got into your uterus?" I asked Mom that evening when she put me to bed. She replied, after a long pause, that Emily had it about right.

"So I have a father?" I knew a couple of kids with two moms, and it had never occurred to me that a man might have played an integral role in my creation. "Where is he?"

It was a few more seconds before Mom replied. "A lot of people have sex with someone special who they're in love with. And sometimes they have babies and stay together. That's what Emily's parents did."

"I *know* that," I said. "What about *my* father?"

"I'm getting to that, kiddo. Be patient!" Mom closed her eyes and took a deep breath. "Your father . . . couldn't stay. But guess what? That's okay, because I was happy on my own. And anyway, I had Hannah to help me. And, I had you, of course." She kissed me on the forehead and stood up to go. "Okay? That's it, kiddo. Good night. I love you."

"But where did he *go*?" I asked.

Mom sighed and sat down again. "Who knows? All *I* know is that I love my big five-year-old girl, and that's enough for me." After counting out five kisses on my forehead, she gathered me up in her arms and snuggled me. "Is it enough for you?"

It was, for a long time.

Ten Years Old

Hannah used to help me make up stories about my dad. "He was tall and handsome," she'd say, "with golden eyes and hair the color of black tea."

Sometimes he was an astronaut visiting the NASA Ames Research Center in Mountain View. Sometimes he was a chef looking to open a restaurant in San Francisco. Once he was a time-traveling Viking disguised as a librarian. But he was always kind, generous, clever, and immensely talented at whatever it was he did. Sometimes he knew about me, and sometimes he didn't, but he always had some cosmic connection to me—he'd see a field of flowers and feel a tug at his heart, or read about me when I became famous, and smile without knowing why.

Then one morning, Mom walked in on Hannah and me in the kitchen. We had decided that my dad was an entrepreneur who was visiting Silicon Valley to pitch the Next Big Thing, and then decided to give it all up to go home to Australia to take care of his ailing granny and her kangaroo ranch.

Mom chased Hannah out, and then sat down across from me at the table with a cup of black coffee. "Listen, kiddo," she said. "I'm telling you this now because you're grown up enough to hear it. Are you ready?"

My heart sped up. Finally, I was going to hear the real story. I nodded, too excited to speak.

Mom took a slow breath and said, "The man who is your father is not going to come back for you, okay? He just isn't. And you need to accept that. Making up stories about him might make you feel better, but it's not going to make him magically appear."

That hit me so hard I almost couldn't breathe.

"Does he even know I exist?" I whispered.

Mom looked out the window and took a long sip of her coffee. "No."

I don't know what my face looked like, but I know that Mom looked at me and added quickly, "But that doesn't matter. Because I chose to have you without him. You don't need a dad to be happy, or successful, or any of those things, CJ."

"Were you in love with each other?"

Another sip of coffee. Another long look, this time at her coffee mug, wrapped in her two hands. Finally, she said, "'Love' is a strong word, kiddo. Don't believe everything Hannah says about it. You're here, and I'm here, and we love each other, and that's all that matters."

She refused to say any more on the subject, and I never asked her about it again.

20

I KNOW THAT MY FATHER DOESN'T LOVE ME. That he doesn't know I exist. I know that Mom has no idea where he is and no desire to find him, and I've learned to live with that.

But one thing I've never quite been able to let go of, despite how badly things could turn out, is the fantasy of finding him myself. I suppose I can blame Hannah and her stories for that. And now Owen and his death grip on happy endings for all.

"Aren't you even a *little* curious about him?" he kept asking as we closed up the shop. Mrs. Ohara and Blake had been gone for hours, but he couldn't stop talking about it.

"Of course I am," I snapped at him. "But I told you it's pointless."

"Just ask," said Owen as he locked the front door. "Maybe

she's been waiting for you to be old enough to handle it."

"She's still pissed at me for taking Hannah's side about selling the shop. She's not going to tell me anything."

"It's been two weeks. She can't still be mad at you."

I thought about it in the car on the way home, and all through dinner. It would be nice not to have half my entire family shrouded in mystery. It would be nice to know *something* about my dad. I bet it would help explain a lot about me and all the ways I'm different from Mom.

So after I finish helping Hannah with the dinner dishes and before I start my homework, I knock on Mom's office door.

"What's up, CJ?" Mom saves whatever she's been working on, closes the laptop, and swivels around in her chair. "What do you need?"

She's doesn't seem angry. Maybe Owen was right.

I start with a long windup about the time when we went out to Tomi Sushi and I couldn't handle the uni that she'd ordered for me. I'd reminded her that I'd tried it before and that I didn't like it.

"Just try a bite," she'd said. "You have to develop your palate. You can't go around refusing to eat things because you think you remember a time when you didn't like it."

I'd managed to choke down one bite. As I chased it with big gulps of water, Mom had frowned at me as if I had chosen to hate raw sea urchin out of sheer orneriness.

"Remember that?" I say, and she nods.

"You ready to try it again?" she asks with a smile, and I

almost wish we could just stop the conversation here, where it's safe.

I shudder. "No. But I was thinking. Maybe it's hereditary. How I don't like uni. Like how some people taste cilantro differently."

One eyebrow twitches, and she uncrosses and then recrosses her legs. Swivels around to face her desk, and then back to face me. She says, "What exactly are you asking me?"

"I just. I just wish you'd tell me who my father is," I say quickly. "I'm old enough to know. I can take it."

Mom exhales slowly, her eyes closed. Thinking about what to tell me, maybe. After a long silence, she opens her eyes and says, "Hon, I'm sorry, but I really, truly don't know."

Impossible. "How can you not know?"

Another sigh, and she looks longingly back at her laptop for a moment before she says, "I was a little out of character that night, Ceej. Granddad was dead, Hannah was pissed at me, I was working my ass off at MVC . . . I was a mess. I wasn't using my best judgment."

"Well, duh."

"The truth is, CJ, I didn't know who he was to begin with."

I feel like I've caught a cannonball in my arms. I stagger around with it, trying to find my footing. "What even . . . does that mean? Are you saying you don't even know his *name*? You didn't even get his *phone number*?"

She shakes her head. "I'm sorry."

"How could you be so irresponsible?" I hear the shrill note

of accusation in my voice, and I'm aware of the hypocrisy in calling *her* irresponsible. But I have to blame someone.

"What do you want me to say, CJ? I said I was sorry, didn't I? I told you I wasn't using my best judgment." I can hear the mounting irritation in her voice, and it pierces me. I'll never know. It's her fault. And she's sitting here all, *Yeah, I fucked up, get over it.*

I gather my memories of a similar conversation from last year, when I was pregnant, and fling them back at her. "You weren't using *any* judgment, sounds like." I hope that hurts.

Mom's expression closes up, shuts me out. She takes a beat before she says tightly, "Nope. You're right. No judgment at all, CJ. All my fault, no one else's. Stupid, stupid Mom." She closes her eyes again, rubs her temples. When she opens her eyes, her expression is softer, her eyes pleading. "But I hope I've made up for it since then. I got pregnant by mistake, but I had you on purpose. Okay? I wish I could tell you more, but I can't."

The dense, hot anger inside me dissipates and then coagulates into something new and unwieldy, and I realize with a shock that it's grief. I'm surprised at how sad I am, both at the frayed messiness of this loose end that will drag behind me forever, and at the hard finality of the fact I've gone as far as I can go with this question. The answer is over, it's done, it's buried forever in the past. I will never know any more about my father than I do now.

I try to go back to being angry at her lack of judgment, and at her hypocrisy about my lack of judgment last year. I try being upset about the unfairness of her expecting so much of me my whole life when I am literally the living embodiment of her giant fuckup. But that backfires: is that how she sees me?

Mom stands and gestures for me to come over. So I do, and she wraps her arms around me. It's an odd, unsettling feeling, standing here like a little girl, loving my mom and resenting her at the same time, wanting simultaneously to offer up my grief and to hoard the tangled roots of my anger.

I wish she knew who he was. I wish things hadn't happened the way they happened. I wish I could be 100 percent angry with her for all the things—for getting drunk and pregnant with a guy she doesn't even remember, for constantly nagging at me to be better at everything, for wanting to sell the thing that matters most to me to the family who betrayed us. I wish I could be 100 percent okay with everything and proud of her the way I used to be when I was little. I don't know why it matters. All I know is that I hate this in-between feeling.

21

AFTER NEARLY TWO WEEKS OF SILENCE, WE finally got an email and a phone call from Geoffrey Acosta from the *Merc*. He's dropping in today with a photographer to interview and take photos of us as we work. Geoffrey thinks this article will "galvanize the community" to take action, and Hannah is delirious with visions of a big community fundraiser that will put our financial woes behind us.

I am not quite as excited. This is because "as we work" is taking place half-past butt thirty on Sunday morning. The sun hasn't even come up yet, and I'm at Heart's Desire, weaving the last of the garlands that will hang from the railings and banisters at the Los Altos Hills mansion where the Feda-Chan wedding and reception will be held late this afternoon. Hannah's prepping the bouquets and boutonnieres for the wedding party.

Usually Hannah books only one wedding per weekend, but early in the scramble to prove Mom wrong about the money situation, she took on a few last-minute clients, which we're committed to despite the fact that she seems to be depending entirely on the news article, rather than the extra business, to save us. This one is a shotgun wedding, which if you ask me, is just asking for trouble. It's also asking for two early weekend mornings in a row—one for yesterday's wedding, and one for today's. I might be just the tiniest bit resentful of the whole situation, especially since Shane texted me last night that his mom asked him to drop by Sweet Emily's this afternoon to pick up a cake and did I want to meet him there—but, of course, I will be draping flower garlands in Los Altos Hills by then. Owen's just brought over coffee and fresh-baked scones from Sweet Emily's, and if today's early morning wakeup doesn't kill me, the irony will.

Today, he's wearing a T-shirt that reads:

If there's anything that the lessons of history have taught us,
   it's that people haven't learned the lessons of history.

Tell that to today's couple. Most shotgun weddings end in divorce. But everyone thinks that history doesn't apply to them, that they're the ones who can buck the trend, that they're special, somehow. So here we are.

At least Mom knew better than to get married.

As I wire one blowsy pink peony after another onto a

central cord, I tell Owen what Mom said about herself and my dad.

"I'm sorry," he says.

"Yeah, well you should be," I reply. "I was perfectly happy before, and now I'm bummed that I'll never know who he was."

"Sorry," he repeats. "But aren't you glad that you know that now? Isn't it better than living in ignorance?"

"No."

He doesn't reply, and I feel a little sorry for being so blunt, but not sorry enough to apologize because gahhh, Owen and his relentless optimism.

We're close to being finished when Geoffrey and Keila Padilla, the photographer, arrive to interview Hannah. Keila takes a million pictures while Geoffrey guzzles coffee and takes notes as Hannah gives him the history of the store, tells stories about my grandparents, and explains what the store has meant to the community.

"That guy was such trash. I hate that we have to go to a *school* named after him," Owen mutters to me, disgust and disbelief amplifying his voice.

"You're telling *me*?" I say.

Geoffrey overhears him. "You two go to McAllister?"

We nod.

"Well, then you'll be interested in what I learned yesterday."

"What?" I ask.

Geoffrey winks. "I'll send you the link to the article when it's live."

"Aw, come on. Tell us," Owen pleads.

"Let's just say it goes way beyond the flower shop," says Geoffrey, and that is as much as we can get out of him. I hate it when people are coy about news, especially when the news turns out to be nothing at all. But this sounds like it could be big.

A few hours later, Emily stops by as we're loading the van to take our floral bounty to the Feda home. She's brought us a dozen lemon sugar cookies this time (my second favorite after snickerdoodles) to trade for more petals to wear in her locket to her Golfland date with Fiona later today. I'm using dried and crushed purple rose petals for enchantment and a pinch of southernwood from Hannah's herb cabinet for charming banter—both of those seemed to work last time—and added a sprig of heather for good luck.

Emily looks so excited and nervous, it's contagious, and as I hang the locket around her neck I feel a rush of something so powerful I could almost believe that it's magic. I just know this date is going to go well for her. I mean obviously I don't *know*. But I have a good feeling about it. I haven't felt this relaxed around her in a while, and I'm so filled with joy at having our old friendship back that I can't help giving her a hug.

"I put in everything you'll need. Good luck. You got this."

She shakes the locket at me, gives it a kiss, and tucks it into her shirt. "Flower magic. I can feel it already."

"Though just promising her a couple of cookies would probably be effective, too."

"I've got a bag of six in my car."

"Then you're all set. Where are you going?"

"Golfland, then a movie at AMC Saratoga, and then . . ." Em clears her throat and picks up a stray stem from the work-table and twirls it between her palms. "I'm not sure."

"Sexyfuntimes?" I do my best to waggle my eyebrows, but I've never been good at that. I have a feeling they just go up and stay there and make me look surprised.

"Shut up! I would never . . . Not on the first date, anyway," says Em, blushing.

"Okay, okay." I hug her again. "Go. Have fun. Remember to be yourself. Don't drink and drive."

"Thanks, Mom. I'll text you later." And she disappears out the door.

By four o'clock in the afternoon, we're putting the finish-ing touches on the arrangements at the Feda mansion, which is on five posh acres of premium real estate in Los Altos Hills. Even Mom was impressed when Hannah told her she was doing this wedding; Obsaa Feda came from Ethiopia as a child with virtually nothing, and now runs a hugely successful AI software company.

Hannah fusses with the flowers on the enormous wedding cake on display in the foyer while Owen and I stroll around the grounds with a checklist. My peony garlands adorn the banisters of the grand staircase inside the house. The view from the covered walkway to an enormous heated tent on the back lawn is partially obscured by more garlands of red chrysanthemums hanging like fringed curtains along the sides. Under the tent, eucalyptus runners stretch across long banquet tables, punctuated by the arrangements of calla lilies we did last night and this morning. Rose petals float in a nearby fountain, and specially procured water lilies bob serenely in the black-bottomed swimming pool.

The bride and her attendants are having their pictures taken, and everyone looks so excited and happy that I can't help hoping that this marriage works out. I catch Owen watching them, too, after he counts the table arrangements and checks them off on his tablet. He's got a goofy little smile on his face, as if he's caught whatever contagious optimism is in the air. Though let's be real: he hasn't caught it. He is optimism incarnate.

He turns and catches me watching him, and suddenly I am aware that I have a goofy little smile on *my* face. *It's not for you!* I want to shout. *It's* about *you and how ridiculous you are!* But it's too late. He grins back and bows like the big doofy doofus that he is, and I shake my head but I can't stop smiling because, okay. Okay. I might think he's a little bit cute, with his ridiculous, unintentionally punk-rock hair and his stupid square jaw, and funny-looking ears, but that's it. That is it. Really.

Thankfully, this line of thought is cut short by a text from Emily:

E: Golf and movie were

Just chilling rn

It's going well. Flower magic doing its job

I type back, Lol 🌻🖤🌻🖤🌻🖤🌻

Owen comes over just as I send it. "What're you smiling at?" he asks. I show him the text.

"I thought you didn't believe in flower magic," he says.

"I don't. But Em does." I adjust a basket full of flax stems and heather on the altar, which is overflowing with symbolic plants. "I guess I figured it couldn't hurt to give fate a little nudge in the right direction."

"Yeah. I think you're a bigger softie than you let on," he says, but he's wrong.

Twenty minutes later, we've finished checking everything off and putting the supplies and extra materials away. Owen turns to me and says, "Hey. You got anything to do after we're done here?"

I wish I could say I was doing something with Shane, but I haven't heard from him since that text last night, so I shake my head.

"You wanna drive down to the coast? We'll be just in time to catch the sunset."

I do love a good sunset. "Fine," I say.

Owen opens the passenger-side door of his truck with a flourish and a bow—he's got to stop that. "Your chariot awaits." He extends his hand, and I take it and step up into the passenger seat, and he shuts the door behind me. I text

Hannah and tell her I'm leaving with Owen.

"Where are we going?" I ask as he settles into the driver's seat.

"Pigeon Point Lighthouse."

22

NEARLY AN HOUR LATER, WE PULL INTO THE Pigeon Point parking lot off Route 1. The sun is already low in the sky, so we hurry down the path, past the lighthouse, past the old keeper's residence, to the end of the point. We lean on the white picket fence and look northwest, up the coast toward Half Moon Bay and Mavericks Beach.

Owen, being Owen, drops some historical trivia. "Did you know that the Montara lighthouse—that one up past Mavericks—was built in Boston in the 1800s, and it was a light-house on Cape Cod for like, fifty years before they shipped it out to California? Then they used it in San Francisco for a couple of years, and *then* they brought it to Montara. I learned that on a field trip in fourth grade."

"You amaze me, you know that? It's like you have a piece of

useless historical information for every occasion."

"It's not useless. That story is a metaphor for how you can start over in life. Or how there's always someone, somewhere, who needs you."

"You can't help yourself, can you."

"It's a gift and a curse."

"Why *do* you like history so much, anyway?"

Owen stares at the horizon, arms folded across his chest against the wind. He says, "I started liking history when I was in grade school. I didn't have a lot of friends, and like, Harry Potter was a great escape, but he's magic, right? He had Dumbledore looking out for him, and Ron and Hermione. I liked reading about real people who made it without magic. Without friends. And then I got interested in all the other stuff."

"Are you saying you didn't have any"—I start off saying it as a joke, but halfway through I realize that it might be true, so the energy fizzles out of my voice as I finish—"any, um, friends?"

"Yeah. I don't blame anyone for it. I mean, I was kind of a shitty kid. It took me a few years to not be an asshole all the time. Not to *feel* like an asshole all the time." His eyes lose their focus a little, and I can tell he's seeing his past.

I'm not sure I should ask what's on the other side of the door he's opening. But I'm so curious. How is it possible that Owen, Mr. Sunshine himself, was a shitty kid whose only friends were history books? I ask hesitantly, "Why?"

Owen puffs his cheeks out. "Lots of stuff. Some of it had to do with having to admit to myself that I was bi, but it was mostly my parents. My mom was having problems with depression and drug abuse—prescription drugs, not like meth or Molly or anything. But it was pretty bad. She'd threaten to kill herself, or threaten to leave us, or . . . other shit like that. I felt like it was my fault, somehow."

"Oh. God, I'm sorry. That sucks." I remember him talking about things getting rocky, but I never imagined anything like this.

He shrugs. "She's okay now. I mean, she couldn't help it, really. It was like her brain was miswired, you know? And I was getting into trouble, skipping school, all that stupid shit. So. Yeah. She had a coupla hospital stays. There was lots of therapy. For everyone. But things are better now. She has good doctors, good medicine. Happily ever after, at least so far."

If Owen's family made it through a nightmare like that, I guess I can see where his optimism comes from. But I can't help wondering. "Do you ever worry that it'll happen again?"

"All the time," he says.

"Seriously?"

"Not like I'm always thinking about it. But like, sometimes my mom goes through a tough cycle, and all the old fears spring right up, like they never left, you know? Like they were sitting there under the surface of the rest of my life, just waiting for something to happen."

"No offense, but that doesn't feel like happily ever after," I say. Ugh, that's so harsh. I lean against him to soften it, to show him I meant to be sympathetic, not critical.

"I said happily ever after *so far*," he reminds me, leaning back.

That is exactly the problem, I realize. "But that's it!" I say. "The *so far* part. Happily ever after, true love . . . True love is supposed to be forever, right? That means by *definition*, if you're always going, 'It's all good *so far*,' it can't be real. You don't have a choice." Wait, that sounds terrible. "I mean, theoretically. Not in your actual life."

But Owen is unfazed. "It *is* about choosing a future, though. You just can't guarantee it, is what I'm saying. It's a risk."

"Too risky for me." I shake my head.

"But you can work to make it pay off. That's when you choose. That's what my parents did."

I still don't buy it. "What if you 'choose' to leave because the other person is an asshole? Or what if you choose a job in New York and the other person chooses a job in LA? Is that like 'true love for now'? Or does it mean it was never really love?" Also, why am I being so difficult?

"Why do you ask such hard questions?" says Owen, grinning at me.

I don't have an answer for that one. I shake my head, and we watch the setting sun and the ocean in silence. There's something about the ocean. Often there's nothing going on that you can see, but people just want to watch it anyway. Maybe it's the waves—even though nothing seems to change; when you look closely, everything is always moving and shifting around. It's kind of hypnotic.

"Why do they call this place Pigeon Point, anyway?" I ask, after a while. "There's no pigeons around here."

"They named it after the first ship to wreck off this coast," says Owen. "The *Carrier Pigeon*. In 1853. It had a pigeon painted on the bowsprit—I guess carrier pigeons were supposed to be good luck back then?—but obviously it didn't work. It foundered out there on the rocks, but a bunch of folks from Pescadero saw it and rescued everyone. After that, there were more and more wrecks, and for years people kept asking for a lighthouse, but they didn't get one until this other shipwreck where almost everyone drowned."

"Seriously, Owen. How do you *know* all this random stuff?"

Owen points at the little information plaque in front of him and smirks. "Read to succeed," he says. I shove him, and he shoves me back. The wind blows my hair around, and—*brrr*—I realize it's starting to get cold out here. I rub my hands on my arms.

"I wish the sun would hurry up and set. I'm freezing."

"Hang on. I'll be right back," Owen says, and he takes off running. A couple of minutes later, he's back with a big wool blanket from the truck. He flings it around us both, and we stand next to each other under it, pulling it tightly over our shoulders like a giant cloak.

"Okay. So if you could go back in time and prevent any

historical disaster, what would you pick?" he asks as if he'd never left.

"Hmm." I think of something Mr. Escalante told us in English the other day. "I think I'd save Henry Wadsworth Longfellow's wife from burning to death."

"What? Who?"

"Longfellow. The poet. His wife—her name was Fanny. I guess she spilled sealing wax on this lacy, ruffly dress she was wearing, and somehow it caught fire and she was immediately engulfed in flames."

"God." Owen shudders.

"Right? He tried to save her by wrapping her in a rug just like this," I tug on the blanket. "And then he just flung his arms around her, but it was too late, and she died of her burns the next day, and he was permanently scarred by burns on his face and hands, so he grew a beard after she died. You know, to"—I realize that Owen is regarding me with a kind of horrified bemusement—"to cover up the burns," I finish, rather weakly.

"Seriously?" he says. "CJ, do you even know what a disaster is? The *Titanic*, World War I, World War II, the Holocaust, Hiroshima, Rwanda, Syria. *Those* are the disasters you could prevent, and you go with Longfellow's wife?"

"What? It's tragic! Did you know he courted her for seven years? For seven years, she said no to him, and then finally she said yes and they got married and had six kids and a blissful life together until it literally went up in flames—and needlessly, I might add. They could have been so happy together for such a

- 178 -

long time! I thought you liked happy endings."

"Yeah, but come on. You could save millions of innocent people in Europe, Asia, Africa, the Middle East, wherever, and you choose to save Fanny freaking Longfellow. Why? Because it's a tragic love story." He smiles at me. "You're a romantic, after all."

"Hey. You didn't say it had to be a great humanitarian choice. Anyway, those other disasters are so huge. Like, one single person could not have prevented World War II from happening."

"You could poison Hitler's coffee, and he could have died. That would have prevented the Holocaust. And possibly World War II."

"You didn't say we got to bring special tools with us and use super sneaky spy tactics. That's not realistic. Besides, I couldn't kill anyone."

"Not even Hitler? Not to save millions of Jewish lives and prevent World War II? Besides, it's not like *time travel* is realistic. We're talking fantasy hypotheticals, here, not actual possibilities."

"Okay, fine. Hypothetically, Hitler would be a prime candidate. A better candidate than the Longfellows." Owen nods, satisfied. "But even with Hitler dead, someone else might have come along and taken over. I mean, there are so many terrible people in the world. Think of Assad in Syria. Or Idi Amin. Or Stalin. Or slave traders. Or the soldiers who were part of the Nanjing Massacre. It's too big. It's too awful. And it'll never,

ever stop because people are terrible."

"Well. That's dark."

"You're the one who brought up Hitler. Anyway, history is dark."

It's even happening in my own small life. The McAllisters—both then and now—are just part of a long history of bullies taking things from people who don't have the power to fight back. Maybe the newspaper article will make a difference, but there will always be other McAllisters, other bullies. How do we keep fighting in the face of that fact?

We huddle together with the blanket around us, watching the ocean crash against the rocks. And then in the process of adjusting the blanket so that it protects us more effectively against the wind, I somehow end up in front of Owen with his arms around me, clutching the blanket under my chin. I lean into him and luxuriate in the warmth of his body seeping into mine, in the comforting solidity of his chest, and the pressure of his arms. I close my eyes and it occurs to me that strangers who see us will assume we're boyfriend-girlfriend. Ha. As if.

And then a funny thing happens. It's like the idea of Owen as my boyfriend takes over the way my body understands things. It changes the way his arms feel, the way his body feels, pressed against mine the way it is. It's still comforting, still friendly, but now, suddenly, it's starting to feel kind of sexy as well.

It's like the color blue. Anthropologists say it didn't exist for centuries—people just didn't "see" it. The sky was sky-colored, not blue. And then somehow, somewhere, someone named it, and suddenly the sky was blue. Suddenly everything is different because I've become aware of a possibility where one didn't exist before. Or maybe it did. In any case, I don't know what to call it, and I'm a little nervous about what to do with it.

We remain suspended in the space between friends and . . . something else, for a long, breathless minute. The ocean rushes and roils below us and the sun trembles on the horizon. I can feel Owen's chest expand and contract with each breath he takes. What if I tilted my face toward his, just a little? What if I turned around in his arms, put my own arms around his neck? Maybe he'd brush his lips against my forehead, then against my closed eyes, my cheeks, and then I'd turn my face to his and feel those lips on my mine. Where would that lead? What could we become?

I feel the rush of Something about to happen, something big, something terrifying, because what if Something did happen, and then what? What if it didn't work out? Or maybe even worse, what if I think Something's about to happen, and Owen doesn't? We work together. We've told each other things. Either way, there would be guilt and awkwardness and we'd never be able to go back to the way things were before it happened. Or didn't happen.

Best to keep things as they are.

I come to this conclusion just as the last molten light of the sun winks out at the edge of the world, which is convenient, because it gives me the excuse to push away from Owen and exclaim, "Well! That was fun. I'm chilled to the bone, though. Let's go home."

The unsettling new whatever it is doesn't go away immediately, but by the time Owen drops me off at home, everything is back to normal. He pushes his hand through that gravity-defying black mess on the top of his head, and I have the sudden urge to run my own hands through it, too. I have to cross my arms so I don't reach toward him by accident.

I guess it's not *quite* back to normal.

"Well." Owen turns to me. "Bye."

"Bye."

And then he's driving away and I'm going into the house and closing the door on him, on how weird it got back there at the lighthouse, and thanking my lucky stars that nothing's changed.

That Friday, the subject of Weekly History Minute is the tragic demise of Fanny Longfellow. When Owen (as Henry Wadsworth Longfellow) looks at the camera and says, "True love. It *does* exist, and despite this tragedy, I am so glad to have experienced it." I know he's trolling me, but instead of being annoyed, I can't help smiling down at the desk. What a dork.

A Brief History of Chisaki Joan Katsuyama's Romantic Learning Opportunities, Part III

Day 45, continued

I sat in the bathroom in a vortex of panic, at the center of a cacophony of voices that swirled around me: *Shit, shit, shit, what am I going to do now? How could I have been so stupid? I am so fucked. What do I do, what do I do, what do I do?* My little chorus of demon wasps screamed at me over the other voices: *Stupid! Careless! Reckless! Worthless!*

I wrapped everything in a giant wad of toilet paper—the box, the test, the instructions—and threw it all into the garbage bin outside the house. Screw recycling. Nothing mattered anymore.

I went to the kitchen and made myself another cup of mint tea. *Shut up*, I told myself. *Shut up, shut up, shut up. Smart, mature decisions, CJ. What's the first decision you need to make? What would a grown-up do?*

As I watched the steam rise and curl around itself, the

voices settled themselves down to an angry murmur. On a lot of websites that I read afterward, they make it seem like the decision to have an abortion is an emotional, agonizing one where the woman is racked with guilt and paralyzed with doubt. But after a few sips of scalding tea, I knew I could never have a baby. I was surprised at how sure I was about it. I'd have to be pregnant—okay, *more* pregnant; visibly pregnant—which was horrifying. I couldn't imagine that Andy would want to be a baby daddy, even though this disaster was partly his fault, that inconsiderate jerk. I didn't want to be his baby mama, either, for that matter. I knew I didn't love him. He'd actually begun to get on my nerves lately—though that could have just been my nerves.

A baby would alter the path of my life forever, and even though I wasn't sure what my path was going to be, mother-hood was not a stop I wanted to make anytime soon. I knew I couldn't be the kind of parent a baby deserved. And it seemed pointless and even cruel to remain pregnant just so I could give the baby away.

So, okay. I needed to end the pregnancy.

Days 46–60

As Mom often says in her "Powerful Woman" speeches and seminars, it's one thing to make a decision and a whole other thing to act on it. I did a lot of googling. I learned that I had enough money in my savings account to afford an abortion. If only it wouldn't send a notification to Mom when I withdrew the cash I would need.

Days passed, and I lived in a haze of low-key panic. Sometimes I thought I could actually feel the thing growing inside me, like an alien parasite. If I could have reached in and clawed it out with my own hands, I would have. I know I sound like a monster. But that's how I felt.

When I finally told Andy, he said with obvious reluctance, "Of course, I'll support you no matter what you choose," and even though I knew I wanted an abortion, his hesitation filled me with disgust. We fought, and I broke up with him. He texted me that he could pay for half, if that's what I wanted. *Fuck you*, I texted back. Thank God I wasn't in love with him. Thank God I was ready to do this without him.

When I first got my period way back in seventh grade, Mom told me a story about the possible pitfalls that lay ahead, with herself as the main character. She was sad, she got shit-faced, she had sex, she got pregnant. Moral of the story: don't have drunk and/or unprotected sex, or else.

I rolled my eyes. "I'm not going to go and get drunk and have sex. That's just gross."

"You better not, or there will be hell to pay, I can promise you that."

"You had me, though."

"I had you. That's true. But I don't want you to ever be in a position where you have to make that choice. So be smart."

"But what if I want a baby?"

"Don't get smart with me, CJ. You know what I mean."

"You said to be smart, though."

Then she put down the coffee cup that she was holding and said, "I'm not kidding, Ceej, this is serious. If you're ever in a relationship, you need to keep your head on straight. You have to know that what a lot of people think is true love is mostly just hormones and infatuation, okay? True love is for fairy tales, so don't sit around thinking it's going to happen to you, because that's what'll fool you into doing all kinds of stupid things, and not just having sex and doing drugs. People move across the country, pass up career opportunities, allow themselves to be abused—all because they think they're in love, or that someone is in love with them. Just focus on your own vision and your own success, and don't fall for anyone just because they say they love you. Got it?"

"Got it."

23

THREE THINGS HAPPENED THIS WEEK THAT HAD
me so jittery with anticipation, I could barely sit still. The first
is that Em set up date number two with Fiona. The second is
that in the middle of my Algebra II homework the other day, I
was able to send Emily a screen shot of the following exchange
between me and Shane:

    S: Wyd?

    CJ: Algebra hw wbu?

    S: Same. Trig hw.

    So wyd Sat? You free to hang?

More about this in a minute, but let me tell you now that
this severely impacted my algebra-doing ability for the evening.

    The third thing is that Geoffrey from the *Merc* emailed

Hannah on Thursday and told her that his article was going live on Monday—the day after tomorrow—and it was going to be a "game changer." But he wouldn't give her even a single hint about why. We spent the rest of the day Thursday and Friday afternoon guessing what it could be: Maybe one of the McAllisters embezzled funds from their fancy foundation. Maybe one of them is a Russian spy. Maybe one of them buried a dead body under the shop during the years that they owned the property. The more outlandish it got, the better it felt; it took my mind off the actual possibilities and their consequences. And it made waiting easier.

Anyway. It is now Saturday night and I am not at Heart's Desire obsessively speculating about what's in the *Mercury News* story with Owen and Hannah like a loser (not that they're losers) because I am in the arcade at Bowl-O-Ramen with Nathan Blessing, Ari Chookaszian, and Shane Morgan, eating gyōza and flirting with Shane like a queen. I mean, okay. I'd only give myself a six or maybe even a six-point-five out of ten on the witty-banter scale. But considering that my default mode around Shane is starstruck silence, I'm totally crushing it. So, yeah. I'm going with queen.

It may be because I broke down and put a pinch of southernwood in my jeans pocket before I came here. Or it might be the hit I took off the pen that got surreptitiously passed around earlier. I rarely vape, but I was feeling so nervous, I figured it couldn't hurt. Flower magic, ha ha—because THC extract is from marijuana, which is a plant—I can't actually think about it too hard, or I'll make myself giggle, and I don't want to look like I can't handle my shit. Especially since Shane, I realize too late, hasn't had anything. "I gotta stay clean and sharp for the next couple of tournaments," he said.

Shane's talking about Sabrina right now, which is weird and just a little off-putting. Also we're watching Nathan and Ari shoot zombies, which makes it weirder. I mean, they're not shooting real zombies, obviously. Fake zombies in a video game. Not that zombies are real. Nathan and Ari are playing a video game in which they pretend to shoot real zombies' brains out. That's not weird. The weird part is that Shane is talking to me about Sabrina, which is weird, and watching Nathan and Ari at the same time. And that makes for a very weird listening experience. Weird. Weird. Weird.

". . . and like everything always had to be *perfect* with her," Shane is saying. "It was like, chill *out*, dude. And she was— BRO! THAT WAS LIT!" he shouts as a zombie blows up. "She was *always* stressed out. Like she'd cry, and she'd be all, 'What if I'm not *good* enough? What if I'm not *smart* enough? What if I don't get *in* anywhere?' And I'd have to be all— OHHH FUUUCK. YOU'RE FUCKED, NOW, BRO— I'd have to be all, 'You're *great*, babe, you're totally gonna get in *everywhere.*' Like, constantly."

"*Sabrina* worried that she wasn't good enough?"

"Constantly," Shane repeats glumly. "It was hard work being her boyfriend."

Ari and Nathan end up dead, or possibly undead, and start

arguing about who should pay for the next game.

"And she always got mad if I wanted to hang with these guys instead of her." He leans into the little game booth to punch Nathan, who gives him the finger. He turns to me and says, "You, on the other hand, are very chill."

He smiles. I smiles. I mean, I smile. He smiles at me, and I smile at him, at his beautiful hair and his beautiful mouth and his beautiful eyes and, God, he's just so beautiful. And did he just imply that he liked me better than Sabrina the Overachiever? Which kind of rhymes? Because I don't have a stick up my ass like her? I think he did. I think I might as well just die right now because there's very little chance that life will get any better than this moment that I'm in right now.

But the moment is very rudely interrupted by—no, not zombies, not Nathan or Ari. It's Lilianna Ortiz, Nikki Henry, and Brynn. For Fucking. President. I knew we were waiting for Lilianna, who is Nathan's girlfriend, to show up so we could bowl. I did not know we were also waiting for Nikki, which is fine. I definitely did not know we were waiting for Brynn, which is not fine.

I get a thrill of pleasure from Brynn's surprised expression when she sees me, which turns into a sour little pinching feeling when I realize that her surprise could easily stem from the fact that I am utterly unqualified to be here. But she very politely covers it up with a friendly smile and an enthusiastic, "Hey, CJ! What's up?"

Nathan and Ari very politely wrap up their zombie killing

spree, and the vape pen makes a second round, and Brynn, Nikki, and Lilianna all very politely decline, which sucks, because I took another teeny hit and now Brynn probably thinks I'm a stoner. Not that I care what she thinks because I have nothing but scorn in my heart for her. I know that Owen and Emily both think I'm being unfair, but I don't care what they think, either, because . . . well, because. Because everything is easier when Brynn is not in the picture. Just like now. Before, it was fun. Now, it's not. Is that unfair?

We walk out of the arcade and into the bowling alley, and everyone is being perfectly nice and friendly and polite, but I am fighting a losing battle against the ever-growing feeling that I don't belong here. And I can't drive home because I'm high. Also Shane drove me here, so I don't have a car. Fuck. I thought that being high was supposed to help you relax and not care about stupid shit like this. I can't even get high properly. I *am* a loser, despite not being at Heart's Desire making table arrangements and talking about secret newspaper news with Owen and Hannah. Who could maybe come and get me. Maybe I should call them. Maybe Hannah could come and pick me up and take me to Heart's Desire, and then maybe we could go home together when she's done working, maybe. I wonder if Owen smokes. I wonder if he would judge me for smoking. It's not like I do it very often. Anyway, I don't care what he thinks.

"CJ? Ceee-Jaaaay!" It's Shane's voice in my ear, but it's Brynn's hands practically in my face, waving.

"Huh? Oh. Oh. I'm sorry, I was uh . . . thinking about something," I stammer, which sends everyone into gales of laughter: *Look at CJ spacing out because she's high.* Which I'm not. I'm distracted because of Brynn. We're lined up at the shoe rental counter, and Nathan and Ari have already gotten their shoes. If I'm going to bail, I need to do it soon.

"I asked you where Emily was," says Brynn when she recovers. To the shoe guy, she says, "Women's size nine."

"She's out with this girl Fiona. They met at the mixer the other week." It may be the most satisfying sentence I've spoken all evening. Brynn for President is single and Emily is on a date. All hail Queen Emily.

"Oh!" The expression on Brynn's face shifts from a gently patronizing smile to raised-eyebrow, pursed-mouth surprise. And then she smiles again, but it's fake. I can tell. Her eyes look anxious. "Good for her! Is it like, a date?"

Then I realize that she's jealous. Brynn Foer-Fucking-Preston for President is jealous, possibly even sad, because Emily is out on a date with another girl. I feel the tiniest spark of . . . wait. Am I—should I be—feeling *sorry* for her? In this, Emily's moment of triumph? That's not right.

"Yeah," I say. "They're really cute together. I think it could become a long-term thing."

"Oh. That's great! Good for her!" says Brynn again, and she smiles her fakey-fake smile and takes her rental shoes from the shoe guy. Nikki and Lilianna look at each other. "Good for her," Brynn repeats, softly, to her shoes. I don't look at her because when I do, that little spark starts sparking and I don't like it.

Now that I've made Brynn sad, the feeling of not belonging is even bigger and more uncomfortable. Even the pressure of Shane's arm against mine as we lean against the counter waiting our turn can't distract me from the thick cloud of tension that's just descended. Part of me wants to stay and bowl out of sheer spite, but while I'm not nice enough to feel sorry for Brynn, I'm also not spiteful enough to stay, and anyway, she'll probably destroy me at bowling. And I am feeling increasingly sleepy. Being angry and uncomfortable is exhausting.

Reluctantly, I text Hannah.

CJ: Hey, I'm tired of being here but I'm too high to drive (sorry I promise I won't do this again)

Can you please please please come and pick me up? And not tell Mom?

Within a few seconds, I get a text from Owen saying he's leaving now.

Great. This won't be awkward at all.

Shane goes with me to the parking lot. "You sure you have to go?" he asks.

"Yeah, I'm sorry. My aunt is freaking out right now," I lie, silently cursing Brynn for ruining my evening.

The Bowl-O-Ramen parking lot is a less-than-ideal place for a first kiss, with its ugly fluorescent lampposts and giant neon sign, but I walk slowly, hoping maybe Shane will make a move anyway. But then Owen—who I am going to strangle later—appears and kills the mood (such as it is) entirely. I imagine that my eyes have lasers in them and I am lasering him into oblivion. But he is oblivious.

Once Owen and I are on our way, I ask him, "Why did Hannah send you? Why didn't she come herself?"

"You're welcome," he replies.

Sigh. "Thank you for coming to pick me up," I mutter.

"She sent me because she was busy with a flower crown that wasn't coming together the way she wanted. She didn't want to stop working on it."

"Oh."

We don't say anything else for a while, and I hope it's just the fact that I'm high that's making me feel like Owen is radiating curiosity, like the air is literally pulsing with it, like—

"So, how's Shallow Shane?" he asks lightly. "You two a thing now?" Gahhhh, I knew it.

"He's not shallow, and we aren't a thing," I say coldly. Shallow Shane, whatever. Owen can just stop it with that. Nicknames are *my* thing.

"Okay," says Owen.

More silence. Please let it last. I start to nod off.

"So what did you and Shane talk about?"

OH MY GOD. "We talked about Sabrina, actually. It was very enlightening. Shane is an interesting person, and very nice, and not at all judgmental, unlike some people I know." I don't know why I'm feeling so defensive, except I feel like

Owen is passive-aggressively trying to shame me for liking Shane. "If I'm not allowed to be judgy about Brynn, you're not allowed to be judgy about Shane," I add.

Owen considers this and nods. "Fair enough."

Thankfully, the rest of the ride transpires in silence. I even manage to get a little nap in.

As we head into the shop, Owen says, "Hannah'll be glad you're here. I'm only good for trimming stems and stuff."

"Urrghh. I just want to go to sleep," I groan, and he chuckles.

"I'll bet."

I scowl at him. Though at least we're talking like normal people now.

"Hey." Owen's voice is more serious now, his face concerned. "Does it seem to you like she's being unrealistic about how much this newspaper article is going to help? Like, I'm not even sure she's planning on doing the sale anymore, and I haven't been booking a lot of new consultations or contracts. Should we be worried?"

I'm so not feeling equipped to handle this right now. I shake my head. "I don't know." I pause, and then say hopefully, "Geoffrey said it was going to be a game changer."

"Yeah. But what's the game?"

I think about that. I had assumed that he meant our fortunes would be reversed—that this was going to help Heart's Desire get out of debt and start making money. But if that were true, wouldn't Geoffrey have said so?

It's too complex to think about right now, and once we're inside, it feels like betraying Hannah to express any doubt about the future of Heart's Desire. But Owen's question keeps surfacing and resurfacing, always unanswerable.

What game is going to change?

24

SUNDAY MORNING IS UNPLEASANT, TO SAY THE least. The bride has planned a sunrise wedding on a hilltop, so apart from the criminally early hour, setup is dark and freezing and frantically rushed. The upside is that I get to go back to bed when I get home. Of course, Mom is already up, drinking coffee and flipping through the *Mercury News*.

"Another Sunday wedding, huh?" she says when Hannah and I practically crawl through the door. "You two are crazy." She shakes her head ever so slightly, no doubt thinking, *How pathetic*.

"Not crazy for long, though," says Hannah with a cryptic smile. "Things'll turn around pretty soon."

"I hope so," Mom says, turning her attention back to the paper.

Hannah winks at me, and I manage a weak smile before heading to my room. I really believe tomorrow's article is going to be a good thing, but my conversation with Owen last night has confirmed my suspicions: Hannah believes that it's going to be *the* thing.

I wake up to a text from Emily that she's craving Sharetea, so I let her drag me to the mall because I'm a good friend. Sharetea makes good boba, I admit, but I'll happily fight anyone who thinks it's worth a trip to Valley Fair on a Sunday afternoon for its own sake.

Once we're finally in possession of our drinks (coffee milk for me and hokkaido pearl for Em), we leave the food court and score two seats on the bench outside Nordstrom, where we can sip in peace.

"I hate Fiona. Why'd she agree to see you a second time if she wasn't ready to start seeing anyone new? She should have told you up front." I chew on a boba ball and take another sip of iced coffee. "I'm going to start an I Hate Fiona Club. Wanna join?"

"Come on, Ceej, be fair. She was up front with me yesterday. She thought she was ready, and then she realized she wasn't."

"I guess." I sigh. "I'm just so bummed for you. You two would've been perfect for each other."

"Eh." Emily shrugs. "Maybe, maybe not."

"What d'you mean, 'maybe, maybe not'? She was smart. She was hilarious."

"What happened to the I Hate Fiona Club?"

"I'm changing it to the I'm Very Disappointed That Fiona Is Unavailable Because She Was Perfect for You Club."

"Well, anyway. I'm totally fine. She *is* smart and funny, but . . . I dunno. It was exciting to meet someone who I maybe could go out with. But, like . . ." She stirs her tea, poking at the boba pearls at the bottom of her cup. She's stalling.

"What?"

"I'm actually kind of relieved that she wasn't ready yet."

"Come on, Em."

"No, for real. I just." One last pause. "So like, no offense to your matchmaking skills or whatever, but I didn't feel that spark, you know?"

"But you were so excited about her before."

"I know. I didn't keep feeling excited, though."

I sigh. "Are you sure you're okay?"

"I'm fine, Ceej. I promise."

She does seem fine. She's not one to hide her feelings, anyway. Em pulls out her phone and scrolls through her Instagram, liking, liking, liking. Suddenly, she stops. "Hey," she says, staring at her screen. "You didn't tell me Brynn was there last night."

"Yeah, she was. She was the whole reason I left early. Didn't I tell you that? Wait, don't tell me you're following her."

"She follows me," says Em, a bit defensively.

"Em."

"She sent me a request, Ceej. She's my lab partner. It would have been weird not to follow her back."

"Whatever. Anyway, you should have seen her face when I told her you were out with Fiona."

"What—why would you tell her that?"

"She asked where you were."

And then I realize that I should have kept my mouth shut, because Em's eyes brighten. "She did?" She must hear the energy in her own voice, because she clears her throat and tones it the hell down. "I mean. Hm. That's weird."

"Uh-huh." I let that sit there, and Em likes about five more photos on her feed before she can't stand it any longer and says with studied nonchalance, "So, uh. What did her face look like when you told her where I was?"

"She was surprised, I guess. She said good for you."

"Good for me?"

"Yup."

"What do you think that means?"

"I think that means she's happy for you, Em." I have to work to keep the snark out of my voice. What was I thinking, bringing this up? I should have known she'd grab it and run with it.

"But like, did she say it like, *Yay, good for her!* like she was genuinely happy for me? Or was it more like—"

"Em. Listen to yourself. You need to chill, okay? That girl is nothing but trouble."

Emily sighs and shakes her tea. "Maybe." She takes a big sip, chews, and swallows. "But like, listen to *yourself.* When's the last time you talked to her?"

"Um, last night?"

"That doesn't count. Like really talked to her, I mean."

"I don't have to talk to her. I know what she did, and that's enough."

Emily shrugs. "Okay. But if the *Merc* story doesn't generate interest, I bet you could get her to help with an awareness campaign or something. I told her about how the McAllisters want to buy Heart's Desire, and she's fired up about how they treated your family. Nikki, too."

"What? When? Why didn't you tell me? Why didn't *she* tell me?" What the hell? Em didn't have my permission. Also: "And Nikki Henry? Since when do you hang with her?"

"Oh. I um. I went to the lacrosse game on Friday night, and I was talking with her afterward. I just dropped by for a second after work to meet a couple of friends," she adds when I stare at her with what probably looks like shock, because it is.

"Who? Aviana?"

"What? No, Aviana had to babysit."

"So who did you go with? And why? Why would you go to a lacrosse game? And why were you talking to Nikki?"

Em recoils a little and I realize that my voice has shot up about six levels, from Irate to Nearly Hysterical.

I take a breath to try to calm down, and Em says in *her* Irate-level voice, "Jeez, chill, CJ. A couple of kids from class asked if I wanted to go, and I knew you wouldn't want to. So."

"Oh. Okay."

"You're not mad about it, are you? It was really no big deal."

"No, I'm not mad. It's fine."

It's so not fine.

But I have to say it's fine. There's nothing wrong with going to a lacrosse game with people who aren't your best friend. Em's right—I wouldn't have gone, even if I could have. The only negative emotion I have any right to feel is concern that Emily's going to end up getting her heart broken by Brynn. But instead, I'm mad. And confused. I feel totally betrayed.

But Em and I are friends. I can't let her know I'm this petty.

25

"WAKE UP, CJ. CJ. COME ON, CEEJ, YOU HAVE TO get up."

It can't possibly be time to get up yet.

Mom flicks on the light, and I wince. Shielding my eyes, I squint at her and mumble, "What time is it?"

"It's four thirty. Get up."

"What the hell, Mom? Why?"

"There's an article in the *Merc* about MVC's offer to buy Heart's Desire, and I don't want to risk being here if the local TV news crews show up. Come on. Get up. I don't want you to have to deal with them, and I sure as hell am not going to give those jackals what they want."

Oh, right. It's Monday morning. "What's it say?" I ask. It

must be serious if Mom's waking me up to avoid television news crews.

"You can read it later," says Mom. "I am so mad at Hannah. Did you know about this, by the way? Did Hannah tell you she was going to the press with this story?"

Fuck. I shake my head, which technically isn't lying because I'm technically not saying anything. I could just be clearing my sleep-fuzzed brain.

"I'm going to kill her. I can't even confront her now because of course she's left extra early for the flower market. On purpose, I'm sure. God, what a baby! Hurry up, CJ. I want you out of here in fifteen minutes."

"Where am I supposed to go? It's four thirty in the morning."

"I don't care. Go to Sweet Emily's—they start baking at four, right? Just don't go to Heart's Desire, because the TV crews could be there, too."

"Where are you going?"

Mom, who's already on her way out of my room, pauses with her hand on the doorframe and says, "I'm going to work. We have some serious damage control to do, thanks to your aunt. God help her if the sale doesn't go through because of this. I swear, I'll murder her."

Wait. What?

"What do you mean, if the sale doesn't go through? I thought you said you were only talking about it," I say.

"We are talking about it. But now I'm less in a position to think about it and more in a place where I'm going to have to beg McAllister not to back out."

The truth opens up before me, and for a moment it blots out everything else. "You never believed we could save Heart's Desire. You've been planning on selling it this whole time."

Mom squeezes her eyes shut and clutches her forehead. "You know what, CJ? Fine. You got me. That store is nothing but a headache, and I can't wait to get rid of it. I don't care how Hannah feels about the McAllisters. Seventy years and three million dollars is enough time and money for us to drop the grudge and move on. Now, please hurry up and get dressed."

Twenty minutes later, Mom's gunmetal-gray Tesla Model 3 glides silently down the street ahead of my old Camry. She heads toward the expressway, and I head to Lincoln Avenue and park behind Sweet Emily's, still stunned. I knock on the back door, and Tim, the head baker, lets me in and gives me a croissant fresh out of the oven. I take a bite and check the *Merc* online. It's eye-opening, to say the least.

A Brief, Backward History of the McAllister Family, as Paraphrased from the San Jose *Mercury News*

The super-short, sanitized version: 1900–present

According to the *Merc* article, the McAllisters—founders and benefactors of institutions like the McAllister Cancer Research Center, the McAllister Educational Foundation, and Eliza McAllister Memorial Hospital—started off as farmers, way back in the early 1900s, before computers were even invented, when the valley was carpeted with orchards and farms instead of strip malls and tech company parking lots. Back in simpler times, when Lennie and George worked the fields in *Of Mice and Men,* and Asians were forbidden by law to enter the country or become naturalized citizens.

By the 1950s, the McAllisters had become one of the largest landowners in the valley, and they went around donating land and money, sitting on city councils, and generally making a name for themselves as the generous, civic-minded pillars of the community that we know today.

Rewind to 1942

Funny thing, though. They came by a lot of that land and money in a not-so-civic-minded way. When Japanese American farmers and business owners were (unconstitutionally) rounded up and shipped off to internment camps during World War II, people like the McAllisters (cue ironic trumpet flourish: *dunt-da-da-*daa!) swooped in and offered to buy their properties for pennies on the dollar. Which I already knew.

What I didn't know was that the McAllisters scooped up way more than Heart's Desire. They bought hundreds of acres of land from displaced Japanese American farmers, in addition to homes and small businesses like my family's. They developed them, sold them, and bought more land, which was developed and sold, and so on, and so on, making the McAllisters richer and richer. And then, finally, they started donating it.

According to Wikipedia, McAllister High School used to be an apricot orchard owned by the McAllister family. At the beginning of the fifties, they donated the land to the city to build a high school on. But, the *Mercury News* article read, that orchard originally belonged to an apricot farmer named Ryōhei Motohara. Robert McAllister Sr. bought it from Motohara in 1942 for 10 percent of its real value, just like he did with my great-grandfather.

Rewind to 1938

That's not even all. Not only did the McAllisters acquire a fortune's worth of real estate in the valley, but it turns out that

Robert McAllister Sr., a true class act, had been pushing to get rid of the Japanese American community for years. He was a board member of the Native Sons of the Golden West, which lobbied Congress to ban Japanese immigration and even to deport everyone of Japanese descent. In one of the many letters he sent to state and national authorities, he actually wrote, "We must rid our communities of the insidious Yellow Peril that looms over honest white farmers and threatens our women and children. If we do not, the white man will certainly lose everything to the brown man." Ooh, those scary Japanese people.

Did McAllister use the war to force his neighbors out of their homes, farms, and businesses specifically so that he and his family could grab it all for next to nothing? Hard to say for sure. But even if the land grab wasn't originally part of an evil get-rich-quick master plan, Robert Sr.'s letters make it clear that not only was he a greedy and unethical one-percenter, he was also deeply, undeniably, and unapologetically racist.

26

WHEN I SUGGESTED WE EMAIL GEOFFREY, MY only goal was to save Heart's Desire. I thought he would write a story about a family fighting over whether to save their history or sell it to the highest bidder, who happened to be descended from an old racist family enemy. I was worried about going behind Mom's back because it didn't seem fair to put the story out for everyone to judge.

But in the space of about thirty minutes, everything's changed. McAllister was not just one unscrupulous man screwing one family out of one business. He was a greedy, unscrupulous racist who built his fortune on the misfortune of others—which he helped bring about. He's not just a bad guy. He's a full-on villain.

And here's Mom, who presented herself as objectively

considering a very tempting business deal, telling me that, in fact, she can't wait to sell our family's hard-won property back to the family of the same greedy racist.

And here I am, going to a school named after the greedy racist, built on land that I now know he stole from an unconstitutionally imprisoned American citizen. I was uncomfortable about the name of the school before I knew who the land underneath it really belonged to. And now? There's right and there's wrong, and I love Mom, but she's dead wrong, and so are the McAllisters.

As I sit alone in the dim storefront of Sweet Emily's, fragments of understanding begin to converge inside me. I've always thought I'd never be good enough for Mom. She wants me to become rich and powerful and have a fancy career in a field that she cares about, which will show everyone how smart I am. I've always worried about what would happen if I couldn't live up to the bar she set for my success. I will never be the smartest, the best, or the most ambitious. I don't care about running a successful tech start-up, or a surgery department at a famous hospital, or the state of California. By those standards, I'll always be a disappointment.

But there are things I do care about. I care about loyalty to friends and family. I care about taking responsibility for our actions and how they affect people. I care about Emily's happiness. I care about Hannah and Heart's Desire, and about the way I feel when I'm there, like I have a purpose, like I can make someone's life a little bit more beautiful, a little bit more meaningful, the way Hannah does, and the way my grand-dad and his father did; I care about the connection I feel to that history, to something bigger than me. And speaking of history and families and responsibility, I care about justice for the Motoharas—the family my school *should* be named after. Those are the things that motivate me. Those are the things that inspire me to act. Which gives me an idea. I pick up my phone and start texting. I'm going to disappoint Mom in ways she never dreamed of.

27

FROM THE BOOTH IN SWEET EMILY'S, I TEXT
Emily and Aviana, and after a brief dither, I put Owen on the
thread, too.

Help me do something about this, I type, and then send the
link to the article.

CJ: I'm in the last booth at Sweet Emily's

Hiding from the press cuz I'm such a hot celebrity

Actually, no. The truth is, I hesitate before putting Emily
on the thread. I feel like she's drifting away from me; maybe
she won't want to be part of this. Maybe I'm being insecure
and irrational, but what if I'm not? What's even worse, a mean
little voice inside hisses that maybe I should keep her out of the
conversation—just for a day—before inviting her to help me.
Let her feel left behind, the way she made me feel yesterday.

In the end, I'm able to mute that voice. My trust in our friendship has to be bigger than my fears of her turning away from me. And even if those fears don't go away, I have to remember that this thing is bigger than my personal issues.

Five in the morning is really early, and after I send the texts, I doze for a while. When I open my eyes again, it's five after six, and there are two text notifications on my phone. One is from Aviana, who has swim practice from six o'clock to seven thirty but still wants in. The other is from Owen, a minute ago.

O: On my way!

fucking autocorrect. I sound like my mom

O M W

How can he already be on his way? I reply:

CJ: Why are you awake right now? Do you even know what time it is?

Three minutes go by, and Owen doesn't reply. He's probably driving. I'm sure he's the kind of guy who never texts while he drives. Two more minutes, and Owen walks in and sits down next to me.

"Hey, I just got your text. I was driving," he says, and I give myself a mental high five. "I was going to go for a run, but plotting the revolution over breakfast pastries sounded like more fun."

Owen gets up to buy some food, but I put my hand on his arm and make him sit down because Emily has just texted. Soon after, she comes in from the kitchen and plunks a plate of muffins on the table. She makes a hot chocolate for herself and a mocha for Owen and joins us in the booth. She looks disheveled and grumpy, but she's my friend, so she's here. I feel like my whole body is smiling.

"So. What do you think about a student movement to change the name of the school?" I say as Em sips her hot chocolate and Owen wolfs down a muffin. "That makes the most sense, right? McAllister basically stole the land he donated, so it should be named after the guy who originally owned it. Robert McAllister High School becomes Ryōhei Motohara High School."

Owen swallows and nods. "Naming it after McAllister is a perfect example of erasing nonwhite history."

Em points out that McAllister's name is technically also part of that history. "Not that it should be," she adds hastily.

"Since when do we name things after racists, though?" I ask.

Owen, of course, has tons of answers: Woodrow Wilson, Andrew Jackson, Peter Stuyvesant. "Leland Stanford was a raging racist."

"As in Stanford University?!" I can't believe it.

"Google it."

After more muffins, more caffeine, and more discussion, we decide to stage a demonstration in the quad and collect signatures to present to the administration.

"We can't do this alone, though," I say. "Who can we get to help us?"

"Zach Webster, obviously. His mom's Japanese and he's super involved in his temple youth group," says Owen. "Aviana's already with us . . . Will and Sam can probably pitch in. How about Mizhir? Or Tulasi?"

Emily and Owen insist on putting Brynn on the list, as well. "She's vice president of the ASB, Ceej," says Em for probably the fortieth time this year. "*And* captain of the girls' lacrosse team, *and* president of the QSA. *And* her mom's on the city council. It doesn't matter how you feel about her, or what she's done in the past. She has tons of experience, and she has access to important people. She has to be on the list."

I try not to feel like Emily's rubbing my own insignificance in my face. On the other hand, there's no denying that Brynn could be an important piece. Whatever. It's fine. This is bigger than Emily's new lacrosse-fan/AP-English squad, bigger than her crush on Brynn, bigger than Brynn's increasingly obvious crush on Emily. I can focus on the big picture. I am not jealous. I don't need to be Emily's protector. I trust our friendship.

28

I EXPECT SCHOOL TO BE A NIGHTMARE, SINCE the Katsuyama-McAllister-Motohara story will be the latest, hottest news, but apart from a couple of teachers pulling me aside to ask me about it, nothing happens. I guess I overestimated how many people know me or care about the news. "That's okay," says Owen at lunch. "It gives us more space to plan."

When Owen and I arrive at Heart's Desire after school, totally ready to take on the world, Hannah calls us over and shows us a video on her phone. While we were strategizing what to do about the McAllister news at Sweet Emily's and at school, Mom and the other partners at McAllister Venture Capital were apparently doing the same thing in the war room of MVC. And while I was learning the subjunctive past perfect tense in Spanish, Trey McAllister, scion of the McAllister family, CEO of McAllister Venture Capital, and Mom's boss, was holding a press conference in the lobby of the McAllister Foundation. Mom's there in the background, with the other partners.

In the video, Trey, dressed in a dapper charcoal-gray pin-striped suit, sapphire-blue necktie, and hipster glasses with thick black frames, steps up to a podium and starts reading from a piece of paper.

"I would like to address the actions of my grandfather Robert McAllister Senior, as reported in today's San Jose *Mercury News*," he begins. "The entire McAllister family, on behalf of the organizations we represent, wishes to express our deepest regrets for my grandfather's actions, as well as their harmful consequences. We condemn the internment of Japanese Americans during World War II. My grandfather's views, like those of many Americans at the time, were mistaken and uninformed. Having lost his brother to the Pearl Harbor attack a few weeks prior to Executive Order 9066, he was probably motivated by justifiable anger, fear, and grief; however, this does not excuse his attitude toward the Japanese American community or his acquisition of their property."

"I think you just tried to excuse him, though," grumbles Owen.

Trey continues, "We are proud to tell you that one of our partners at McAllister VC, Michelle Katsuyama, is a descendant of one of those local Japanese American families." He turns slightly and gestures at Mom, who smiles back at him, and then at the flashing cameras. She looks glamorous and sophisticated—like an actress playing a high-powered female business executive. The usual pride in my beautiful, accomplished mother clashes with indignation that she would align herself with these douchebags.

"Look at her hair," says Hannah. "She probably hit the salon and got a professional blowout."

"Michelle is a prime example of the incredible resilience, motivation, and work ethic of the Japanese American community," says Trey. "They were able to overcome people's racist attitudes, let their resentments go, focus on the positive, and succeed despite everything that history threw their way."

At this, I groan. I'm so sick of the model-minority thing. There are kids who actually believe it's true, that Asians are better and smarter than everyone else. And it makes kids like me feel extra defective, like I'm disappointing not only Mom but also the entire world. No wonder I have issues.

Trey doesn't care about my issues, though. "Michelle's grandfather started with virtually nothing and built a flourishing small business, and Michelle herself has risen through the ranks of our firm and is one of our most talented and hardworking people. I couldn't be happier to work with someone of her fine caliber." The McAllister people clap and smile, and Mom nods modestly and holds up her hand: *Oh, no applause, really, you're all too much.*

I swear, if she says something in support of the Mc-Allisters . . . But she doesn't. I'm both relieved that she hasn't gone full hypocrite, and angry that she's agreed to be a silent prop.

Trey winds up his speech. "The McAllisters have long been committed to building a legacy of investing in organizations, research, and technology that make the world a better place. Moving forward, we intend to stay focused on our mission to actualize a brighter future for everyone."

The video ends there and Hannah closes the window and looks at me. "Sweet pea," she says, "your mother has sold her soul to the McAllisters."

A Quick and Eerily Relevant History of Asians in America

Mid-1800s

Asians, mostly Chinese men, started immigrating to the United States in large numbers for the first time. They were seen as uneducated degenerates and criminals, here to steal jobs from hardworking white folks. (Sound familiar?)

White Americans blamed unemployment and declining wages on Chinese workers and demanded that Congress put an end to Chinese immigration.

1882

The Chinese Exclusion Act kept out all "skilled and unskilled laborers and Chinese employed in mining" and stayed in effect for the next forty years. Chinese in the US weren't allowed to apply for citizenship, and they could be deported for pretty much any reason. Again—oddly familiar, right?

Paradoxically, a lot of the people who wanted to keep the Chinese out were okay with the Japanese laborers who started to fill the vacuum . . . , until Japan began gaining power in Asia. Then folks lobbied Congress to amend the Chinese Exclusion Act to cover Japanese and Korean immigrants, too.

1907

It's complicated, but basically, Japanese immigration was restricted to parents, spouses, and children of immigrants who were already here. (Yeah, you've heard this one, too.) To make up for this restriction, the US government generously allowed children of Japanese immigrants to attend neighborhood public schools. No kidding. Those were the actual terms.

1924

A new law severely restricted the riffraff coming over from Southern and Eastern Europe, as well as from Africa. Asians, South Asians, and people from so-called Arab nations got the boot completely. No more. Go away. All of you.

1942

Japanese Americans got sent to prison camps. We've been over this.

1946

At the end of World War II, the American government released Japanese Americans from the camps and encouraged them to start fresh and let bygones be bygones. They produced videos showing everyone how well we were integrating back into society and how happy we were. Japanese Americans, for all kinds of reasons—shame, pride, optimism, resignation—went along with it and essentially pretended the internment never happened.

1950s

The baby boomers became teenagers and people began to worry about "delinquent youth." Chinese American leaders saw a public relations opportunity and told everyone who would listen that Chinese kids were respectful, studious, and well behaved. The white media ate it up. News segments were aired, magazine articles were published. "Hooray for Chinese Americans!" turned into the Official Truth About Asians, and the model-minority myth was born.

1960s

The myth really took off with the civil rights movement. White Americans saw us as safer than those angry, uppity black folks who were demanding change and equality. We were praised for our "cooperation" and hard work (Katsuyamas never quit!), offered jobs, and allowed to buy and rent homes that were off-limits for black Americans.

And white people got to say to black people, "We're not racist. Look how well the Asians are doing! Why can't you be like them? Something must be wrong with you." (Something like centuries of slavery and violent systemic racism, maybe?) At the same time, they said to Asians, who still experienced plenty of racism, "Why are you complaining? Look at how much more you have than black folks!"

A lot of Asians believed the myth that we were working harder than other minorities, and we accepted less than full equality for *us* because it was better than being treated like *them*. Black Americans resented Asians for getting a boost that we didn't deserve (false), and bailing out of the fight for equality (often true, sadly). And no one got the equal rights and opportunities that we *all* deserved.

1970s–present
The rest, as they say, is history. Each new wave of Asian Americans and Asian immigrants has fallen for the myth and made it bigger, more elaborate, more constricting, and more insulating. And the myth keeps doing its job: giving us nearly equal social privilege, pitting us against black and Latinx people, and erasing everyone who doesn't fit into the myth.

29

HANNAH AND I ARE WATCHING THE NEWS FROM the couch and eating kettle corn right out of the bag, which drives Mom nuts. Hannah is also shouting at the TV, which also drives Mom nuts. "Fuck you, Trey!" Hannah shouts when they show footage of him reading his statement earlier today. "You privileged prick!"

According to KRON, the *Merc* article about Mom, Hannah, and the McAllisters—and the McAllister family's press conference afterward—got lots of people riled up. Experts have been arguing about whether the McAllisters' philanthropy makes up for Robert Sr.'s racism, and if anything is owed to the Japanese Americans he cheated. They're going in circles around whether the McAllisters' statement was a "robust acknowledgment of responsibility" or a flimsy excuse for racism.

"I vote for flimsy excuse," I say.

"Exactly," agrees Hannah. Then she turns to the TV and addresses the newscasters. "Robust acknowledgment, my ass!"

Mom sticks her head out of her office, where she's been holed up all evening. "Can you two *please* be quiet? I'm trying to get some work done in here. My day has been a shit show, no thanks to you, and I haven't finished half the stuff I need to do."

"I didn't even say anything!" I protest.

"Anyway, you're the one who wants to sell out to a bunch of racists," says Hannah.

"Trey is not racist."

"Mom. He said it was okay for his grandfather to be racist because he was sad and scared."

"He also said that was no excuse."

"But he *implied* that it *was* an excuse," says Hannah.

"Look," says Mom. "Everyone has racist relatives. That doesn't mean that everyone should be punished for it."

"Trey used you as proof that he's not racist. That's right out of the racist playbook," I point out.

"Okay, you know what? I'm pretty sure I've heard it all. In fact, I had to have my contact info taken off the MVC website because of abusive emails from people screaming at me for being a traitor and a racist bootlicker. I don't have the time or the emotional bandwidth to continue this argument with my own family."

"Yeah, well I've had abusive emails from actual racists

screaming at me to stop being a whiny bitch and to go back home to Asia, so I think I have you beat in the 'I'm tired of this shit' department," says Hannah.

Damn. I've heard of that happening to people. But it's never happened to anyone I know. I feel an adrenaline spike, as if someone has actually, physically attacked me.

Mom looks stricken. Then she lets out a heavy sigh and says, "Fuck. I'm sorry you're dealing with that. People are assholes."

"Thank you," says Hannah. On TV, the James Bond guy drives a Range Rover across a creek and over a bunch of boulders on his way to some fancy gala in the city. "Oh, Daniel," says Hannah dreamily, and I think maybe we're on our way to some kind of truce.

But then Mom says, "You shouldn't have started this, Hannah. I don't want you or the shop getting attacked by a bunch of white supremacists."

"I didn't start it, Mimi. You did. You and the McAllisters."

"Okay, fine. You know what? Say whatever you want. I'm *worried* about you, Hannah. Can't you see that? You're the one who went public and brought them all out from under their rocks. Can't you just tone it down until they—"

I can't take it anymore. If anyone is responsible, it's the racists. Or me. It was my idea to go to the *Merc*, after all. "Mom, I don't think the racists are Hannah's fault."

Mom looks surprised that I've spoken up, and then irritated. "CJ, you stay out of this."

"No."

Mom stares me down and says, "I'm sorry, CJ, did you just flat-out defy me?"

I stare back at her. Defiantly. I can't let her blame Hannah for being attacked by racist trolls. "It was my idea to contact the *Merc*. If you want to blame someone besides the actual racists, blame me."

Mom's eyes widen in shock. "You?"

"Thanks for the vote of confidence," I mutter.

"CJ. I mean it." Mom's voice is cold and level. "Good for you for taking some initiative, okay? But this is none of your business, and I want you to stay out of it."

She has no idea who I am anymore. She doesn't know what I value, she doesn't know what I think, and she doesn't know how I feel. And she has no right to tell me what I can and can't do about stuff that matters to me. I take a big breath. "It *is* my business. I love Heart's Desire. And my school is named after the guy who stole it from us. He hated people like us, Mom, and the school is *named* after him and it's built on land he *stole* from another Japanese American. It's totally my business."

"Um, Ceej, I have to agree with Mom on this," says Hannah, and I find myself doing an actual double take.

"What?"

"I mean, stay engaged, sweet pea. Stay aware. But keep your opinions offline. Don't start anything at school or say anything to the press. I don't want any trouble coming your way because of this. Okay? I don't want you becoming a target."

"Finally, something reasonable," says Mom. And when Hannah side-eyes her, she mumbles, "Thank you, Hannah."

"I can take care of myself."

"No," says Mom. "Hannah's right. You can't get publicly involved. I forbid it. I'm going to have the publicist for the firm let all the media outlets know that you're off-limits."

"You can't do that. What about my First Amendment rights?"

"I can, and I will. Your First Amendment rights are hereby waived; you are my daughter and I will not allow you to put yourself at risk. If you have a problem with that, you can sue me."

I turn to Hannah, but she shakes her head. "I told you I'm with your mom on this. Sorry. You'll have to work behind the scenes."

"Or not," says Mom, glaring at Hannah. "I want you to stay out of this completely, CJ."

I'm struck suddenly by the irony of this situation. All that talk about Having a Vision, Getting Involved, Making a Plan, Being Proactive, blah, blah, blah, and now when things really matter, she wants me to check out. Too late. I *do* have a Vision, I *am* Making a Plan, and I am going to Proactivate the shit out of it.

30

IT'S HARD TO BELIEVE THAT PEOPLE HAVE managed to overlook or excuse the racist roots of the McAllisters' money until now, but I guess it's a little like those statues of Confederate leaders that stood for decades before people finally united to demand they be taken down. It's not nearly on the same scale, of course. But it's proof of how willing lots of people are to forget—or bury—stuff that makes them look bad.

But no more. Owen is going to use *Weekly History Minute* to talk about the history of discrimination against Asians in the United States, ending with a call to sign a petition to change Robert McAllister High School to Ryōhei Motohara High School. We're calling our movement STORM: Students for the Original RM. I know. It's not great. But it could be worse.

We're having a working lunch to plan the demonstration for

Friday; Aviana, Zach, and Owen are here already; Em should be here any minute. I watch Owen as he works on the *Weekly History Minute* script for Friday. He does this funny thing where three little vertical lines appear between his eyebrows when he's concentrating, and I'm kind of mesmerized by it.

My enjoyment of the forehead show is ever so slightly spoiled when Emily arrives with Brynn, Nikki, and Lilianna. I mean, okay. Brynn has been helpful. She got Owen extra airtime for *Weekly History Minute* on the video announcements. She's checked out tablets from the ASB office so we can have kids sign an electronic petition at the demonstration. She's been in touch with every club president on campus and told them to get their members to the demonstration, and she's brought Nikki and Lilianna on board.

But the more we talk, the clearer it becomes that something serious is brewing between Brynn and Emily, and that I can't trust Em not to fling her heart at Brynn's feet. What's worse, the old protective feeling keeps getting pushed out by my new sense of betrayal, which scratches at my heart and at the back of my brain like sandpaper, and makes me passive-aggressive and disagreeable. Like as soon as they sit down, Brynn announces that she and Nik and Lili are going out Saturday and do any of us want to come; Em looks at me and says, "Wanna go?" and I smile and say sweetly, "No, thanks. Seems like you've already made up your mind, though. But whatever, you don't need me, right?" I know it's not a great look on me, but it keeps happening.

"I put the Robert McAllister stuff in the daily announcements for the rest of the week, to raise awareness," Brynn says. "For people who don't have Traudt and Mangin for English and history." She cracks a smile at Emily, and Emily laughs, *Oh, witty Brynn.* Okay, it's not just Emily. Nikki, Lilianna, and Aviana laugh, too.

"I don't see what's so funny," I say.

"Oh, it's just that Traudt's brought it up twice already in English," explains Emily. "Most of us have her, right?" She looks around at everyone to confirm. "And Brynn and I were telling Nik and Lili on the way here about how Mangin is super easy to sidetrack. We talked about the McAllisters practically the whole period yesterday in AP US, instead of the Federalist Papers."

Nik and Lili. She's using nicknames, like real friends. "I get the *joke*," I say irritably, even though I hadn't quite, "but it's not funny. We're talking about my great-grandfather's life. And other people's lives."

"Oh," Brynn says, "I didn't mean *that* was funny. I was joking about how easy it is to distract teachers with social issues."

"Okay," I say. "So, they're just a good excuse to get out of doing work?"

Brynn blushes. She glances at Aviana, Zach, and Owen, who avoid her gaze. "That's not how I meant it."

"Whatever. It's fine."

"Are you sure?" asks Em. "Do you want to talk—?"

"I said it's fine, Em," I say, maybe a shade more harshly

than I need to. Em and Brynn exchange looks, like they're a team, and I feel the hot, sharp scrape of betrayal on my heart.

"Don't worry about it," says Owen. "We all want the same thing, so let's focus on that for now." He beckons me over to look at his Chromebook screen and says, "Help me out with this part, Ceej. Will and Sam say they like it, but I'm not sure if it works."

I lean over to check what he's written. That faker. On the screen, he's typed, *Let it go, CJ. We need to work together.*

"What do you think?" he asks out loud, and nudges me. "Does that work?"

He's staring at the screen with that cute little Roman numeral three between his brows, like he's thinking really hard, and then he breaks his stare to grin at me for just a moment—*How clever is this?*—before he looks back at the screen all serious again.

"Clever," I answer. I nudge him back. Doofus.

"I thought so." And he nudges me back, harder, and we engage in a brief but intense battle for shoulder space until I'm actually laughing, and I realize that Owen's literally nudged me back into a good mood. So good that I remember that I've told myself to trust Emily to take care of herself. So good that when I notice her giving me a sly little *wink-wink-nudge-nudge-isn't-he-cute* smile, I don't even care that she's got it all wrong, and I just smile back.

Script for: *Weekly History Minute*, page 3
Submitted by: Owen Takasugi
Approved: R. Adams

(cont. from page 2)
Ryōhei Motohara, the farmer who owned the
land that later became McAllister High
School, sold it to Robert McAllister Sr. for
pennies on the dollar when he and his family,
along with over a hundred thousand Japanese
Americans, were sent to inland prison camps.
One year later, he joined the army and went
to Europe with the all-Japanese American
442nd Regiment. He died in battle three
months later, fighting for the country that
had imprisoned his family and thousands of
others for having the wrong last name.
~~This has been *Weekly History Minute*. Brought~~
~~to you by the History Club.~~

[The unofficial, unsubmitted, unapproved addendum to the
script for *WHM*]
Robert McAllister Sr. was a racist and a thief, and I, for one,
don't think he deserves the honor of having our great school
named after him. Join me, the Asian Student Coalition, the South
Asian Student Association, the Muslim Club, the Black Student
Union, and La Raza in the quad today to sign a petition to

change the name of the school from the name of a racist to the name of a true American hero: Ryōhei Motohara.

This has been *Weekly History Minute*, brought to you by me, Owen Takasugi.

31

SOMEONE FROM THE *MERCURY NEWS* CAME TO
school to cover the lunchtime demonstration, so I can't be part
of it, or Mom and Hannah will kill me, one right after the other.
In a rare moment of solidarity, in order to make sure I don't get
involved, they both showed me some of the uglier messages
they've been receiving and reminded me that some people
would see my involvement as a mission of personal vengeance
against the McAllisters, and that would turn me into a target.
So I'm lying low, at least for now. I compromised by wiring
stonecrop cuttings and cedar twigs together for perseverance
and strength. I pin the charms onto Owen, Aviana, and Zach,
and melt into the crowd, where I see Will and Sam standing
together.

Brynn takes the mic and introduces the three of them,

which—wasn't part of the plan, was it? Then she stays right up front, waving and cheering; I suspect that she's just using us as a way to show everyone what a great, progressive leader she is. This is not her issue.

On the other hand, shouldn't it be everybody's issue? Maybe I'm just feeling left out, standing down here instead of up there. And pissed off, because she invited Em and me to hang and I said no, and Em said yes. I know. Petty.

Owen, Aviana, and Zach take turns on the mic and tell stories about their families' internment experiences. Baseless FBI interrogations, buses, barbed wire. Lost pets. Broken friendships. But also baseball leagues, poetry clubs, and choruses. Flowers and vegetables coaxed from the unforgiving, arid land.

The four of us are pretty different: Zach and Aviana are total #winners; Owen is a history nerd; I'm me. But we're linked by our histories in a way that makes me sad and angry and proud at the same time. I'm not *happy* it happened, but the history and the link are part of me, so they're precious.

Owen's voice rings out over the sound system as he delivers the final message: "We demand that the city rename this school after the rightful owner of the land that it stands on. If you care about justice, if you care about respect, not just for Japanese Americans, but for all black and brown people in this country, then sign our petition"—he raises an iPad above his head—"to let the authorities know that public schools should be named after heroes, not racists."

Will, Sam, and I start clapping and hollering along with

the kids around us, and the guys push forward to sign the petition. I stay where I am, watching Owen, feeling pride well up in my chest, warm and bright as a little sun. Owen catches my eye and smiles, and my heart aches slightly. I wish I could be up there with him.

Soon I notice that in a few pockets of the crowd, the vibe is different—less "Woo-hoo!" and more "Ohhhhh, damn." Some kids are laughing, rolling their eyes, or outright sneering. Even the Asian kids. It shakes me up a little, especially when I see the more hostile reactions. I hear one kid saying, "Zach and Aviana aren't even full Japanese," as if being "only part" automatically disqualifies a person from claiming a heritage, and my world goes cold and gray.

But I'm not going to let a couple of ignorant assholes ruin my day. I look at Owen and I struggle to find my way back to the warm, bright pride and solidarity I felt before. I've almost got it when I see Sabrina Dang—*what?*—rush up to Owen and put her hand on his arm. She beams and says something, and he tilts his head and rubs the back of his neck the way he does when he's nervous, but he looks pleased. He says something back, and it's her turn to look pleased as she tucks a lock of hair behind her ear. She tosses her head and gives him a little swat on his shoulder, and he laughs, and—oh my god, they're flirting. Suddenly my admiration for Owen, my sense of ethnic pride and civic duty, and my angsty self-doubt are completely hijacked by the implications of this stupid flirty interaction that I shouldn't even care about.

The kids lined up in front of Owen are starting to get restless, so he stops making googly eyes at Sabrina and turns his attention back to the line. Sabrina stays at his side, and they continue to talk and laugh as kids take turns entering their names and contact information. This is messed-up. I *want* things to stay the same between me and Owen. I am *not* interested in a romantic relationship with him. And yet I'm watching him and Sabrina like I'm a jealous ex-girlfriend. I need to get a grip.

I'm so intent on their budding romance that I don't notice Shane standing next to me until he says, "Watcha looking at?"

I look around. No Nathan, no Ari. Did Shane come over here just to talk to me? Or—to sign the petition? "Nothing. I mean, I was watching the line. For the petition."

"How come you're not involved? Isn't your family part of the whole scandal?"

He knows. He cares. "My mom and my aunt are kind of on opposite sides, and they want me to stay out of it. At least in public. They think I'll be putting myself at risk of getting trolled or something."

"Yeah, but . . ." He trails off uncertainly.

"What?" Oh no. He thinks I'm an apathetic loser.

Shane tilts his head, looks at the ground and sighs, as if he's thinking about how to put this delicately. He says, "So I know this is totally cynical, right, but think of applying for colleges next year. You could put links to newspaper articles about how you're involved. And if you get trolled, you could write about that in an essay about, like, the risks of social activism or something. I mean, you don't want to fake it. You have to care, obviously. But if you do care, you should go all in."

"Hmm." Sigh. Am I trash for being excited that he cares enough about me to give me advice, even though it's cynical? It's smart advice. Exactly what I would expect of Mom, which . . . sigh.

"Are you going to sign the petition?" I ask.

He shrugs. "I wasn't going to. I mean, it's not that I'm *opposed* to it. But lots of my friends think we should keep the name, because of tradition, and like, school loyalty and shit like that." Oh no. Please, Shane, don't say that you don't want to change the name.

He regards the people signing the petitions and continues, "*I'm* okay with changing the name . . ." Whew. "But it does seem like a lot of time and money for something that only affects a few people. Like it really doesn't matter that much to *me* what we call this place. It has nothing to do with me." He wrinkles his forehead. "Wait, that's not racist, is it?"

"I mean. Kind of?" It's not KKK-level racist, but it still definitely feels, well, *wrong*. But if I say that, it still sounds like I think Shane is racist. Which I don't.

"Wait, seriously? But I don't hate anyone. It's not like I'm like, 'Fuck the Japanese Americans' or some shit like that. I think what McAllister did was fucked up, and I totally get why you don't want to go to a school named after him. But the name doesn't affect me, so I'm not upset about it. How does that make me a racist?"

"I'm not saying you're a racist. It's just. Like. If you say that it doesn't affect you . . ." How do I explain? I've never really thought about it that carefully. I wish Owen was here. Or—

"I hope you don't think I'm racist. I'm just trying to understand." Shane's whole handsome face is concerned, his blue eyes blinking earnestly at me, and I feel a little surge of affection for him. "I don't want you to feel weird about going to school here because of some stupid asshole's name—ohh." I see a glimmer of understanding dawn on his face. "I get it. Tell you what. I'll sign the petition. For you. And I'll get all my buddies to sign it, too."

"Oh. I mean. Don't sign it just because of me." I mean. *Do* sign it because of me? But also don't?

"I want to. You've convinced me." Shane smiles at me. "Come on." He takes both my hands in his and walks backward, leading me toward the petition signing line. "Come with me. You have to sign it, too."

I almost don't tell him. I don't want to be snotty, and he's trying so hard right now. And he's holding my hands in his. Like he's my boyfriend or something. Shane Morgan. But I'm getting frustrated with fading into the woodwork. "Oh. Uh. I wrote it, actually."

Shane stops walking, his expression confused, then—I swear to God—joyous. "Why didn't you tell me? Damn!" He puts his non-handholding fist up and I put mine up and we bump fists and he says, "And here I was all, 'Get more involved! It'll look good on your college apps!' Why didn't you say something? You're a fucking rock star!"

Shane Morgan: sexy, talented, admires strong, smart women. Thinks I am a rock star. Could he be more perfect? I don't think so.

Shane is still holding my hand when we reach the crowd. I consider letting go as we approach the front of Zach's line, because I can see Owen out of the corner of my eye. I don't care, though, because Owen is not the boss of me. And who was just flirting with Sabrina instead of taking signatures? Anyway, it's not like I'm *with* Shane or anything.

"So. You guys here to sign the petition or get married?"

Zach's giving us this arch *I know what's going on here* smirk, and I wish I could tell him to shut up and not ruin the vibe by calling attention to it. Instead I give him a look that I hope effectively communicates stern disapproval of his petty gossip-mongering.

"Signing the petition, bro," says Shane with a sunny Shane smile. "Down with perpetuating the dominant narrative!"

"Right on," says Zach, and hands the tablet and stylus over, another victim (thank goodness) of Shane's boundless charm and complete faith that everyone is on his side.

Though it doesn't even matter, because Owen is basically right there in front of us. I can feel him watching us, so I smile at him, but I barely catch his eye before he turns away. Now I'm totally sure that he's observed the entire thing, from the bashful handholding to congratulatory fist bump to jovial petition signing. Well, good. I mean, I don't care.

Shane and I thread our way back through the crowd (yes, he's still holding my hand, yes he is divine, and yes, I am now divine by association) and pass by the kid who was complaining that Owen, Aviana, and Zach weren't Japanese enough to credibly protest Robert McAllister's name. He's now arguing that no one really has a reason to protest anymore. "You can't punish people for something their great-grandparents did seventy-five years ago. If someone robbed my great-grandfather seventy-five years ago, I wouldn't have to go to prison for it."

Nuh-uh. I hear myself butting in and saying, "Okay, first of all, if my great-grandfather robbed someone and I'm still benefiting from it, I owe that person's family something. Second of all, having your racist great-grandfather's name taken off a school is not a punishment."

Oh, shit. The kid looks at me like I'm nuts. Then he turns to his friend and snickers. "Someone's triggered."

It's such a nothing comment, but it infuriates me, and I realize I'm shaking from the shock of hearing something so . . . is it fair to call it racist? He didn't say anything about my race, technically.

I take a couple of breaths to collect myself, and then I take one more breath and say—

"Fuck you, you little shit. Apologize."

Oh my god. It's Shane. He's let go of my hand and stepped forward and is now locked in a stare-down with this kid, a scrawny, weaselly looking dude who Shane could probably break in half with his bare hands. It's like something out of a superhero movie.

It's kind of thrilling.

But also a tiny bit . . . well, I had a comeback for once in my life, and I didn't get to use it.

Ah, fuck it.

"If anyone's triggered, it's the dude who can't handle credit going to someone besides a white person."

Both Shane and the kid look at me in astonishment. Other kids are starting to notice us and take their phones out—hoping for a fight they can post somewhere, I'm sure. The kid sees this too and backs down pretty much immediately, probably because he doesn't want the entire school to see a video of himself getting trounced. He rolls his eyes and looks at me and says in a voice spiky with resentful sarcasm, "Sorry."

Shane turns to me and says, "That wasn't a very sincere apology, CJ. Do you need a better one?"

It was a shitty apology, but there's no point in drawing this out. Even if the kid apologizes again, he won't really be sorry. "It's fine," I say. And to the kid, pointedly, "Goodbye."

He vanishes, muttering to his friends.

"Holy shit," says Shane. "What a fucking prick. CJ, you okay? Does that kind of thing happen to you often?"

"I'm fine," I say. "And nothing like that has ever happened to me." I mean, I hear bigoted comments all the time. Don't we all? But I don't make a habit of arguing with the random douchebags who make them.

"Well, you're a fucking badass! I'm sorry I jumped in like that. I bet you could have kicked his ass."

"Oh. Well," I say, smiling modestly, and then I run out of things to say.

"Anyway, I get it now, for real," Shane says. "I'm all in on STORM. Let me know if you need any help with anything, okay? I don't have time for meetings and stuff, but like I can show up for fund-raisers or whatever. Anything."

"Cool. Thanks."

In the long pause that follows, I look over at Owen to see if he's witnessed my badassery and Shane's admiration. Big mistake. He is totally captivated by Sabrina, who is putting her arm on his shoulder and rising up on her toes to say something private, presumably. He leans down to listen. Then she steps back and waves, and Owen tucks the tablet under his arm and mimes texting, his hands holding an imaginary phone. Sabrina smiles and nods and practically skips off, perfect hair swinging back and forth, back and forth, just over her perfect butt, which is also swaying back and forth—for Owen's benefit, I'm sure. Owen watches her for several seconds before turning back to the petitions.

"Looks like those two are getting pretty friendly," observes Shane, who seems totally unbothered by the sight of his ex-girlfriend blatantly flirting with another guy.

"You jealous?" I can't help asking.

"Of who—that dude? Nah."

"Why not? What's wrong with him?" I ask. Owen's

thoughtful, passionate, principled, sweet . . . Ugh, what's wrong with *me*?

"Nothing's wrong with him. It's just that Sabrina doesn't usually just run up and flirt with guys she barely knows. She's probably trying to make me jealous."

I don't even know what to do with that information.

My phone buzzes. "Hang on a sec," I tell Shane.

It's Owen. Still right over there. Not even looking to see if I got his text, which reads:

O: Hey, we don't have to work tomorrow night, right?

CJ: No. Why? You got big plans?

O: K cool. I might be going out w some people.

CJ: Who?

O: . . .

. . .

. . .

What's taking him so long? I wish he'd just come over here.

Finally, a reply:

O: Brynn and Co. And Emily, I guess.

Sabrina. Sam and Will.

You're welcome to come, obvi

Oh, obvi, I think. Doesn't seem that *obvi* to me.

I type, *No, it's okay. Knock yourself out. I'll just be at home alone with my Netflix queue,* and hit send.

Wait. Seriously, what is wrong with me? I quickly add a winky face and a smiley face and type, *JK it's all good.*

That's better. I push the phone and all the weirdness into

the depths of my bag and smile at Shane. If Sabrina can ask Owen out, I can ask Shane. Because I am a badass who has an admirer and who is not jealous of anyone. "Hey, um." Here goes. "You busy tomorrow night?"

Shane's face falls. "Aww. I'm gonna be at a tournament in SoCal. I'm actually leaving school early today to drive down there with the team."

"Oh. Okay. No worries, I was just, you know. Wondering."

Next weekend is Valentine's Day, followed by February break. But I'm spared the awkwardness of having to pretend I don't know and "accidentally" ask Shane out for Valentine's Day because he groans, "I can't do next weekend, either, because we're leaving for training camp over February break. Weekend after next, maybe? At the end of the break?"

"Perfect."

"Sweet. It'll be just you and me this time. No one else. Cool?"

"Cool." SO COOL.

The bell rings, the crowds disperse, and Shane gives my hand a squeeze before loping off to join his friends. So what if Owen is hanging with Sabrina—and Em . . . and Brynn—without me? So what if my supposed best friend hasn't even invited me? I've got a bona fide date with Shane Morgan in two weeks.

Aviana and Zach see me from across the quad and pump their fists, and I feel a twinge of guilt that this relationship stuff has elbowed STORM out of my head. I need to be better than this. I need to be stronger. I will be stronger. So, fine. While Emily and Owen are out socializing on Saturday night, I will stay home and work on STORM's next step. I will be a behind-the-scenes leader of a movement and I won't even feel a little bit jealous or pathetic.

McAllister or Motohara: What's in a Name?
Land Donated by McAllister Family for High School Was
Originally Owned by Japanese American Farmer
by Geoffrey Acosta

19 Comments

SharksFan

I think our Society definitely owes victims of Racism, but no one owes Asians anything. Asian Americans are killing it. They're richer than whites. They're taking over Silicon Valley. I'll probably lose my spot to an Asian kid at every College I apply to.

Forknife2005

YOUR spot?? I'm Asian, I work my ass off to get A's in AP classes and I'll probably lose MY spot to an affirmative action kid who didn't work even half as hard as me. Colleges are totally racist against Asians.

ZombieNation

Hey Forknife2005 privileged much??? Racist much??? Black and Latino kids (we all know that's who you mean) deserve to get a good education just as much as you do. Just because they can't afford private school and fancy enrichment activities doesn't mean they don't work hard.

SailorMoon2003

The only reason Asians are "killing it" as you say is because we work harder than your lazy white asses. We value education and we respect our elders. Maybe if the rest of you stopped whining and got your shit together you'd be killing it too.

ricerocket69

YASSSS AZN POWER
SUCK IT YT PPL

coolstoryhansel

Not all Asians are "killing it." Some Asian groups are stuck in poverty even worse than Blacks and Latinos.

realAmerican

These Asian kids are just like the blacks. Oh, my great-great-grandfather was a slave so I should get special benefits! It's not my fault I'm a lazy crack addict, it was the white slave owners! Why don't minorities grow up and TAKE SOME RESPONSIBILITY?!?

FlowrChylde

I hope you die you racist pig

lonestranger

There were hundreds of laws passed AFTER SLAVERY

ENDED that prevented blacks from owning homes, going to school, getting jobs, and even getting healthy food. Political candidates literally MADE UP the war on drugs and scapegoated blacks and Latinos. I'd say that it's time for whites to take some fucking responsibility.

realAmerican
lonestranger what race are you?

lonestranger
Why does it matter?

coolstoryhansel
Racist xenophobes like realAmerican are exactly why we need to rename the school. Keeping the name shows that we think it's ok to round up people just cuz they share an ethnicity or a religion with overseas enemies.

realAmerican
In wartime you have to take all necessary precautions to keep your nation safe. That's the price we pay for liberty. If you don't want to pay it then get out of my country.

coolstoryhansel
Our nation is NOT safe for its own citizens. That's my point. We're attacking innocent Brown and Black citizens because

racist cowards like you have painted them as monsters.
You're the real monster.

Bravagrrl

The McAllister family profited off the oppression and illegal
incarceration of innocent people. Trey McAllister's entire
career—his entire life—is built on other people's suffering.
What's wrong with changing the name of the school to honor
the man who really owned the land, instead of the man who
stole it?

realAmerican

Are you triggered, snowflake?

Bravagrrl

Not triggered. Just explaining why I support the name change.

DubNation35

Well if that's where you're going with it, why not name it after
the Mexican rancher who owned it before him? Or the Native
Americans who lived here before that? You gonna name
every school around here Ohlone High School? How about
the hospital? Or the library?

Bravagrrl

All of that is fine by me.

32

TODAY'S WEDDING WAS FOR ONE OF HANNAH'S friends, so she stayed to party after we set everything up. Owen took off to get ready for his date or his nondate or whatever it is with Sabrina and Co., and I came home and spent the rest of the afternoon alone. I brainstormed a list of ideas for a presentation to the school board meeting next month. After that, I meant to make flyers to put up around Japantown and Willow Glen, saying why we need to rename the school. I did not mean to spend the afternoon messing around making flyers advertising a student line of flower magic. But somehow it happened.

I also did not mean to end up on the couch with Mom, eating ice cream and binge-watching nineties sitcoms. I meant to keep hating her forever. But at seven o'clock, I was done designing flyers, I had liked everything on my Instagram and

Snapchat, and I'd watched YouTube until I could actually feel my brain frying, sizzling gently around the edges. I went to the kitchen to get a bowl of ice cream, and while I was there, Mom called me from the family room.

I am proactivating a plan to save Heart's Desire, rename my school, and bring you and McAllister down, I wanted to say. But it felt too rude to refuse to bring her a bowl of ice cream, especially since she'd brought home a pint of my favorite flavor (chocolate malt) from Tin Pot. She hates chocolate malt. But there was a pint of raspberry sorbet for her sitting next to it, so I scooped some into a bowl and brought it to her.

"Sit down with me, Ceej," she said, and patted the cushion next to her. And now I have become one with the couch as Mom and I watch six white twentysomethings in New York City drink coffee and have hilarious misunderstandings.

I can see why this is Mom's second favorite de-stressing activity after running on the treadmill. Everyone is beautiful and thin and well dressed. There's a joke for nearly every situation. Even when things go horribly awry, you know it will all work out in the end. No conflict goes unresolved, no resentment unraveled, no transgression unforgiven.

I wish our lives could be like that show. I wish I could be certain that we could save the store, that Mom and Hannah would forgive each other, that I'd find a way to make Mom proud of me. I wish I could talk to her about it without it turning into a fight.

I giggle at something on the screen, and Mom looks at me

and smiles. And I know that Mom's happy that I'm here, now, on the couch with her. It's like we've never fought about anything in our lives. I wish we could stay in this moment forever, all the ways we've hurt each other forgotten, all our future mistakes blown away on a puff of air before we make them. I wish, I wish, I wish.

33

IT'S VALENTINE'S DAY, AND BUSINESS IS BOOMING.
Or should I say *blooming*, ha ha.

I, on the other hand, am wilting from exhaustion.

I was up until two o'clock this morning helping Hannah
with arrangements and bouquets for Heart's Desire *and* for
school, and then back up again at four o'clock.

I wish I could say that business has been brisk because of
the publicity we've been getting on the news, or the flyers I put
up around the neighborhood for the store and at school for my
own little side hustle. But Hannah says it's hard to tell, since
the week leading up to Valentine's Day is always crazy. In what
little spare time she's had, she's been on the phone with the
JACL and the National Japanese American Historical Society,
trying to convince them that this new angle on the McAllisters

justifies her request for funds. I get the feeling it's not going well, which is worrisome. April is only six weeks away and if this week isn't going to give us a cushion, I don't know how we're going to manage to keep the store.

I'm actually glad for the distraction of financial woes, since things have been a bit strained between me and Owen and Emily ever since they went out with Brynn and Sabrina last weekend. The whole thing's been pricking at me like a burr in my sock, but I can't be angry because, technically, I was invited and I said no.

But like, Owen didn't text or DM me all weekend. It's not like we text all the time, but still. And Em was super weird about it, too. "Oh, you know," she said, when I called her on Sunday to ask how it was and what they did. "Nothing, really."

I waited for her to elaborate, but she didn't, so I said, "Nothing? What, you didn't go anywhere? You didn't do anything? At all?"

"No, seriously. We hung out at the Creamery for a while, and then Sabrina had to go home. Literally, that's the only interesting thing we did."

And when I tried asking Owen in a general, roundabout way about it on Monday, he changed the subject.

It feels like the three of us are in a badly acted play where the actors haven't quite memorized their lines or figured out where to look or how to stand on the stage. Emily keeps hinting that I'm secretly into Owen, probably to distract me from whatever is going on with her and Brynn. Owen pretends that he's not hiding this Sabrina thing from me. I pretend I don't feel resentful and hurt. We all pretend everything's cool, even though it's not.

Hannah wrote me and Owen a note to get us out of school, which, yeah, it's wrong, but there's no way she can handle Valentine's Day all by herself. Owen's been doing deliveries, and I've been filling orders in the back and serving customers in the front all day. No one's had time to stop to eat lunch or dinner, or even a snack. There are two lemon LUNA bars and a box of stale crackers in the little food cabinet in the back room, but that's it. Last year, Emily brought two dozen heart cookies and some day-old muffins, but today she's been AWOL, so we've been left to starve because naturally neither Hannah nor I remembered to buy any extra food. By the time we finally usher the last desperate customer out and lock the doors at seven o'clock, I'm ravenous.

Hannah collapses onto her desk chair and groans, "God save me, CJ, I am wiped. Out."

"I just want to eat a bowl of something warm and carby and fall into bed," I add from the stool by the worktable, just as Owen returns from his last delivery.

"You're in luck." He holds up a white plastic takeout bag.

I leap up. "Please tell me you've got—"

"Ramen from Orenchi." With a flourish and a smile, Owen extracts three Styrofoam containers. He bows and deposits them on the table next to me.

"Oh my god, bless you." The thought of Orenchi ramen momentarily erases all my problems, and I fling my arms around Owen, who obligingly hugs me back. Then I grab my tonkotsu ramen with an extra boiled egg and extra sesame seeds—exactly how I like it—and dig in.

Owen hands Hannah a bowl of her favorite, shōyu ramen, and starts in on his own tonkotsu. He takes an enormous slurpy mouthful of noodles and murmurs, "Brains . . . ," as he chews and lets the ends splash back into his bowl.

"Grow up," I say, but I'm pretty sure he saw me grinning. It was such a stupid joke—I mean, what are we, twelve?—but this ramen is magic. It's making me feel generous and forgiving: the Valentine's Day Ramen Truce of 2019. Kidding aside, it's a relief to let go of my resentment for a moment. No tension, no awkwardness. Just friends being friends. As familiar as comfort food and corny jokes.

As I watch Owen, I imagine his arm around my back, the way it was when I hugged him a second ago, imagine the gentle pressure of his hand on my waist. Hannah cracks a joke and he laughs, and for a moment it's like the camera of my eyes can only see that strong jaw and those lips, and . . . Holy shit, am I fantasizing about kissing him?

Stop it. Just stop it right now. I'm clearly delirious with gratitude for the ramen. I close my eyes and concentrate on the taste of the rich, salty pork broth and the chewy-crunchy texture of the bamboo shoots in my mouth.

And the buzz of my phone in my pocket.

Hey, wyd?

It's Shane, texting from somewhere down south. That
training camp thing starts tomorrow.

CJ: Eating takeout ramen at work after filling the world with
hearts and flowers lol

Wbu?

S: Eating leftover Olive Garden pasta in a hotel room with my
mom while she watches old movies on her iPad 😳🙁

CJ: Sounds romantic 🖤

S: Ya

Wish I was with you instead 😊

I sneak a glance at Owen, who's busy draining the broth
out of his ramen bowl. I don't need to feel weird about texting with Shane in front of Owen. Owen and I are not a thing.
Shane and I are not a thing, not really. I start texting a reply: *So
do I*, then delete it, and type it, and delete it again.

"Who're you texting?" Owen's finished guzzling his broth
and has evidently been watching me type, delete, type, delete.
He leans over to see my phone, and I turn it off so he can't see
the screen. "Is it Emily? What'd she say?"

"No, it's not Emily."

"Then who is it?"

I start to say that it's none of his business, but his nosiness
irks me. As if he has any right, after being so secretive about
what he, Emily, Sabrina, and Brynn did last weekend without
me. Which reminds me that Emily is not here tonight, having
offered the gossamer excuse that she "just felt like staying at

home for some reason," which I can't help thinking means, "I don't feel like hanging with you for some reason." The resentment springs back to life, and I feel the need to spread it around. So I tell him, because I know it will bug him. "Shane."

"Morgan?" I can hear a tiny splinter of annoyance in his voice. Score one for me.

"The one and only."

Hannah knows about Shane, she's made no secret of the fact that she still massively ships me and Owen. She doesn't say anything or even look over at me, but I swear to God I can actually see her romance radar turn on, as if little invisible antennae have sprouted from her skull. She's so alert with curiosity, she's practically vibrating.

"What'd he say?"

I shrug. "Nothing worth talking about."

"What'd you say?"

"Seriously?"

"It—"

"Oh my god, Owen, why do you care? Why the third degree?"

"Whoa, easy there, killer! I was just making conversation. No need to get defensive." He's smiling, but it's fake, and I don't even feel a little bit sorry. Now he knows how it feels to be curious, upset, and denied.

"I'm not being defensive. You're being nosy."

"CJ! He's allowed to ask questions. I'm curious, too. What are you and Shane discussing?" Hannah looks decidedly disgruntled now, which, seriously? It's none of her business.

"Nah, it's okay, Hannah. Don't worry about it. It's cool," says Owen. I'm sure it's not cool with him at all, but his face is blank, and he's currently working very hard at getting the dregs of his ramen into it, so I can't tell what he's feeling. I don't exactly know what I'm feeling, either.

Another text comes through, this time from the STORM committee. Owen checks his phone at the same time that I do.

Hey, guise. Ugh, it's Brynn. *I'm with Nik and Lili, and I just had a great idea to get some press for the movement.*

Double ugh. *Let's wait until after February break,* I reply.

I watch Owen read it. He looks up and I can tell he's going to scold me for shutting Brynn down, but I am not in the mood to have an argument about her motives or my issues with them, and anyway, Hannah's not supposed to know I'm involved in STORM, so I glare at him and bend over my phone.

Almost immediately, I get a bunch more texts on this thread, but I'm out of patience. I remember something I read over Hannah's shoulder last week in some *BuzzFeed* article on self-care. "Block anyone who makes you feel less than. At the very least, turn off notifications from that person. Don't allow them to disrupt your life every time they have a thought they want to share."

Perfect. I just need some time when I don't feel like I have to deal with Brynn and worry about what she's scheming. I don't have the guts to flat-out block her. But I go to Settings on my phone and turn off notifications for this thread.

Immediately, I feel lighter. In fact, I should just cut this entire evening short, in the name of self-care. I put fifteen dollars on the table and push it toward Owen. "Thanks for the ramen," I say. "I'm gonna go home."

34

EVER SINCE OUR STORY BROKE AT THE BEGINNING
of the month, I've taken to reading the newspaper and googling
for news about McAllister every morning. Today, on our first
day back from February break, I flip to the Lifestyles section of
the *Merc* and see this:

"I Couldn't Just Sit There and Do Nothing"
A White Student Explains Her Efforts to Rename
McAllister High School
by Geoffrey Acosta

What?

The article talks about how Brynn has always been a student leader, how she's an outspoken advocate for LGBTQ+
rights and women's rights, and how totally amazing it is that

a white girl would be so eager to play such a "crucial role" in the movement.

"I've had a lot of experience organizing events and going to protests and marches," it quotes her as saying. "My mom does a lot of fund-raisers for progressive causes, so I feel like it's important for me to contribute as much as I can that way."

Furious as I am at Geoffrey for writing this article, I'm even more furious at Brynn. I text a link to the article to the rest of the committee, except for Brynn, and add, *I'm sorry but wtf?*

Within minutes, Nikki, Mizhir, Lilianna, and Tulasi text back.

Nikki: Oh shit

Mizhir: fr tho

Lilianna: wtaf

Tulasi: 😡

I don't hear back from Owen and Aviana, or from Zach or Emily.

I want to drive over to Emily's house and shove this article at her and say, "Look! Look at how she's taken our cause and made it all about her! This is the girl you're falling for! You knew better!" It's probably too late, though.

I'm so angry that I'm tempted to contact the *Merc* and call bullshit, or maybe call KRON and tell them to send a reporter and a camera to interview someone who actually has personal experience with the actual issue, instead of experience organizing events. Though let's face it. It's too late for that, too.

★ ★ ★

When I get to school, still simmering with rage and—let's be honest—a dash of despair and a pinch of jealousy, I see a news van with one of those telescoping antennae parked in front of the administration building. I pick up my pace and walk over to see what's going on.

I can't believe it. There's Brynn, Owen, and Aviana, talking to a reporter. Brynn is doing the talking, naturally.

I can't hear what she's saying because she's too far away, but she is Holding Forth. Aviana is nodding soberly, and Owen is, too. Eventually, Brynn shuts up and the reporter asks Owen a question. He speaks for a little bit, and then looks at Aviana, who starts talking. But she's only been talking for a few seconds when Brynn, who's been nodding along vigorously, appears to have a huge epiphany of some kind. Mid-nod, she opens her mouth and holds up her finger: *I have something to say that is so important, I can't even finish nodding!* The reporter shifts her attention back to Brynn, who launches into a speech so impassioned that I can actually hear her voice now, though I still can't make out the words.

She finally winds down and the reporter turns to the camera, ostensibly to sign off. This has been Vicky Nguyen for KRON with Owen Takasugi, Aviana Fong, Brynn for President, and Brynn's enormous fucking ego. And now back to the studio.

Suddenly I know what the expression "it makes my blood boil" means. I feel as if my heart is pumping outrage, as if it's flowing through my arteries, hot and poisonous and bubbling, flooding my brain, my lungs, my arms, my legs. I knew it. I knew it. Brynn, true to form, has managed to make this whole thing about Brynn.

Then I feel ugly. Is some of this plain old green-eyed jealousy? Do I just want to be in the spotlight? That could be me with my picture in the newspaper, me being interviewed on TV, me being the #winner for once. Instead, it's Brynn getting all the attention, as usual. I don't know.

The camera crews head back to their vans and Owen, Aviana, and Brynn are swallowed by the herd of kids who had gathered to watch them being interviewed. I follow them onto campus at a safe distance. Once we get to the quad, individual human beings materialize and separate themselves from the mass, heading off toward their classes. Tulasi, who's at the edge of the crowd, sees me and walks over, calling, "Hey!" I wave back and look for Emily, who ought to be close by. I wonder if seeing Brynn take over the television interview will be enough to convince her that I'm right.

Just as Tulasi reaches me, I spot Emily. Standing with her, deep in conversation, are Owen, Aviana, and Brynn, along with Zach and Sabrina. And no one looks angry or upset at all.

35

WE'RE IN MR. HARRISON'S CLASSROOM FOR OUR
STORM meeting, which doesn't officially start for twenty
minutes. But I called an emergency premeeting meeting about
Brynn, so here we all are. Except for Brynn.

"All I'm saying is maybe we should give her another
chance," Emily says. "I don't think she meant to overshadow
anyone."

"Are you kidding me? You know she engineered that feature in the *Merc*. I'll bet she got KRON to come to school today.
How come the rest of us didn't know about it?"

"We did. Didn't you get the text?" asks Emily.

"She never texted me about it."

"She did," says Owen. "On Valentine's Day. She was with
Nik and Lili; she sent that group text? You said to wait till

today?" The others nod, and suddenly I remember that I turned off notifications on that thread. I check my phone. Dammit.

"It doesn't matter, though. She did completely center herself. I watched her interrupt you, Aviana," Nikki says. "She's my friend, but that wasn't okay." I feel a wave of gratitude toward Nikki, who I wasn't sure would support me on this.

Aviana nods slowly. "I *was* kinda pissed about that."

"I say we make her resign," I add, encouraged by Nikki and Aviana's support. "What she did was bullshit."

"We can't just kick her off. That's not the way this works," Owen says sharply. I look at him incredulously, and he's looking right back at me. He's annoyed with me. With *me*.

"CJ, I hate to say it, but Owen's right. I'm not saying what she did was okay, but we can't afford to kick her off," says Zach.

"We can," I say.

Zach shakes his head. "We can't. The administration loves her. Her mom's on the fucking city council. She used to be on the school board."

"So?"

"If we kick her off, we'll be accused of reverse racism. We have to get this past the school board, and the school board is all white. They need to see white kids involved, or they'll brush this off as another minority issue," says Mizhir, who I was hoping would be on my side. I stare at him and he shrugs. "I'm just saying."

"Brynn has so much to offer, Ceej," Emily says, which doesn't surprise me. "She led the March for Our Lives walkout last year. She headed that fund-raiser to help the families whose houses burned down in the wildfires. She organized LGBTQ-plus Education day. I know she's not perfect, but can't you just let this go?"

"No." I'm sick of people—especially Emily—going on about what a #winner Brynn is, like that makes her special, like that's a reason to forgive anything she does. Bullshit. She's not that special. "Nikki led the Black Lives Matter protest last year, *and* she was sophomore-class president. Lilianna organized those activities to educate people about undocumented immigrants, *and* she cochaired that wildfire fund-raiser with Brynn. And Mizhir, weren't you involved in that charity basketball tournament thing?" Mizhir nods. "But people who saw him on the announcements were like, 'That's the dude who did Ask a Muslim Day.'"

Lilianna sees where I'm going and jumps in. "It's true, though. We can be involved in anything, but people pay the most attention when we're leading 'minority groups' and 'minority causes.' They only see us as 'minority leaders.'"

"Right? You're all total leaders," I say. The gray ache of inadequacy pulses briefly in my chest—*I'm* not a leader. I ignore it and press on. "Brynn's no better than any of you. Why should she get all the airtime? Why does she think she gets to be in charge?"

"Brynn is a minority leader. Queer people are marginalized, too, you know," Emily says quietly.

"The QSA is like, eighty percent white," counters Tulasi.

Emily swallows. "She knows that. She told me the other day she wishes it was different, but what's she supposed to do if only white kids come to the meetings?"

I see the others exchanging looks, and my heart sinks. "Emily. Come. On," I groan. Em blinks at me, and I wonder if maybe I've gone a step too far.

Zach slaps his palms down on his desk. "Okay, whatever, you guys, it's not worth fighting about. I say we let Brynn know she fucked up, but we stick together. I'm telling you we need her."

"I agree," says Owen. "We have to be bigger than her mistake."

"No!" I shout. "That's the problem! It doesn't matter if we're bigger than her mistake because *Brynn* is not bigger than her mistake. She's always been this way. She's not going to change just because we talk to her! What?" I demand, when I see people's shocked faces. No one says anything.

"I'm with you guys," Em says to Owen and Zach, ignoring me completely. To everyone else, but really to me, she says, "I think you're being really unfair if you kick her off."

Nikki chews on a fingernail. "She's my friend and my teammate, but I am not here for any white-savior bullshit."

"*Thank* you!" I say. Finally.

Nikki nods at me, but then she says, "I think it's only fair to let her state her case, though."

"Maybe she'll apologize. Maybe she'll figure it out and back off," says Mizhir.

Emily looks at me. She doesn't say anything, but I can read her eyes. *Please*, they say. *You know what it's like to fuck up. She's only done this one thing. She doesn't deserve to be punished for it.* But I know that this "one thing" is one in an entire series of things.

Brynn arrives a few minutes later. "Oh, did I get the time wrong?" she asks when she sees the rest of us sitting somberly in a circle.

Owen tells her what we've been talking about, and her eyes grow large.

"So, uh." Owen clears his throat. "What do you think? You wanna say anything?"

For a moment, the only sound in the room is the clink of Tulasi's bangle against her desk as she spins it on her wrist. Then Brynn straightens up and takes a breath. "You guys have it all wrong. I was trying to bring *more* attention to the issue, not take the focus off it. I would never do anything to sabotage you guys. I mean you can see that, right? How I got the press here, how Owen and Aviana were both able to make really good points on TV?"

Aviana says, "You interrupted me."

Brynn winces a little. "Ohh. You're right, I'm sorry. That was rude." Aviana relaxes visibly, but Brynn's not done. "It's just—we agreed we were going to try to appeal to everybody, and you were talking a lot about being Asian—which is so awesome, right? But there were only a few seconds left, and I wanted to bring it back on message, that's all."

"That's not what—" Aviana stops. It's clear that Brynn's not going to get it.

Then I try. "That article in the *Merc* was all about you, Brynn."

"But that's the *point*," Brynn protests. "To show that it's everybody's issue. You'd think it would be like, minorities against whites, but if a white girl like me thinks it's important, that's a powerful statement."

Explaining to me that you've generously announced to the world that my cause is worth supporting is not the way to win me over, I want to say. She's so clueless, I almost feel sorry for her. Either that, or she's super devious, which I'm tempted to believe. But holy shit. Either way, she can't stop being the star of The Brynn Show.

"So, you're not sorry?" I ask.

"I'm saying I don't see why you're upset. I'm trying to *help* you."

I look at her sitting there, so sure of herself and her power. I remember the one time when I dared to challenge her, about a week after she'd humiliated Emily behind her back on Valentine's Day in eighth grade. "Hey," she'd said, "I'm *protecting* her right now. People were making fun of both of you, and I made them stop. You should be grateful."

Only that time, she had all the power. This time, the power belongs to me. It expands inside me and I feel like I'm literally growing to accommodate it, tall and strong and bright as a sunflower. I say, "Brynn, I really think you should resign."

Brynn looks stunned. "But I— Why? I didn't do anything wrong! Why are you being so mean to me?"

"Brynn," says Nikki gently. "You're not the victim here. No one's being mean. We're just trying to tell you something you're not used to hearing. You need to stop putting yourself at the center of everything."

"I'm not putting myself at the center. I told you I'm trying to help, and I don't understand why you guys can't see that."

"You're not listening to us," says Tulasi. "You have to try to listen."

"No, *you're* not listening," Brynn insists.

Enough of this. I turn to the rest of the group and say, "It's time to vote."

When I've counted the votes and recycled the scraps of paper we voted on, Brynn comes back in, her features arranged in a benign, neutral sort of smile. Nikki jiggles her knee. Mizhir spins his pen and Lilianna picks at the edges of a sticker on her laptop. Tulasi plays with the strings on her hoodie, which used to say McAllister Girls Soccer and now says ~~McAllister~~ Girls Soccer. Owen watches me, and Emily never takes her eyes off Brynn. It's really, really awkward.

I face her and say it. "It was really close, Brynn. I'm sorry, but you have to go."

Brynn's eyes fill with tears—a sight I never thought I'd see. But I can't allow myself to feel bad about it. She did this to herself.

36

YOU'D THINK THAT WITH BRYNN OFF THE committee, everything would be easier. But Brynn was supposed to share tips from her mom today about how to perfectly target our presentation for the school board meeting next Thursday. And it felt weird to call her and ask her to share her notes after she left. So we waded around in our ignorance for thirty minutes, bickering over slides versus posters, facts versus testimonials, and whether we should make a last-minute video, all the while secretly wondering who voted to keep Brynn on and who voted to kick her out.

I'm in no mood to go to Heart's Desire after the meeting, where I'm sure Owen will skulk around the store and disapprove of me all evening, so I beg off work and drive home.

Mom's Tesla is parked in the driveway, which is strange. It's not even five o'clock yet.

When I poke my head into her office to say hi, she shuts her laptop and turns around. She does not look happy to see me.

"I got an email from Mr. Harrison," she announces.

Oh no. This has to be about what just went down at the STORM meeting.

"I thought I asked you to stay out of this mess. I know you're planning something for the school board meeting next week, and I want you to stop." And there it is.

But I'm ready for it. "Mom, McAllister was a racist. He stole that land from Motohara. He stole our store. How could I stay out of it?"

Mom leans back in her chair and closes her eyes. "I'm not asking why you got involved, kiddo. I'm asking you—again—to back off. I know you feel strongly about Robert Senior, but the rest of the family and all their good work don't deserve to suffer because you're mad about my selling Heart's Desire."

As if this whole thing is a little temper tantrum on my part. Every time we argue about Heart's Desire, I'm reminded that she really doesn't know me anymore. She doesn't know that I'm finally on my own path. Maybe now's the time to tell her. I take a steadying breath and start. "Mom, you're the one who's always telling me to have a vision and a plan and to fight for what I believe in. Well, I believe in Heart's Desire. I like it there. I'm good at choosing flowers for people. I'm good at arranging them. But you want to take it away from me so you can make some money you don't even need. And now that the school-renaming movement is getting in the way of you and your company, you want me to back off that, too? You're such a hypocrite."

Okay, that did not end the way I meant it to. But I'm not sorry I said it.

Anyway, it's like she didn't even hear me; she says, "CJ, that flower shop does not have a future, with or without MVC. I will not allow you to become a florist, for crying out loud. You are literally throwing your future away working with Hannah."

"I'd rather work with Hannah and be happy and poor than—"

"Hannah wasn't born until after the store started making money. She has no idea what it's like to be poor, and neither do you. She didn't have to eat rice and Spam every day. She never had to get her clothes from the church charity closet. But I did. And there is nothing wrong with wanting a little financial security and a little comfort, CJ. There's nothing wrong with success."

That stops me a little, picturing my high-powered, sophisticated mother wearing secondhand clothes and eating Spam for lunch. I knew that her childhood wasn't as easy as mine, but she's never told me before just how hard it was. I lean against the wall and flick the corner of the area rug with my toe, thinking about that.

"Listen, kiddo. Hannah has never in her life considered anyone's point of view besides her own, and she takes everything she has for granted. As do you, I might add. Not all of us can make a living on a hobby, CJ, and not all of us can just stick by our lofty principles twenty-four-seven. I know Hannah's told you that you can. I'm telling you she's full of shit."

With that, the sympathy I had begun to feel for Mom evaporates. "You know what, Mom? Maybe Hannah can't afford her own fancy house, but who cares? She's always done what she thought was right. She's taught me to stand up against racism and sexism. That's more important than how to get into a fancy college and make a lot of money, which is all you seem to care about teaching me." Bam.

Mom looks like she might explode. "Are you fucking kidding me, CJ? Is that really what you think—that I don't fight against racism and sexism? Do you have any idea how many assholes assume that the fucking twenty-one-year-old male intern is my boss? Or think that it's okay to try to follow me into my hotel room after a business meeting? Or that I'll be flattered when they tell me that their fantasy is to see me in a geisha costume? And that's just the shit they say to my face, CJ. I won't even tell you about what I've heard that they say behind my back." She's sitting straight up now, eyes blazing, her hands gripping the armrests of her chair. "My entire *career* has been a fight against racism and sexism."

Oh. I'd seen some of her speeches about fighting to get recognized and promoted and demanding an equal salary. I didn't know about the other stuff. Only, "Why do you put up with it, if it's so horrible? Why don't you do something? Or tell someone? Or quit?" I feel inexplicably angry at her—why can't she be the warrior I thought she was?

Mom taps her fingers on the armrest for a moment before she says, "First of all. Never, ever blame the target. No one asks to be harassed."

"You blamed Hannah for her racist trolls," I mumble.

Mom sighs. "Well, I was wrong." She gives me a stony look and asks, "May I continue?"

I nod.

"I put up with all that bullshit, CJ, because if I report it, I'm a whiny bitch who can't take a joke and isn't a team player, and that's the end of my career in the industry. And I want to stay in the industry. I put up with it because Katsuyamas never quit. I put up with it because sometimes you have to shut up and do what's smart instead of what's right, because that's the only way that you can get ahead and achieve your goals." She pauses and sighs again before going on. "It sucks. I hate it. I know you probably don't understand, but for most of my life, it's been the only way. But success is the best revenge, CJ, and I am successful. I'm giving you what I never had in my life: an ambitious, powerful female role model."

I don't know how she does it. I feel like I've been bungee jumping the whole time I've been listening to her: Righteous outrage. Remorseful sympathy. Outrage. Sympathy. And here I am again, back at outrage. "If you wanted to be a role model, you'd spend less time sucking up to Trey McAllister so that you can be 'successful,' and more time being honest about what his family did to ours. All you care about is what you want."

There's a long silence that I hope is the sound of my point hitting home. Mom closes her eyes and takes one yoga breath, but I can tell it's not enough. She laser-eyes me and says, in a voice as cold and sharp as a steel blade, "You're the one who needs to think about your family, CJ. You and Hannah playing at being social justice leaders—"

"I'm not playing at it, Mom. I'm working hard at it. It means something to me."

But once again, she brushes my goals aside. "Even worse then. You're working to make the McAllisters look bad so you can get what you want. Have you thought at all about how that affects anyone besides yourself? How it affects me, for example? Have you ever considered for a moment what the money from the sale could mean for us?"

I'm pissed enough now to sneer and say as nastily as I can, "A yacht?"

Mom looks like I've just slapped her. She swivels her chair back and forth for a moment and looks silently up at the ceiling. When she speaks again, her voice has lost its sharp edge. "I've hung on to Heart's Desire ever since your grandfather died because he loved it so much. I hung on to it because I felt responsible for his death and because it felt like the only way I could make amends for accepting the job at McAllister. But let me tell you something, CJ. Heart's Desire wasn't doing well when he died, and it's been hemorrhaging money—*my* money—for years. And did you think Hannah's been living with us rent-free all these years just to keep you company? I pay for everything, CJ. I've been supporting her and what is essentially a hobby that costs tens of thousands of dollars a year. And I'm tired. I'm so fucking tired of it."

I feel as if the ground under my feet is crumbling. I have nothing to say.

Mom continues. "And I haven't told anyone yet, but I'm thinking about starting my own micro-VC firm, specifically to fund women-owned and -run companies. Do you know how many start-ups get turned down solely because they're run by women? Especially women of color. No one will ever admit that's the reason, but it is. Once the sale goes through, Hannah will be taken care of, even if she never gets off her lazy ass for the rest of her life. And we'll have a safety net if my firm fails."

Now what? How am I supposed to stay angry at Mom for being a money-hungry sellout when she's actually trying to start a rad feminist venture capital firm? Only—can you be a feminist if you play along and don't complain about sexism and harassment and all of that? I poke the now flipped-over corner of the rug with my toe, trying to get it to flip back again.

Mom leans forward in her chair and says, "Please, CJ. I'm really impressed that you and your friends are taking this on. But it would mean a lot to me if you could come up with a compromise. Have a plaque dedicated to Motohara. Or have a page of your school website dedicated to him. Put it on Wikipedia.

Something that doesn't involve marching around screaming about Robert McAllister being a racist, because it's so much more complicated than that. Okay? That way, the shit storm dies down, MVC can buy the property without a huge public outcry, and I get a chance to start something new."

All I wanted was to work at Heart's Desire. Why did things have to get so hard?

As if she can read my thoughts, she adds, "And you and Hannah will still be able to do your flower stuff on the side. I have to be in Denver for a conference next week during the school board meeting, so I'm trusting you to do what I'm asking. I know you can do it. Don't let me down."

The whole thing is falling apart anyway, I want to tell her. *I may as well do what you want.* But that feels like admitting defeat, like quitting, and if I quit, this will become just another one of CJ's Many Failures. But if by some miracle I succeed—if I prevent the sale of Heart's Desire, if this renaming thing goes through—I'll be betraying Mom and crushing her dreams. No matter what I do, no matter what happens, I lose.

A Brief History of Chisaki Joan Katsuyama's Romantic Learning Opportunities, Part IV

Day 60

Mom, who'd noticed me dragging myself around the house and not eating, took me to the doctor. I couldn't think of a good way to say no.

No fever. No swollen lymph nodes. Nothing wrong with my lungs or my heart, no noticeable swelling of any of my organs. Dr. Shumba turned to Mom and said, "Could you just step into the hallway for a minute? I'd like to have a private conversation with CJ here."

"Oh, sure. No problem!" Mom stood up and left with a fake smile on her face.

Once we were alone, Dr. Shumba went over her notes for a few seconds before asking me, "When did you say your last period was?" She lifted her gaze and looked me in the eye, and I knew she knew.

After my inadvertently weepy confession, she gave me a tissue, went over some options, and said gently, "You have a few more weeks. Think about it carefully, and then do what you're comfortable with. If you decide to tell your mother and she disagrees with what you want to do, feel free to contact me and we can figure it out together."

"Okay."

Think about it carefully. I had just assumed I would end the pregnancy. Shit. Did that make me a bad person? That it was never even a question?

But Mom couldn't possibly want for me to have a baby. Right?

On the other hand, Mom decided to have me.

Day 60, continued
Once we were in the car, Mom asked, "So what did you and Dr. Shumba talk about?" in a voice that was so casual, it sounded forced.

"It's confidential."

"Nothing I need to know?" Her voice was still light, but a note of suspicion curled through it, acrid as burned coffee.

"Nuh-uh," I said, and pretended to fall asleep, so Mom wouldn't ask me more uncomfortable questions.

Still Day 60
We had my favorite takeout for dinner: pomegranate apple

mango chicken bowl from Aqui. I did my best, but halfway through, I had to suppress the urge to gag. Which was when Mom pounced.

"CJ, are you pregnant?"

I wanted desperately to lie, but the lie was too big. It lodged in my throat along with the cumulative anxiety of the past few weeks. It was thick and heavy and I thought I might choke on it. "It's, um. I, um."

Across the table, Hannah froze, her fork halfway to her mouth.

"CJ. Answer me. Is that what you and Dr. Shumba talked about? Are. You. Pregnant?"

"Yes," I whispered.

Mom took in a sharp breath and looked off to the side. Hannah lowered her fork to her plate. I tried not to cry.

"Let's remember that we're a family," said Hannah, a little too brightly. "We support each other. Good times and bad times."

"Are you sure?" said Mom, as if Hannah wasn't even there. I nodded.

Mom closed her eyes and massaged her temples, taking another breath in. She released the breath in a long, slow puff, her eyes still closed. Then she opened her eyes and asked, "How? I mean, what— Okay, I'm sorry, CJ, but how could you let this happen? After everything I've told you about being careful, about being responsible—did I not make myself clear? Did I fail you somehow? Why didn't you tell me you were having sex? I would have gotten you on the pill, at the very least! Jesus. Were you even using a condom? Did he pressure you into not using a condom? Because if he did—"

"Mimi!" Hannah cut in. "Calm down. It doesn't matter how it happened. What matters is that she's pregnant *now*. I mean, you of all people should understand how she's feeling."

"Well, okay, Miss Therapist," Mom snapped. "CJ, how are you feeling? Because if you're feeling how I felt, you're beating yourself up for being stupid enough not to insist on using a condom. If you're feeling what I felt, you're ashamed and disappointed in yourself because you let some idiot talk you into doing something you knew was a bad idea." Mom was practically snarling now. "That better not be it, CJ. Please at least tell me you weren't as stupid as I was. Please tell me you used a condom, and it was an accident."

I opened my mouth to snarl back at her, but something sharp and bitter and formless as smoke rose from the lump in my throat and filled my head, and all I could do was cry. Because what Mom said was exactly how I felt. Furious with myself. Destroyed over having failed and disappointed her in such epic fashion. Unmoored and adrift in the face of an oncoming storm.

And terrified about facing her and telling her that no, it wasn't the condom's fault. It was mine. Well, mine and Andy's, but I felt like I was having to own it way more than him, even though I knew I shouldn't. I was literally carrying the consequences of our mistake. The thought made me cry even harder.

"Oh, Ceej." I could hear the remorse in Mom's voice, and it washed through me and released even more tears. She came over and put her arm around me. "Don't cry, kiddo. I'm sorry. I shouldn't have yelled at you, I just—" She sighed. "You know, I'm still mad at myself for screwing up all those years ago. And now I'm mad at myself for not doing a better job protecting you from the same mistake." She paused, and scowled. "Though your shit boyfriend bears plenty of responsibility, too."

"He's not shit." I sniffled. Why was I defending him? He *was* shit. "Anyway, we broke up."

Mom scoffs. "Thus proving my point. And he *is* shit if he thought unprotected sex was a good idea."

"It wasn't just him. It was both of us. I mean, I didn't think it was a *good* idea. But I thought—"

"You didn't think," she snapped. "That was the problem. Neither of you were thinking."

I started crying again.

A pause, a sigh. "I'm sorry, CJ. That was uncalled for." I could feel her willing herself to shift modes. "So. How many weeks?"

I shrugged and wiped my eyes. "I don't know. Six? Seven?"

"Okay." I recognized her problem-solving voice: mode-shift successful. "So . . ." She pulled out her phone and looked something up. "Good. That means you still qualify for an abortion pill. I'll call my gynecologist and we can take you in tomorrow to get a prescription. Okay?"

"Okay." I allowed myself to relax just a little bit. Maybe

things would turn out okay, after all. Mom was on my side. She was going to help me through this.

"Mimi, stop!" Hannah put her hand on Mom's arm. "Have you even asked CJ what she wants?"

Mom shot her a withering look. "Hannah. Are you fucking kidding me right now?" She turned to me. "You don't want to keep the baby, right? I mean, that would be—"

"No. I don't," I said hurriedly. I didn't want to hear all the terrible things she might think of that decision.

"Okay then." She took a sip of wine and addressed Hannah. "CJ has made a tough, smart, mature decision, and I will not allow you or anyone else to make her feel guilty about it. Wanting an abortion and not collapsing with angst over it doesn't make her a bad person."

Hannah pushed her food around her plate and nodded at it. She spoke slowly and deliberately, the way you might talk someone through defusing a ticking time bomb. "I'm not trying to make anyone feel guilty about having an abortion. But you've just made this huge deal about what a terrible mistake it was to get pregnant. I want to clarify that you don't necessarily think that having an unplanned baby is a mistake."

"It *is* a mistake, Hannah. It would be like . . . like breaking a vase she could never repair."

"But not *always*." She looked hard at Mom.

What the— Oh.

Mom figured it out at the same time that I did. "Well, obviously, having CJ wasn't a mistake," she said impatiently. "But her situation is different from mine. Jesus, Hannah, could you please stop complicating things?"

I've replayed that conversation over and over in my head. I'm grateful to Mom for taking control and basically being cool about everything after her initial reaction. I'm grateful to her for being so totally behind my decision, and for calling bullshit on anyone who thinks I should feel guilty for not feeling guilty. But I wonder if she secretly still feels angry at me for screwing up so profoundly. Sometimes I think I'll never do anything impressive enough to make up for it, to make up for a lifetime of disappointment, really. Sometimes I wonder if, deep down, she does regret her decision to have me.

I know how I felt when I realized I was pregnant. How frantic I was to not have a baby. She must have felt the same way. Someone must have convinced her that she'd have an amazing daughter who would grow up to be worth the sacrifice and the extra work. Was I worth it? Was I?

Mom has always said that having me was a deliberate choice, that even if the pregnancy was a mistake, I was not. But if having me was really the right decision, why would she still be so angry about having gotten pregnant with me in the first place? That night planted a seed of doubt in my heart, and the doubt put down roots and sent out tendrils that have been growing ever since, a tangle of thorny vines that coil themselves around me and draw blood every time I reach for her.

37

IT'S NOW NEARLY THREE WEEKS AFTER VALENTINE'S Day, and maybe it's just me, but business feels a little slow. But Hannah says it's normal and not to worry, and anyway, I've been too immersed in the drama around STORM to pay a whole lot of attention lately.

The school board meeting is coming up tomorrow, and tensions are running high. Rumors have been circulating that we kicked Brynn off the committee because she's white. Mizhir couldn't resist saying, "I told you so," although he didn't look happy to say it. Despite our lack of access to Brynn's insider tips, the STORM presentation is ready to go and, if you ask me, it's freaking amazing—this is a committee full of #winners, after all. But no one else feels confident about it. Even if we make it past the school board, the next hurdle we face is the city council, one of whose members is probably mad at us for kicking her daughter off the committee.

I know that Owen blames me for everything, and I've discovered that I really don't like living with that. So despite being frantic to finish the flower-magic pins I've promised everyone for tomorrow, here I am at his house after work, trying to talk things over. His mother directed me to the backyard, where he's mucking around with a hoe in their little vegetable garden.

"Brynn was shitty and totally insensitive," I tell him. Instead of answering, he chunks at the dirt with the hoe: *chunk, chunk, chunk, chunk.* "Come on," I say. "You were there. You heard her. She didn't think she did anything wrong."

Owen looks up. "Maybe, but your vibe felt really hostile. It wasn't like, 'We get that you want to help, but you're hurting us.' It was more like, 'Fuck you, get out.' That wasn't cool. And how do you think the school board is gonna take the news that we kicked Brynn off the committee? At best, we look disorganized and fragmented. At worst, we look like we hate white people. Is that the image you want to present?"

I roll my eyes. "They don't have to know. And they're not going to believe we hate white people."

"We booted the only white kid on the committee, Ceej, and that's all some people need. I get that she was shitty, but it would have been worth trying to educate her and work with her."

He goes back to hoeing: *chunk, chunk, chunk.*

Frustration scribbles itself into a knot of tangled thread in my skull. "It's not like I don't get that. I'm not an idiot. In fact, if it was anyone else, I probably *would* have given them another chance."

"Anyone else?" Owen stops chunking and stands the hoe upright. "Are you saying it's about Brynn and not about what she did?"

"It's about Brynn not caring who she uses or who she hurts as long as it makes her look good. She wasn't going to stop just because we asked her to. Believe me, I know. I did us a favor."

"So it's personal? You compromised the entire movement for *personal* reasons?"

I wish he would stop obsessing about that. "Owen. Nothing's been compromised. Stop obsessing about our image and stop blowing things out of proportion. Anyway, if you're worried about how we look to white people I'll ask Shane to join us. He said he'd be down to help with anything. He has tons of white friends, and he can get them all to come to—"

"You didn't answer my question. Did you ask us to vote Brynn out for personal reasons or not?"

"I mean . . ." Yes? Kind of? "I wasn't the only one who voted her out."

"The others voted on principle. They like Brynn, but they didn't have patience for her ignorance. I can respect that. But I think you're more . . . obsessed with your own shit and your own grudges. Sorry, Ceej, but that's the truth."

Ouch. But . . . well. When he puts it that way, of course it looks bad.

"I'm sorry, Owen. I just. I'd had enough. She's done this before and I was tired of putting up with her. Anyway, we don't need her. I told you if you want white people, I'm sure that Shane and his friends will go to the board meeting. I know that's cynical, but you're the one who's worried about optics."

"Yeah, about that." Owen's hand strays to the back of his head. "Being cynical. It's pretty obvious that Shane signed the petition because of you. He'd be going to the school board meeting because of you. He's trying to impress you."

"What even—that's the stupidest thing I've ever heard." I think back to that afternoon in the quad. He did say he'd sign the petition for me. And then he held my hand and I kind of lost my mind. But then he was ready to beat up that little punk, and he said he *got* it. That couldn't possibly have been about impressing me. Even if it was, isn't that a step in the right direction? "Anyway, who cares why he's there? Brynn wasn't in this for the right reasons, either."

"I think she was."

"I know she wasn't."

"You can't know."

I suppose not. But I've seen Brynn's dark side, and until I personally see evidence of something different, I refuse to change my position. "Agree to disagree."

Owen starts hacking absently at the ground again. Without looking at me, he asks, "So are you and Shane like, a thing?"

"Oh my god, *what*? What does that even have to do with any of this?"

"You are, aren't you?"

"No, of course not!" Well, probably not. Not yet. No, probably not ever, even. Not really. "Why even does it matter?"

"It matters because—" Owen stops hacking, drops the hoe, and paces in a little circle. He takes a deep breath and grabs two fistfuls of his hair as he lets his breath out in a huff. "God, CJ. I don't— I can't—" He lets go of his hair and shakes his head. "I don't know. You're right. It doesn't matter."

"What. Tell me what you were going to say."

Owen sighs. "I dunno. I guess I'm feeling a little protective, is all. You know he doesn't date girls for very long. I don't want you to be just another bead on a string, you know? You deserve better than that."

"Owen, okay, that's super sweet of you, but I'm not in love with him or anything, so you can stop feeling protective or whatever. And I don't need your approval or your protection." I realize with a guilty start that I've had nearly this identical conversation with Emily about Brynn. I push that thought aside. I need to focus on what's happening here, now.

Owen doesn't respond. He starts hacking again, and I let the silence expand, because it feels good to know that he doesn't know what to say. Finally, he stops hacking and switches to pushing the loosened dirt around. He says softly, "You're right. You don't need my approval. I don't have any right to butt into your relationships, as long as no one's getting hurt."

"Thank you."

He kicks a pebble on the ground. "I know I'm being a dick. Sorry."

"It's fine."

He flips the hoe up, scrapes the dirt off the blade, and wipes it clean with a rag. Then he leans it against the shed and tosses the rag into a bucket. "I just. I'm kinda into you, Ceej. In case you hadn't noticed. I guess I'm jealous."

Well. This is a shocking turn of events. Inside me there's a burst of something disturbingly sparkling and hopeful—nothing like the big, blingy exclamation marks that Shane inspires—but quite possibly better. It's delicate, shimmering, achingly perfect. The thought of taking care of it freaks me out. And how dare he present it to me at the same time that he accuses me of ruining everything? So I crush it. "Oh, who's petty now? Who's obsessed with their own shit now? Is that what this is really all about? Anyway, you have no right to be jealous, what with all that flirting you've been doing with Sabrina."

Owen looks stunned. "What even . . . are you talking about?"

Suddenly I realize that if I keep going down this road, I'll look jealous, which I'm totally not. "Whatever. That has nothing to do with this, so forget it."

"Okay."

"I'm sorry."

"Don't be sorry."

"Okay."

"Okay." Owen raises his hand to rub the back of his head, realizes it's dirty from the hoe, and lowers it. "Well. I guess I'll see you at the school board meeting, then. Hopefully it'll go okay."

He turns and heads into the house without another word, and leaves me standing there, rooted to the ground and unable to figure out what just happened, or what I can do to reverse it.

38

STINGING NETTLES ARE ONE OF THE WORST plants you can touch. The silky hairs on the leaves and stems are actually tiny little hypodermic needles full of toxic chemicals, and one touch can release hundreds of them, which burrow into your skin and make it feel like it's going to burn right off. When the burning subsides, it's replaced by an unbearably itchy, bumpy red rash.

The conversation I had with Owen is a lot like that. His accusation about my being too wrapped up in my personal issues with Brynn (I can't even allow myself to think about his stupid confession and the awful way I ended things) has been bothering me constantly, and it's still irritating me when I leave Heart's Desire and pick up Emily to go to the school board meeting.

It's a long shot, but if I can get Em on my side, maybe some of this yucky feeling will go away.

"I'm not too obsessed with my own shit to see the bigger picture, am I?" I ask her when she gets in.

"What?"

I tell her what Owen said about me and Brynn.

"But she literally—like, actually literally—put herself in front of the movement. Do you see that? All she cares about is herself and her own success."

Em looks out the window for a moment before she says, "Ceej, I know you don't want to hear this, but he's right. You're still mad at Brynn for something she did to me in middle school. I don't know why it's such a big deal to you, but from here, it really looks like that's the main reason you kicked her off the committee."

"Em. You don't understand."

"You're right, Ceej, I don't."

I don't want to hurt her right before the board meeting, but I have to get her to see things my way. The time has come to tell her the whole truth. "Okay, listen. There's more to it than just an ugly eighth-grade breakup."

Em puts her hand up. "Can you just . . . not? I feel like whatever you're going to tell me is going to make us fight, and I don't want to fight with you. Not right now."

We spend the rest of the drive in silence. Emily texts like mad the whole time. When we park and get out of the car, she sighs, loudly and heavily.

"What, Em?"

"You can tell me about it tomorrow, okay? Whatever it is that's making you so mad at Brynn."

"Okay. Whatever." The car chirps as I lock it, and we start across the lot.

"I don't need a ride home, by the way."

"Okay . . . ?"

"I'm going home with Brynn."

Seriously? "Brynn's here? What's she going to do, stage her own protest?"

"She was going to come and support you guys, but I told her not to. And she listened. She's picking me up afterward as a compromise." Emily tilts her chin and looks at me like *See? Brynn's trying to be better.*

But I'm not convinced. "Is she staying away because she doesn't want to upstage us? Or because she doesn't want to make us mad?"

Emily doesn't answer.

"Yeah, that's what I thought."

I want to ask her why she's going home with Brynn, and why she waited until now to tell me, but I don't want to let her turn that into evidence that I'm obsessed. Screw her, anyway.

I've been telling everyone that our presentation is fine, that we don't need Brynn, but I'll admit the stress has gotten to me, so when it all goes well, I could cry with relief. Everyone's wearing tiny little bunches of iris leaves and heather that I gave them for eloquence and good luck. Owen (wearing a T-shirt that reads, *Don't make me repeat myself. —History*), Zach, and Aviana talk about the history of the land, and Mizhir, Nikki, Tulasi, and Lilianna talk about how keeping the McAllister name feels like an endorsement of racist government policies today. Shane and a passel of his white friends are there as promised, to show that it's not just a minority issue, and I refrain from telling Owen I told him so, but I can't help raising my eyebrows at him when Shane's squad whoops and hollers right along with everyone else at the end of the presentation. The all-white school board seems impressed by the entire show.

After a brief round of hugs and high fives with STORM, Owen goes over and shakes Shane's hand and thanks him for coming. I hate that he's so freaking ethical and fair-minded and all "let's do this for the greater good." It makes me feel bad about myself.

Owen, Aviana, and Zach answer Geoffrey's questions for his *Mercury News* article and pose for pictures; I notice that Emily is nowhere to be found. She must have left with Brynn before the rest of us even made it out of the boardroom.

It started raining during the board meeting, and I'm making my lonely, wet way back to my car when Shane breaks away from his pack and jogs over to me. "So, hey, I know we talked about getting together, right? I just found out that the Hoas are having a party on Saturday," he says. "They live up in this ginormous mansion in the hills, and it's gonna be like the party of the century. You should go."

"Oh. Um, okay." Only, party of the century? It sounds like a mob scene. I'd rather not spend another evening hanging with the bros and getting high.

"Don't say okay. Say hell yes." He grins. "The house is a legit palace. With like, grounds and everything. And there's this private gazebo thing with flowers and stuff in the backyard that we can hang in. Just you and me. You'll love it, I promise." He takes my hands in his—mine are cold; his are warm. "Come on. Say you'll be there." Now our fingers are clasped together, and he bends down and tilts his head a little so he can look me straight in the eye. "Please?"

There's something thrilling about having a physically perfect human begging you to meet him in a private gazebo on the palatial grounds of the party of the century. So I say yes.

39

I'VE BECOME SO USED TO WAKING UP EARLY ON Saturdays to help Hannah with weddings that when I wake up and it's light out, I have to think about what day it is. I smile and stretch and snuggle back down into my covers, but it's bittersweet. Sleeping in means that we don't have a wedding, which means we're not making money.

Hannah confessed to Owen and me when I arrived at work yesterday that February was not as good as we'd hoped it would be. The *Merc* article did generate some interest and some extra walk-ins, but business has already dropped off again to pre-article levels. She closed the shop early and declared it closed for the weekend, saying we might as well take a break.

"CJ, will you be okay on your own for tonight and Saturday night? I'm just going to take myself to Asilomar and do some self-care. That way I'll be fresh and rested on Sunday when your mother comes back from Denver." Spending two nights at a hotel on the beach seemed like an odd way to face impending financial disaster; on the other hand, you could also say it was the perfect way.

I do have one thing to do at the shop today, which is to make a custom hairpiece for Sabrina Dang for some dance competition, probably, made of tiny pink, white, and purple roses entwined with jasmine leaves to enchant and charm the judges. We agreed for her to come by Heart's Desire at two, so I drive over at one to put the piece together.

As I wire the roses to a plastic hair clip, I wish I had someone to talk to about how well we did on Thursday. I felt weird bringing it up with Owen yesterday afternoon, especially in front of Hannah. I can't talk to Emily. Aviana's busy with a tae kwon do tournament or a swim meet or something. And I obviously can't tell Mom. How sad is that? I wonder how she'd feel about it. I wish I could feel confident that she'd be proud of me.

40

THERE'S A LOCAL ORDINANCE WHERE LIAM AND
Brendan Hoa live that says the lots can't be smaller than an acre,
"to preserve the rural atmosphere," according to something I
read somewhere. "To keep the riffraff from buying in" is more
like it, if you ask me. But it makes for some good party houses:
spacious, plenty of on-site parking, often with swimming
pools, and little chance of the neighbors calling the police to
complain about the noise.

I pull into the driveway, which is so big and full of cars that
it's really more of a parking lot. It reminds me of the parties
you see in movies. Small, quiet hangouts are the norm in Silicon Valley, so I imagine everyone jumped at the opportunity
to go to a big one.

The palatial front hall (Shane wasn't kidding) opens onto

the living room, which features an enormous picture window that overlooks the valley. In front of the window, a girl sobs on a couch, surrounded by a huddle of cooing friends—sophomores, I think. I feel a pang of loneliness—where are my friends? I didn't even bother to find out what Em was doing tonight.

I follow the sound of the bass down a staircase to the left, which deposits me in what is clearly the main party room. It is cavernous; I mean, it must span the entire length and breadth of the house. There's a pool table and a foosball table, and a bunch of kids are piled on a couch in front of a giant television screen playing the Warriors' game. There's an actual bar with bottles of hard alcohol and what looks like soda and maybe even beer on tap. Liam is serving people and bawling over the crowd noise, "It's gluten-free! It's good for you!" Only . . . is beer really gluten-free? Who knows? Some kid I've never seen before has set up a table where he's selling THC cartridges, batteries, edibles, and weed.

The house is built into the hill, so the basement that I'm in is actually the first floor of the house on the back side. Sliding glass doors open onto a pavilion that glows with fairy lights. When I slip through the doors, I understand why the inside of the house didn't smell like weed. It's not as crowded as inside, but it sure is . . . smoky.

In one corner of the patio, Shane, Nathan, and Ari are having an old-school chugging contest around a miniscule teak deck table laden with a vape pen, a JUUL, and two pitchers—

one empty, one half-empty. Or half-full, I suppose. Shane wins by a mile and punches the air, crushing his cup in his massive hand. "Three in a row, bitches! Yeah! I am the king!"

Deep breath. Ready, steady—

"CJ!" Shane's face breaks into a delighted smile, and he bounds over to me and envelops me in a muscular hug that literally sweeps me off my feet. He puts me down and settles his arm on my shoulders.

"Hey." I try for a sexy-hair swoosh, but my hair is stuck under his arm, so I end up doing a weird sort of half jerk.

"Oh—sorry!" He sweeps my hair over my left shoulder, then carefully replaces his arm. "Better?" I nod, and melt a little inside. He gives me a small, private smile and whispers, "I'm so glad you're here. I've been waiting for you forever."

I'm just a pile of mush right now. I don't even know how I'm standing upright.

"All right, my dudes," Shane announces to the patio, "I'm out." After a couple of sloppy fist bumps, he tucks me under his arm again and says, "Too many people down here. Wanna go upstairs?"

What—no gazebo? Oh well. It's probably wet from yesterday's rain, anyway. I swallow my disappointment and say, "Okay."

We make our way over to the stairs. Shane stumbles once about halfway up, and for a moment his arm seems to be hanging on to me for support more than pulling me close to him.

"You okay?" I ask. Maybe this wasn't such a great idea.

"I think I might be a little drunk," he whispers in my ear. He smiles at me adoringly and adds, "You saved me from breaking my neck. You're my guardian angel." His gaze lingers on my face as he strokes my cheek with the back of his fingers, and I think maybe this is an okay idea after all. Shane steadies himself before pushing the hair out of his eyes and squinting up the stairs. Then he squares his massive shoulders, points up with renewed purpose, and declares, "Arright. Onward." I feel like I'm on the arm of a very drunk, very polite Viking, which is . . . good? Bad? I'm having to recalibrate my expectations so quickly, I can't keep track anymore.

We make it into the front hall without further incident and hang a left into the living room with the window over-looking the valley. He guides me to the right, past Sad Drunk Girl and her sophomore posse on the sofa, into a little alcove tucked away in the corner. It's sort of the opposite of a window seat, with a bench piled high with cushions, and it's lined with bookshelves—a reading nook.

Shane presents the cushioned seats with a sloppy bow, which reminds me of Owen. I shut that thought right down.

We sit down, and I snuggle in next to him. "Comfortable?" he asks.

"Yeah." Oh yeah.

He leans toward me and rests his forehead against mine. He murmurs, "You're so pretty. I've been wanting to kiss you for like, weeks. I really want to kiss you right now."

Well. A little shiver of excitement skims up my spine. And

suddenly I'm curious. If you know, as Shane must, that no matter who you want to kiss, no matter when you want to kiss them, they will absolutely want to kiss you back, how do you choose who to kiss?

"Why me?" I ask.

"'Cause you're pretty," he says again, and the corner of that gorgeous mouth quirks up, and I so, so, so want to kiss it, I mean *I've* been waiting for weeks, too, but something inside me suddenly, perversely wants more. Owen said that pretty was all that Shane cared about, and I am going to prove him wrong.

"Why else?" I lean into him.

"Um . . . 'cause you're sexy?"

"Oh. Okay."

He mistakes my disappointment for insecurity and puts his lips to my ear. "I wouldn't be here with you if I didn't think you were totally hot," he whispers, and part of me is still going, *Yes!* but part of me is going, *Oh no,* and maybe he doesn't mean it the way it sounds, but still. Dammit.

"I guess I meant besides my looks," I say, pulling away just a tiny bit.

Shane looks taken aback, but he plays along. "You're . . ." He concentrates for a moment. "You're a really good listener. You're like, super chill. And . . . oh, I know!" He brightens. "You're like, this badass social activist and . . . hang on." Shane holds up his finger, blinks a couple of times, and says again, "Hang on. I just gotta . . ." He closes his eyes and breathes

- 307 -

in and out a couple of times and stands up. "Whoa, shit." He sways and grips the edge of the alcove. "I think I might be sick. Hang on a sec, okay? I'm just gonna go puke."

He stumbles back through the room, toward the front hall, distracting a couple of Sad Drunk Girl's friends as he passes them. Shit. "Where's the bathroom?" I ask them as I run after Shane, but they just shrug. Private Dreamy Evening with Hot Shane in the Gazebo has officially devolved into Public Drunken Evening with Vomity Shane in the Reading Nook. It's like a fucked-up version of Clue.

Shane is fumbling with the latch on the door, and I figure the front steps are a better place to puke than the front hall, so I step in and help him. He lurches through the doorway, nearly falling as he forgets about the steps. He reels off to the left, bends over double, and empties the contents of his stomach onto the roots of a hydrangea bush. I hope he doesn't kill it.

By the time I've reached his side, Shane is half standing, hands on his knees, spitting into the grass. "Shit," he says, "That was a lot of beer."

"Yeah."

He stands upright and wobbles on his feet. I can't leave him out here. "Let's get you inside where you can lie down."

His brow furrows and his perfect lips gather into a frown as he considers this option. He looks down at me, and his half-lowered lids rise suddenly, as if he's surprised to see me there, then sink back down again. "Fuck, I'm sorry."

"That's okay. Come on, let's go inside."

He allows me to lead him, like a beautiful, barfy, repentant Siberian husky puppy, back through the front hall. "I'm so sorry," he keeps repeating.

We find a bathroom where Shane rinses out his mouth, and then I settle him in the reading nook on his side and find a wastebasket (leather, but beggars can't be choosers) and put it next to the bench.

"I'm so sorry," he slurs one last time. He takes my hand and squeezes it and gives me a sweet, lopsided smile. "Thank you," he says.

Now that my encounter with Shane is officially over, I don't really want to be here anymore. So I slip out the front door again and head to my car.

As I walk down the driveway, something blooms inside me—an understanding that's been unfolding for a while now, I realize. Shane's not right for me. He's beyond not right for me, in fact. Shane is sexy and good-natured and bound for glory, and he thinks I'm pretty and sexy and badass and a good listener, and those are all good things, but I think . . . I think I want more than that.

The reality is that he just doesn't get me. And I don't get him. Not really. There's no spark, as Emily would say. No magic. I think I liked it better when my relationship with him was a fantasy from afar. And I want someone who I can appreciate up close. Someone I really connect with. Who likes it when I listen, but who also wants to listen back. Who thinks I'm badass, but challenges me and holds me accountable when

I fuck up. Who has seen me at my shitty, petty, selfish worst, and still wants to hang around with me.

At least, I hope he still wants to hang around with me.

I need to find Owen and tell him I'm sorry for being a jerk and for letting my stupid personal issues with Brynn get in the way of the big picture. I wonder if he'd be willing to listen to me, if he'd be willing to forgive me. I wonder if he still— Hey, is that his truck?

41

OWEN'S HERE. HE'S PARKED SEVERAL CARS BEHIND me, so that means he got here after I did. A wave of joy ripples through me, followed immediately by another wave of apprehension.

Did he see my car? Does he know I'm here? Did he see me helping Shane? I have to tell him what happened. I can't let him think—as I'm sure anyone who's seen me with Shane tonight will tell him—that Shane and I are together. I have to let him know that he's the one I choose.

Please let him choose me back.

I send him a text:

Hey, I'm at this crazy party in the hills. Saw your truck. Where are you?

No answer.

I rush back inside. Where could he be? A quick tour of the first floor reveals nothing. Shane is sleeping peacefully in the reading nook; Sad Drunk Girl has recovered and is dancing furiously with her friends in front of the picture window. I go down to the basement, and before I've even made it to the bottom of the stairs, I spot him near the bar.

"Owen!" I shout as I wade toward him through the crowd. I'm shameless. But who cares. He doesn't hear me, so I stand on my tiptoes and shout again. "Owen!"

This time he does hear. I watch him scan the room, looking for me. Some guy as big as a wall steps in front of me on his way to the bar and finds it necessary to stop and talk to a friend. I've barely nudged my way past him when it happens.

I emerge from behind Wall Guy's triceps and catch Owen's eye, and it's like watching my life in slow motion. I can see what's coming, but I can't stop it. I can only stand and watch, horrified, as one of the beneficiaries of Liam Hoa's bartenderly generosity turns away from the bar . . . trips . . . staggers . . . and empties a cup full of purportedly gluten-free alcoholic beverage all over my shirt.

A collective "Ohh, shit!" goes up from the crowd, and the staggering drink spiller, one hand over his mouth, the other hand outstretched in apology, repeats over and over, "Oh, fuck. Sorry! Sorry! Sorry!"

I shake him off—there's nothing he can do about it now. I wring my shirt out and wonder if this humiliation will at least win me a little sympathy from Owen, despite everything.

In the end, the person who comes rushing over to help me is not Owen.

It's Sabrina.

"Oh, CJ! Oh my god, are you okay? What is that, beer? Oh, you poor thing."

"I'm fine. I'm fine. Really, it's okay. Don't worry about it," I babble, and I sidle past her and Owen, holding my soggy shirt out away from my body. I just want to get out of here as quickly as possible, and it's not simply because of the spill.

Because the spill is bad enough. But it's the other thing that happened—the out-of-my-control, unchangeable thing that happened in the moment between the one where Owen's eyes met mine, and the one that left me drenched in alcohol and humiliation. I had just squeezed my way around Wall Guy and turned toward Owen, a tentative smile on my face, fear and hope battling in my heart.

Only it wasn't just him. Sabrina—perfect, beautiful, brilliant Sabrina—was snuggled under Owen's arm, her own arm splayed across his chest, her dainty face tilted up toward his. She saw me and her face lit up and she pointed at the flowers in her hair. And I realized that she didn't order the flowers to enchant the judges at a dance competition. She ordered them to enchant Owen. And it looks like they're working.

42

FLOWER MAGIC ISN'T SUPPOSED TO *WORK*. IT'S all romantic hocus-pocus.

This is what I tell myself as I spin and duck back into the crowd, holding my shirt out in front of me. On the other hand, if the magic doesn't work, that means that Sabrina has captured Owen's attention purely on her own merits.

Neither option is pleasant to think about, and I focus my energy on getting the hell out of there and back home so I can mope in peace. Naturally this means that I bump right into the world's biggest fan of flower magic: Emily.

"CJ!"

"Hey, Em."

Well, this is awkward. I didn't text her, she didn't text me. And yet here we are.

"What happened to your shirt?"

I consider saying, "Nothing," which would be an obvious lie. Instead, I say, "Um." And start to cry. I mean, not sobbing or anything. Just low-key weeping. A couple of wayward tears and a closed-up throat.

Em takes me to an empty bathroom and I unload on her like the pathetic lovelorn loser I have apparently become. Dammit. I don't want to be sad about Owen. Not before we even get together. Which will probably never happen now.

"I'll be okay," I tell her. "I'll be fine."

"I know you will." She smiles. "Hey, Ceej?"

"What."

"I'm sorry I've been a butt. I don't like being all weird and uncomfortable with you. I miss telling you stuff."

I sniffle and wipe my eyes. "I've missed telling you stuff, too." I hug her, and she lets me, despite my disgusting shirt. I smile. This is one good thing from tonight, at least.

"So, um. Can I tell you something?" she asks.

"Sure."

"Okay. But don't be mad at me. Promise?"

It's never a good sign when people begin a confession with "Don't be mad." But I need us to keep being okay, so I say, "Promise."

She takes a deep breath. "I think I'm in love."

"Ha ha."

"No, really. I mean. Not *really*. But yeah . . . seriously in like, anyway."

Oh no. My heart contracts.

Keep it together, CJ. Emily was here for you. Be here for Emily.

Emily looks down at her index finger, which is now wound tightly in a hair bandage, and lets the coil of hair go before starting on a new lock. "Look. I know you don't trust her. I know you hate her for hurting me and screwing up with the whole *Mercury News* interview and all that. But can you please give her a chance? For me? I've never been this happy in my whole life."

Emily's eyes are sparkling and her cheeks are flushed. She really does look happy. I can't not be happy for her. I give her another hug—it's a big night for hugs, I guess—and say, "If you're happy, I'm happy."

"Really?"

"Really." I will put aside my feelings about Brynn. I'm not the boss of Emily. She can see whoever she wants.

Em smiles again. She's so happy to have me back on her side. I can totally do this. I can be the supportive friend she needs right now. To prove it, I say, "So. You and Brynn. When . . . I mean, how long . . . ?"

"Um," says Emily, playing with the edge of her shirt, "Since Valentine's Day." She smiles shyly. "That's a pretty high-stakes first date, huh?"

I smile and nod. "For sure." But—wait. Hang on a sec. Valentine's Day? "You told me you went home and crashed early on Valentine's Day."

"Yeah . . . I'm sorry. I should have told you. I wanted to, but I was afraid you'd be upset."

"So . . ." I don't want to ask, because the answer is going to make me sad. "You lied to me about Valentine's Day?"

Em drops her shirt and goes back to her hair. "Yes. But—"

I knew that was a bad question. I shouldn't have asked it. I should be asking questions like *What did you talk about? Did you do anything besides talk? Did you kiss good-night? What was it like?* I try hard to reset.

"Hang on." I've just remembered something else. "Brynn sent a text that night that said she was with Nikki and Lilianna. Was that a lie, too? Was she with you?"

"Oh. We were all out together—just as friends—when she sent that text. Brynn and I . . . we kind of hooked up after Nik and Lili went home." Em blushes.

It shouldn't matter. I should be happy for her. But I'm trying to dig myself out of this weird sense of double betrayal: If it was supposed to be just friends at first, why didn't she invite me? Is that who she's here with at this party? Why is she here with them instead of me?

I know. I *know.* I know I got invited anyway. I didn't invite her, either. Maybe she even knew I'd be here.

"CJ? You've had this thing about Brynn ever since eighth grade. I know it's because she was shitty to me, and I appreciate that, but you've gotten a little out of control lately." Emily's got this condescending, kind-but-firm thing going on in her eyes, and that condescension changes everything. I stop feeling hurt and start feeling angry.

Angry at Brynn for manipulating Emily. Angry at Emily for skipping blithely into disaster after all I've done to keep her out of it, for running off with her fancy new friends as if *our* friendship doesn't matter. Because why should it matter being compared to Brynn for President, future leader of the free world, and her posse of #winners?

It's time she knew the truth. Then she'll see who her real friends are. "Do you even know why Brynn broke up with you in eighth grade? Did she even tell you?"

"She did tell me, Ceej. She didn't *want* to break up with me. She was afraid of her parents, and she freaked out. She apologized for the way she handled it, and I'm okay with that. It's really hard to stand up to your parents about being queer."

"Yeah, I know she freaked out. But did you know that Brynn tried to get me to turn against you in eighth grade? She asked me in front of everyone if I was afraid to be friends with you. I could have pretended to be afraid. But I didn't. Because we were friends."

This gets her. Emily fires back at me. "Shut up, Ceej. Telling people that you're friends with a queer kid is nothing like telling people you're queer. It's not even close. You're just jealous of Brynn because you hate everyone more successful than you, and you can't see that the only reason *you're* not doing better is because you don't even try. And now you're jealous of me because I have a great, amazing girlfriend and all you've ever had is a couple of lame, shallow relationships with guys you don't even really like. Oh—except the one nice guy you keep refusing to go out with because you're too afraid to risk another failure. And now it's too late, but that's your own fault."

She's right. I shouldn't have compared my loyalty to her in eighth grade with Brynn's decision to stay closeted. And congratulating myself for it was fucked up. But I'm still nursing the ache of being left out and left behind, and she doesn't know about my abortion, but she's rubbing my face in every other failure I've ever had to carry, and the only thing my pain doesn't blot out is my need to hurt her back. "Well, at least none of the guys I went out with told their friends that they thought I was gross. At least none of them let people laugh at me behind my back."

"What the hell are you talking about, CJ? You're not even making sense anymore."

I tell her the whole story: Austin waving her Valentine's Day cookie in the air; Brynn laughing and passing it around; Brynn asking me if I was afraid to be friends with Em. "She's a manipulative, backstabbing hypocrite, Emily, and all she cares about is making herself look good. I bet she's only going out with you so she can bring you to prom and get in the newspaper for being McAllister's first prom queen to bring a girl as her date."

Something in the back of my head is whispering, *Reel it in; shut it down*, but I'm on such a roll, and it feels good, too, in a horrible, mean way. It feels good to tell my version of the history of Emily and Brynn, to finally reveal to Emily who she's been hung up on all these years. What Brynn really did.

But that high is short-lived. Emily's entire face droops. All except her eyes, which are now bright with tears. I can tell she's hoping I'll take everything back, but I can't. Not now, anyway. Not yet.

She turns and leaves without a word, and I'm overcome by a desire to run after her and take it all back like I know she wants. Maybe I'm being childish, hanging on to the past like this. But the fact is that Brynn did something awful. And I looked out for Em, I tried to protect her, and she paid me back by prioritizing a crush—a doomed crush, I might add—over her common sense, over her best friend's advice. And now she thinks she's too good for me. I try to let that delicious sense of self-righteousness fill me up again, but it sputters and goes out.

43

TWENTY MINUTES LATER, I'M STILL DRIVING aimlessly around in the hills. I've rejected a potential boyfriend; and I don't know what Owen even is anymore, but I've lost him, too; and now I've lost Emily.

I can't let things continue this way. I need to make a change.

There's no point in trying to win Owen back, now that Sabrina's got her claws into him. But maybe I can fix this mess with Em. Our friendship is more important to me than anything. Anyway, if Brynn breaks her heart, someone needs to be around to help her pick up the pieces.

So I send Em a text.

Hey, I'm sorry I yelled at you

I'm still hurt, but I shouldn't have been so mean to you. I was just venting. It's not how I really feel.

Let's try to figure this out, okay?

I stare at the screen, my heart galloping, galloping, galloping while I wait for her reply. Time, on the other hand, seems to slow down. The seconds plod endlessly by.

Finally, Emily:

Clearly it IS how you feel bc you're not really taking anything back

I've been beating myself up over not telling you right away about Brynn, feeling like such a bad friend

Brynn kept encouraging me to tell you about us, she said it wouldn't be that bad, and if you were a good friend you'd be happy for me. For us.

Guess she was wrong

Any additional apology I offer now would just be groveling. It would have to be an it's-all-my-fault-please-take-me-back apology, and it was definitely not *all* my fault.

I look at our conversation. The words in their speech bubbles on the screen are so small, and everything else is so big. My pain and confusion, her anger, my regret, her rejection. The chasm that those tiny letters have opened up between us. I put my phone in my bag and head home.

44

NEEDLESS TO SAY, I'M A MOPEY, WEEPY MESS when Hannah arrives home from Asilomar.

She takes one look at me and hauls me out of bed at one in the afternoon and makes me go on my second walk of the year at the open-space preserve. "It'll make you feel better," she promises. "Spending time in nature always makes people feel better. That's why I went to the beach this weekend."

Hannah sets a much more leisurely pace than Mom (go figure), so I have enough breath to tell her everything as we walk. Another bonus: we're not hot, sweaty, and gross when we reach the meadow at the top of the hill. The preserve used to be Spanish-Mexican ranchland, and a lot of the hills are covered in meadows instead of trees and chaparral. The grass is still fresh, green and new, punctuated here and there with splashes of yellow-orange California poppies and swaths of purple bush lupines. It's easy to feel hopeful here.

We sit on a bench, and Hannah says, "Enough with the sad stuff, sweet pea. Take a break from that. Tell me something happy."

The only happy thing that I can think of is how we rocked the school board presentation. I hesitate at first—partly because she's not supposed to know about it, and partly because I'd rather wallow in my misery—but eventually I tell Hannah all about it, and by the time I'm finished, Hannah is beaming at me, and I do feel better.

"I'm so proud of you, Ceej," she says.

"Yeah, I'm proud of me, too, actually," I reply. Then I ask her something that's been plaguing me ever since the meeting ended. "Do you think I should tell Mom? Do you think she'd be proud of me, or mad and, like, disappointed?"

Hannah shakes her head. "That is an excellent question. I know this is a cop-out answer, but I think she'd be a little of both."

It's a sad question, really. "The first time I do something she might be proud of, and I'm afraid to tell her about it."

"Oh, love. She's already proud of you. She's your mother," Hannah protests.

"No, Hannah. I don't get great grades. I'm not a great athlete. I don't do music or computers or art or theater or anything." I'm aware of how pathetic I sound, but it's like I'm on a greased slide—once I start down it, I just keep slipping downward, no matter how hard I work to stay up.

"You do great work at Heart's Desire. You should be proud of that."

"I know. I am. But Mom isn't— Come on, Hannah, it's true. Name one thing I've done in my whole life that Mom's proud of."

I watch Hannah search for something she can say that won't break me.

"Your mother is one of the smartest, most talented people I know, sweet pea. She expects everyone to be as driven as she is."

That's not an answer. "One thing, Hannah. Or just tell me, honestly. Is she proud of me?"

"She believes in you."

I knew it. "So that's a no. She's not proud of me. Say it, Hannah."

Hannah stands up, puts her hands on her hips and turns in a slow circle, taking in the view of the hills around us. "Ceej. I know it's tough to have Mimi Katsuyama as your mom. But you have to stop feeling sorry for yourself about it."

"Damn, Hannah," I say. "That was . . . uncharacteristically harsh."

Hannah shrugs. "I mean, she's not proud of me, either—not in the same way she would be if I were more like her. But I'm not going to change, and moping about it isn't going to change anything, either."

"Yeah, I guess." I watch her extend her left leg behind her

and stretch. I wonder if it's easier with sisters. How do I not care if Mom's proud of me?

"You have so much, sweet pea. Talent, brains . . . you have the luxury to define for yourself what you want out of your life. So do it." She switches legs. "And then embrace that definition and believe in it so fiercely that it doesn't matter if Mom, or I, or anyone else believes in it with you. You have to do things that make *you* proud of *yourself*. Got it?" Hannah stands up straight again and looks at me expectantly.

"Got it." I smile. "Wow. What a speech."

"Thanks. I read it online this morning," says Hannah, and we both laugh till we cry.

"It's true, though," says Hannah, finally, wiping her eyes. "Especially when you live with someone like your mom. Take it from someone who knows.

"Look at these wildflowers." Hannah sweeps her arm around. "They're not fancy, they're not prizewinning orchids or roses. But they don't care. They're just wildflowers, doing their thing, and they're beautiful. Be like them, sweet pea. Just be you and be happy."

I think back to what Mom said about Hannah, that she's basically a self-absorbed freeloader. Maybe that's true; maybe it's not. But I don't care either way. I'm glad she's my aunt.

We walk back down the path into the trees and eventually out to the parking lot, where I ask Hannah as we get into the car, "What are we going to do about Heart's Desire, though? Is it doomed? Are we going to give up?"

"Katsuyamas never quit, sweet pea, you know that. I'm going to talk to your mom today, actually, and see if we can figure something out. Don't worry. We'll be okay."

I'm not so sure. Mom has to know about Heart's Desire's February numbers. I can't imagine anything but a lot of arguing, or at the very least, a few barbed comments, when she gets home and figures out where Hannah spent the weekend. But there's no point in arguing, so I nod my head.

We drive home, and before she goes to take her shower, Hannah kisses me on the forehead and says, "Your mom really does believe in you. She believes you can do great things."

"What if I don't want to do great things? What if I just want to do everyday things?"

"*You* decide what's great, remember? Figure that out, and then do it."

As if achieving greatness—or success, or even the best version of myself—were just that simple: Define it. And then do it.

Right. Of course. No problem.

A Series of Screw-ups: The Chisaki Joan Katsuyama Story, Part II (Or Maybe It's a Prequel)

When Mom found out she was pregnant with me, Hannah was ecstatic. She had always loved babies and children and wanted to be a mother, but had just undergone a hysterectomy after being diagnosed with uterine cancer at twenty-two years old. Mom was thirty-four. My grandfather, who had always longed for a grandchild, had died of a heart attack a few weeks earlier. How much clearer could it be? "It was fate," she likes to say.

"You know how much Dad wanted grandkids," she'd told Mom. "You could make him happy by having this baby. Imagine what her life could be like with you as her mother! Imagine how far she could go!" Hannah would hire a temporary extra assistant at Heart's Desire and take care of me there, and Mom could keep working. I would have two strong working women as my role models, and I would have the best of everything that each of them could offer. I would fulfill Hannah's dream of having a child to raise, and—I wonder now—maybe Mom's desire to make up for disappointing her father, and maybe even to atone for his death.

So I guess depending on your perspective, Mom either saw the light, or she fell for it like a sucker.

45

IT'S PROMPOSAL SEASON, AND IN A CRUEL TWIST of fate, I've become the go-to person for promposal flowers. The combination of the Motohara story and my flyers around school seems to have worked; also a couple of kids have told me that Sabrina referred them, and I can only guess that it's because she and Owen are hitting it off.

If there's one thing I'm learning from promposal orders, it's how boring people are. Everyone wants a dozen roses to whip out at the moment the target understands they're being promposed to. And then there's the promposal ideas themselves: it's like everyone's read the same "Nine Groan-Inducing Promposal Ideas She'll Love!" article online. There are the themed promposals: pizza (this is cheesy but . . .), doughnut (please doughnut say no), and sports (let's kick it/make a racquet/have a ball at prom!). There are the ones that spell out PROM?: seashells on the beach, cupcakes on the lunch table, Post-its on a bank of lockers.

But by far the most popular request is a dozen roses and a bunch of violets to go with a variation of Roses are red, Violets (which I've had to substitute with irises because violets are an expensive pain in the ass) are blue; kids tell me what to write on the card or the poster (which it was my idea to offer, thank you very much), all excited by the rhyme, like they think they're Shakespeare or something:

Roses are red
Violets are blue
I sure would like
To go to prom with you!

A few of them go wild and change it up with something like

Roses are red
Lilies are white
I sure hope you'll be
My date on prom night!

Okay, that one is better, but only in the sense that dying of old age is better than being eaten alive by a pack of rabid hyenas. It's still terrible. It makes me want to scratch my own eyes out.

Hannah says I'm being mean-spirited and uncharitable and I need to remember to embrace my pain and also embrace others' joy and hope. She's probably right. But if I died and went to hell, the devil would make me sit in my brimstone-and-sulfur cell and embrace writing horrible punny promposal cards for all eternity.

A few kids have asked for consultations about which flowers would be best to use for the specific person they want to ask. It costs more, so I get why people avoid that option. But you'd think people—especially the ones who haven't already done a soft ask (which I always recommend, because rejection is doubly humiliating if it's a promposal)—would want to do everything they could to ensure a yes and a happy prom experience. Holy shit. What is happening to me? I'm becoming Hannah.

The worst part is that Owen and Emily aren't here to laugh with me. Or at me. Or scold me for being a grouch, because to be honest, they'd both probably be on Hannah's side. But Emily hasn't spoken to me since the party, for obvious reasons, and Owen quit working at Heart's Desire the week after for less obvious reasons. Hannah says it's because spring is super busy on the nursery and supply end of things, so his dad needs him for that. But I keep wondering if it's also because of me.

Usually I can get lost in my work when I'm putting together a bouquet or a table arrangement. But now I can't even enjoy work anymore. I keep finding myself grinding through my arguments with Emily, then with Owen, over and over, until

I'm left with nothing but dust and resentment and confusion and loneliness.

That's when I start missing them. I want to tell Owen to do a *Weekly History Minute* on vanilla, which comes from an orchid originally cultivated by the Totonacs, who were conquered by the Aztecs in what's now Mexico. I wish I could tell Emily that lilies of the valley are technically part of the asparagus family. I want to complain to both of them about the horrible punposals. I want them both to tell me to have faith in love and romance and parents and friendship. I want them to tell me that the committee falling apart wasn't my fault, that us falling apart wasn't my fault, that Mom and me falling apart wasn't my fault. I want things not to be the huge mess that they've become.

I don't know. Maybe it was my fault. If it was, I wish I could see how. I wish I knew what I could have done differently. But it's too late, anyway. I can't change what happened.

46

BRYNN ASKED EMILY TO PROM WITH A PROMPOSAL that left the entire school agape. I mean. It was out of control. For starters, Geoffrey Acosta and Keila Padilla, the photographer, were there, presumably covering it for the *Merc*.

The marching band came out of the music building and arranged themselves on the quad, playing the reggae version of "Can't Help Falling in Love." As the last notes faded out, they turned to the roof of the administration building and we followed their gaze to see Emily and Brynn. It became clear the band was standing in a formation that from Emily's vantage point must have look like: P R O M ?

Once the cheering subsided, Brynn pulled a multi-colored bouquet of roses out of her backpack—a bright bunch of crimson, sunny orange, lemon yellow, and blush pink—handed them to Emily, dropped to one knee, and said into a micro-phone, "Emily Baxter, I can't help falling in love with you. Will you go to prom with me?"

It was all very romantic, if by romantic you mean public and spectacular and completely over the top. I have to admit I was kind of impressed by the time and effort it must have taken to plan the whole thing. Because, let's face it, you don't organize an event like that unless you care a lot. Like, a *lot* a lot.

Brynn held the mic up to Emily.

Emily stood there for a moment, taking it all in, I suppose. Curling her hair around her finger.

Then she said, "I'm sorry," and turned around, ran to the stairwell, and disappeared.

A big "Ohhhhh" went up from the crowd, and Geoffrey scribbled in his notebook; Keila stopped taking pictures. I waited for a shiver of schadenfreude, that feeling of low-key satisfaction you get when someone else experiences failure, humiliation, or bad luck. But it didn't come. I just felt sad and confused. Emily said I ruined everything. Maybe it's true.

47

HEY, CJ, THE TEXT READS, *IT'S BRYNN.*

    B: Can you meet me today after school? I need to talk to you

It's important

    CJ: I have work, sorry

    B: After work then? I can meet you wherever you want

Please

I need your help

    CJ: Okay. I get off at 6. Meet me at 6:30 at Purple Onion

    B: Perfect

Thanks so much

I'll pay for dinner

When I arrive at the café, Brynn is already waiting for me. She's Using Her Time Wisely by doing her physics homework, and she doesn't see me until I sit down across from her.

"Hey, I'm so glad you agreed to meet me," she says, without the usual exclamation point, I notice. She looks terrible. I don't say this lightly, because even on a bad day, Brynn is make-you-jealous pretty. She's got rich red hair, intense gray eyes, and adorable, Cupid's bow lips. But today she's a faded-out version of her usual self. Everything looks smaller and just—*less*, as if someone turned the dimmer switch down on whatever energy source keeps her at her usual gazillion watts. But it's her eyes that really throw me. They don't light up at all, and it's not because she's fake smiling. In fact, they actually start to fill with tears, and the corners of her smile tremble and collapse, and she presses her lips together and wipes her eyes. She takes a couple of shaky breaths and tries for another smile. "Sorry."

"It's okay."

"It's just—" She looks away, struggling to regain control, but I can see more tears gathering. Another breath. I'm starting to get uncomfortable. Finally, she blurts, "Emily broke up with me," and she gives up trying to stay calm and starts crying for real. Not blubbering or sobbing or anything, but she is definitely deep into weeping territory.

"Oh. Um, I'm sorry," I say. What should I do? I start to get up to move to her side of the table because I feel like I should hug her, or rub her back or something, but I mean, I hardly know her. *And* I thought I didn't like her. *And* I thought I wanted Emily to break up with her. This is all quite distressing. I hover and bob uselessly, like a worried helium balloon.

Brynn shakes her head. "It's okay," she says, and it occurs to me that we're about eight sentences into our conversation and half of them have been "I'm sorry" and "It's okay." What is it about apologies that make them fall out of our mouths like pennies in some situations and stick in our throats in others? There's so much we don't need to be sorry about—like crying in front of someone—that we apologize for automatically. Me saying I was sorry to Brynn just now was different—I feel bad for you—but still. And it's clear that Brynn is *not* okay.

"Um," I say. I'm still in balloon mode. "Uh . . ."

"Here." Brynn holds out two twenty-dollar bills. "Can you get me the sidewalk baguette sandwich? And the blood orange lemonade and a Nutella twist? You can get anything you want, and keep the change. I'll be okay by the time you get back."

How does she manage to be totally pathetic and totally condescending at the same time? It's like a superpower. I take the money, place the order, and wait around the counter until it comes up. By the time I'm back, Brynn has managed to pull herself together, more or less, though she still looks terrible. "Sorry about that," she says again. "I don't want to make you feel uncomfortable."

I nod once and wonder if she has any idea that I'd feel uncomfortable no matter what. That I haven't felt comfortable around her since middle school, that, in fact, every moment in her presence in the last few months has been an excruciating exercise in discomfort.

"Though I guess maybe it's been kind of uncomfortable

lately anyway." She smiles wryly. Okay, so she does have an idea.

My instinct is to deny that this is true, but I figure if Brynn can be honest, I can, too. "You could say that." Then I add, "Is it about to get even more uncomfortable?"

"I just—" Brynn's voice quivers again, and she squeaks, "I mean, I don't understand. She won't speak to me. She's blocked me on everything," before she loses it again. "Things were going so well. I thought she was happy. I thought we were in love with each other. I mean, I know I was in love with her—*am* in love with her." She takes a crying break and I hand her a wad of tissues from the box at her side.

"She said you told her why I broke up with her in eighth grade. What I did."

"She deserved to know," I say.

"If it makes you feel any better, I hated myself for it," says Brynn.

"I don't know if it makes me feel better. Either way, you can't change what you did."

Brynn hesitates, then says, "I know what I did was fucked up, but I was thirteen, CJ. I had stuff going on that you don't know about. Why would you hang on to it for so long? Why would you use it to try to break us up?"

"Because what difference does it make what you had going on, or how old you were? Because you could have just been like, 'Oh, how nice of her,' but instead you humiliated her and then totally abandoned her. How was I supposed to know you weren't going to screw her over again?" Only I'm having trouble summoning the old rage, now that I'm face-to-face with her remorse and her pain. What was going on in her life that I didn't know about?

"I know. I get that there's no excuse for what I did. But that's still a pretty judgy thing to say about the kid I was back then. Like I know that people around here are super accepting of queer folks, but it's still fucking terrifying in middle school. Emily had tons of family support. She had you. And you know who I hung with back then."

I do. A bunch of homophobic bro wannabes and boy-crazy Mean Girls. I'm starting to wonder how it felt for her to be with those kids all the time. People are so trash in middle school.

"And my parents . . . My dad, actually. He's like the biggest homophobe on the planet. I already felt like I was failing him because I'd just found out that I didn't get into the gifted math program, and he's this like phenomenal engineer, and he was so disappointed in me. And then Em let me know she liked me, and I was so excited, but then I *knew*, and it scared the shit out of me because of what it would mean to my dad and my friends. So when Austin pulled out that Valentine cookie . . ."

"You panicked." I remember it so clearly, the animal fear in her eyes.

Brynn nods. "It was so obvious to me who I was and how much I liked her. I felt like if I didn't do something drastic right then, everyone would be able to see it."

"So you sacrificed Emily." I'm having a hard time letting go of how cruel it felt. Am I being unfair?

"I told you I'm not proud of it."

"Why didn't you just say you weren't interested, and leave it at that?"

"You still don't get how scared I was. My dad, I mean. He thinks I'm going to hell. I felt like I had to hide—like I had to be the opposite of myself, like I had to be like my dad—for it to count. You wanna know the most fucked-up thing, though? I thought it would make him love me more somehow. I didn't even tell him what I did. Like just secretly acting homophobic would send vibes to him that I wasn't queer and he'd love me for it. If I could take back one thing I've done in my life, that would be it."

A few minutes ago, I would have said, "Good choice," but I can't anymore. I still hate what she did, but now I can see how trapped she felt, and that she was doing the best she could. Instead, I ask, "So what does your dad say about you being McAllister's first lesbian prom queen?"

Brynn shakes her head and gives me a tight-lipped smile. "We don't really talk anymore. He just kind of pretends I don't exist, except when he prays for me."

"Oh."

"I don't regret it. I mean, I pray every day that he'll change how he feels. But I can't take it back, and I don't want to. I was dying, pretending to everyone all the time. And knowing my dad would probably hate me. I just got to a point where I figured his attitude would be the same no matter what, but if I came out, the rest of my life might get better. So I did."

"But now your dad—"

"I know. Emily's so lucky. I know it's selfish, but I love being at her house and having her parents accept me the way they do."

"Yeah. They're pretty awesome." *Look at me*, I think. Getting to know Brynn. Having things in common. Emily would be proud. Only. Right. She hates me right now.

"She had a great best friend, too."

"Oh, horsefeathers," I say, suddenly jokey and uncomfortable. Empathy is all well and good, but we don't need to throw ourselves a touchy-feely goop party.

"No, seriously. I would have loved to have a friend as loyal as you. I don't blame you for seeing me as your enemy. I didn't mean to mess up your friendship."

It crosses my mind that Brynn was Em's enemy, too, for a while, and that crystallizes something for me. Emily and I had been best friends for years, but it felt like an important part of our bond was forged in the crucible of eighth grade. I'd stuck with her through one of the most traumatic events of her life, and my rage against Brynn became part of the way I defined my relationship with Emily. Casting myself as her protector was messed up in some of the same ways as Brynn's white-savior act.

"You didn't mess up me and Em's friendship. I did. I could have given you another chance, but I dunno. I guess it was easier to be mad at you."

"Are you still mad at me?"

I think about it. Can I look past what Brynn did all that time ago? How much do our actions in the past define who we are in the present? And how many of Brynn's actions, even her legitimate screwups, have I warped with the lens of the past, and of my own resentment? I know the roots of my anger are justified. But can I justify hanging on to them?

"I don't think so. Not anymore."

Brynn smiles again, the first real smile I've seen on her face today. She actually looks relieved. I can't believe this. Since when does Brynn Foer-Preston care about what I think of her? For a second I think she might be contemplating hugging it out, and I steel myself to accept her embrace, but instead she wipes her eyes and asks me another question.

"Do you think you could help me with Emily?"

"Ah." The reason I'm here.

"So apart from the eighth-grade drama, she said she broke up with me because she thinks I'm just using her to get publicity for myself for prom."

Oh. "Um. I may have given her that idea."

"Why?" asks Brynn, her voice full of reproach.

I feel a stab of guilt—we're not enemies anymore, after all. But I don't think I was wrong. "Aren't you, though? I mean, are you telling me that you invited the press to cover your whole big promposal so you *wouldn't* get publicity for being McAllister's first lesbian prom queen?"

"Okay, fine. But it's not just about attention. Visibility is important, CJ. People still don't see queer couples as normal, so it's important to show everyone that we are. That we do normal things like become prom queen and make promposals."

"Yeah, okay. That makes sense."

"I mean I know she's kind of an introvert, and I get how she might feel embarrassed," she continues, "but I really thought that she would like it. She's not closeted, so I don't understand what's wrong with telling other people how much I like her. It's not like it's a secret."

"But if you really loved her, you'd do it the way *she* wanted. And anyway, can't you see how it would look to her? It was you taking the spotlight from STORM all over again."

"You know what, I still don't get that. You guys kept saying I made it about me, and I told you I was only trying to help."

Wow. This again? Though I guess I'm the one who brought it up. Okay, fine. "When you called the paper and got them to do an interview featuring you, who did you think it was going to be about? You said it was about calling attention to the movement, but who came out looking like a hero? And don't even tell me you don't plan to use this whole experience as a college application essay. About how instrumental you were, even though you didn't have to be. Have you ever heard of the term, 'white savior'?"

Brynn looks aghast. "I didn't mean to be! I really was only trying to help."

Oh, Brynn. Well, here we go, then. "And I don't know if you saw the newscast of that interview you did with Aviana and Owen. Were you even aware of how much more you talked than them?"

"I was excited. The news lady gave me the mic first. And I let them speak when I was done."

"Yeah, so that was her fault. But did you even consider giving Owen the mic *before* you started talking? You *let* them speak. Shouldn't they have been letting *you* speak, considering their families were actually, like, directly affected by the internment?"

"But everything I said—"

"And you kept saying at the meeting that you did us a favor."

She still looks puzzled, so I cast about for something that would make her understand. "Imagine if a straight person grabbed the mic from the main speaker at an LGBTQ-plus marriage rally and made a big speech about how they were so stoked when their gay uncle finally got married, and how it's really important to support LGBTQ-plus marriage rights. And then they wanted you to thank them for being a good ally."

"Oh." Her eyes open up a little wider as the understanding sinks in. Finally.

"Like, it's cool to support us, right? But it's not cool to take over and expect us to be grateful." Now that I'm not furious with her for everything she ever did, I find that I can be a little kinder.

"I'm sorry. That was fucked up. I should have known better."

"Well. Yeah." I can't bring myself to say, "It's okay," because it's not really, even though she didn't mean to do wrong. But I can say, "Apology accepted," which feels right.

And now I'm ready to wrap a ribbon around this encounter with Brynn, just tie it up in a pretty little bow, walk out, and maybe engineer a reconciliation with Emily. Only I have this nasty little grub of a feeling that's still bothering me, and I can tell that ignoring it won't make it go away. Ugh. I'm going to hate this.

"Hey, Brynn?" I say. She smiles at me. Ugh. "Um. I may have let, um . . . How I was so mad about you and Emily? I may have let that influence the way I reacted to the STORM thing."

Brynn's smile fades. But she doesn't look surprised, which . . . Ughhhhh. This is not fun.

"I mean. You shouldn't have done what you did. And kicking you off was a pretty harsh punishment, but I'm not going to apologize for the group. But I was kind of, um, operating on my anger at the old you. What I thought was the old you. Mistakenly."

Brynn nods slowly. Okay.

Big breath. "And-maybe-I-was-a-little-resentful-about-how-awesome-you-are-at-everything-and-maybe-I-was-worried-that-Emily's-going-to-ditch-me-for-you-and-your-elite-little-crew-and-maybe-that-might-also-have-been-a-big-reason-why-I-wanted-you-off-the-committee." Whew. There.

"Wow," she says. "That's . . ."

"Yeah." I'm tempted to throw it back to her white-savior

thing. But instead I push an apology out of my throat. "I shouldn't have let that drive me. I'm sorry."

I fold my napkin in half, quarters, eighths as I wait for Brynn to respond. Sixteenths. Thirty-seconds. I'm trying to force it into sixty-fourths when she says, "That's okay, I guess."

Whew. I put the napkin down and tell her, "It doesn't have to be okay."

"It kinda does, though. I want it to be."

"You're a nicer person than me, then."

I want to do something to make up for my pettiness, but I can't let her back onto the committee—that's not up to me, and I'm not sure it makes sense, anyway. There's really only one other thing I can do.

"So," I say, "do you want me to talk to Emily?"

48

THERE'S ONLY ONE WEEK LEFT IN MARCH, AND Hannah is in an unusually good mood, considering she bailed on the sale and Heart's Desire is teetering on the brink of collapse. She smiles as she checks inventory on her laptop, half humming, half singing as she scrolls and clicks.

Sweet dreams till sunbeams fiiind you
Dum, dum-da-dum-da worrieees behind you
Dum, dum-da-dum whatever they be
Dream a little dream of me

Waiiit a sec. I know why she's so happy.
"Hannah."
"Hm?"

"Who's the new boyfriend?"

"What?"

"I said, 'Who's the new boyfriend?'"

"What?" she says again. She looks up from her work and glances at me just long enough for me to see the guilt in her eyes. "Hmph," she says, tossing her hair and looking away. "I don't know what you mean."

"Hannah, you're humming that song."

Now she's full-on blushing, but she still pretends not to know what I'm talking about. "So?"

"You always hum that song when you're into a new guy. You *only* hum that song when you're into a new guy. So who is it?"

Hannah gives up and breaks into a bashful smile. "Richard."

"Who?"

"Richard. You know, the guy with the first-date boutonniere. Remember? He came in the beginning of December, and he needed flowers for his first date with someone? You recommended pansies and white violets."

"That guy? Didn't he come in like two more times for other dates, though?"

"He did," Hannah says. "And we tried a new combination of flowers every time, but always with the pansies: think of me. Remember?"

"But they didn't work."

"What do you mean, they didn't work? Of course they did, sweet pea! Just not the way we expected them to."

"Why, because— Ohh. Because he thought of *you*."

Hannah nods. "Uh-huh. It was after the third time he came in. We got to talking while I made his boutonniere, and when I gave it to him I got that little fizz that I get when the magic is working. But it was a little different than usual—it sort of wrapped itself around me instead of passing through me, if that makes any sense."

It does, but only because it reminds me of when Owen had his arms around me at the Pigeon Point Lighthouse. I wish I'd recognized it then.

Hannah sighs and her gaze loses focus, as if she's reliving the moment. "Richard says that he kept thinking about me, even during his date that night. He says she was pretty and smart and nice, but being with her just wasn't the same as being with me. And then his friend set him up with someone else. So he went on that date last night, mostly just to make his friend happy. And he didn't even want the boutonniere. He only bought it as an excuse to see me."

"Did he tell you that when he got it?"

"No! And I was so sad. But I was a little bit hopeful, because I felt the magic again, but even stronger, and I knew why. He came in today around noon and asked for a fifth boutonniere, and I said, 'I'm sorry that your date last night didn't work out,' and he said, 'I'm not,' and I said, 'Who's your date tonight?' and he said, 'You.'" She sighs. "Isn't that romantic?"

"It is. It's very romantic."

She hums a few bars of the song again and says, "'Dream

a little dream of me.' That's what the white violets told him to do, essentially."

"White violets say 'think of me,' not 'dream of me.'"

"Same thing, in this context."

"Maybe. Whatever. Congratulations, I guess."

"Thank you, sweet pea."

Hannah goes back to her inventory and her humming, and I go back to the tulips I've been preparing to put on the floor out front.

I don't understand how Hannah can go careening head-long into every relationship that comes her way. She's like a dandelion seed. All it takes is a breath of wind, a whisper of possibility, and she's floating untethered into the future without a single thought as to what might happen next. She doesn't think about the past, either. Nothing weighs her down or holds her back. It's like she leaves every failed relationship, every hard lesson, every painful memory behind her on the bare stem of the dandelion. I wonder what it takes to live like that.

As I puzzle over this, it strikes me again how calm she is. I don't know what Hannah and Mom talked about after Mom got back from Denver—Hannah told me she had to wait and figure out just one thing before she could tell me, but not to worry. Even so, and even with the prospect of a new romance, it's strange. I've been so preoccupied with the promposals and with my own misery that I haven't been paying attention to Hannah at all. Guiltily, I ask, "Hey, I forgot to ask you this week—what's going on with Mom and the store? Remember you said you had to figure one thing out? Is she giving us more time? Or was there something else?"

"Hm? Oh, right." Hannah shrugs. "I met someone in Monterey who gave me the idea of putting together a donations fund-raiser, so I asked your Mom for a couple of contacts and three weeks to talk to them. You know she has a lot of wealthy friends."

"You were going to borrow money from her friends?" That sounds humiliating.

"No, no! I asked them for pointers on putting together a fund-raising event. Like one of those fancy dinners that cost five hundred dollars a plate. Or an auction party, you know, where people donate plane rides and vacation weeks, and guests bid on them."

"That sounds fun." It sounds like a lot of fun, actually.

"Yeah." Hannah has put down the tablet, and she's peeling a scrap of tape off the counter. "So I met with these people, and— Oh, I don't know, CJ. We went over the numbers together, carefully, and I realized that there's no way we'll be able to raise enough money to pull it off. I guess I was just in denial before—I love this place so much, I couldn't be reasonable about it. And there's a boatload of tax issues I don't want to deal with. And the kind of work it would take to keep things running once we're back on our feet . . ."

Hannah's using the voice she uses to explain why her last boyfriend was, in hindsight, a mistake. She's essentially breaking up with the store. "So that's what I've been trying to figure out. Remember what we talked about? About defining yourself? I had an epiphany about myself. I can't worry about money. It's not who I am. So I've decided that it'll be better for everyone if we just do what your mom wants and sell the property. And if things work out with Richard, I might just move in with him, which will get your mom off my back about rent."

"But you've just started dating," I say stupidly. It's not even the main issue here, but I'm so stunned I'm having trouble thinking straight.

"Yeah, but I really think he might be the One."

Why didn't I notice it before? Hannah's always been my refuge from Mom's momness, and I think I'll always need her that way. But she's the same way with the rest of her life as she is with her relationships. How can she be so self-involved? Why doesn't she just act like a grown-up for once? Impatience and disappointment seep into of my image of her, like the brown rot on the edge of a decaying flower petal.

Mom was right. Hannah gets so worked up about things like pride and family and being connected to our history, but in reality, she's just floating on dreams and stories. Mom's the one who's been carrying the weight of it, alone, holding on to our tiny corner of history for Hannah's sake—maybe even for her own sake, or her father's. I can finally see why she wants to let go.

49

WHEN I ARRIVE AT EMILY'S HOUSE, MRS. BAXTER greets me with a big hug and a sad smile and points me to Emily's room. Em is sitting next to her bed with her arms wrapped around her knees, her forehead resting on top. Without looking up, she says, "What do you want?" She sounds pretty hostile.

This is not going to be easy. I sit down next to her and clear my throat.

"I came to apologize."

"Not to gloat? I broke up with Brynn—isn't that what you wanted? You were right, I was wrong. You must be so happy."

The venom in her voice is overwhelming. I hardly know what to say.

"I'm not happy. I didn't want you to break up—"

Emily scoffs. "Ha."

"Okay. Maybe I did. I didn't want you to be with Brynn. But I was wrong." When she says nothing, I add, "I was wrong about a lot."

"Yeah, well. We both were." Em lifts her face. Her eyes are red from crying. She still won't look at me.

"I'm sorry."

Em shakes her head. "Sorry doesn't do any good. It doesn't change anything. Brynn still threw me under the bus in eighth grade and never told me. You only told me out of, like, spite or something."

I hate that I can't defend myself. I hate that she's right.

"Why did you wait till it was going to really hurt me?" she asks. "Why didn't you tell me before?"

"I tried, though. The night of the school board meeting. You told me you didn't want to hear it. Remember?"

"No," she says, exasperated. "Like way before. Like when it happened."

I sigh, thinking back. "You were already so sad. What was I going to do—say, 'Oh, and also, people are laughing at you behind your back'? That would have been cruel."

Em pulls at the carpet. "Maybe."

"And then, I dunno. It's not something you just bring up randomly. And when you and Brynn started talking, I thought . . . I guess I thought I was holding back and not being petty."

"Until you told me for completely petty reasons."

"Yeah, well. Go big or go home, right?"

Emily rolls her eyes.

"Brynn said that you broke up with her because of the promposal, though."

"Well, yeah. Because I was already upset with her about what you told me. She explained her reasons, and everything, but I wasn't ready to forgive her yet. And then she went and did that huge promposal, with newspaper reporters and everything, like using me as a prop for her big historic first-lesbian-prom-queen moment was going to make up for humiliating me and lying to me."

"Yeah . . . about that." I take a breath and get ready to make a case for Brynn. I'm still not sure I can do it, but I said I'd try.

But now that Em is talking, she's on a roll. "I can't believe I stood up for her on that white-savior thing. I knew she screwed up, by the way." Em shoots me a sharp look. "But I was too crazy about her to see straight. And I was mad at you for trying to hurt her." She sighs into her arms and says, "You know the worst part? I'm so angry at her for all the things she did. But I also wish we could forget any of this ever happened and be happy together again. Is that pathetic, or what?" She smiles wryly and wipes a few stray tears off her face.

I smile back. "I don't know what it is. I'm sorry it sucks so much, though."

"Yeah. Don't ever fall in love. It's the worst."

"Well." She doesn't need to tell *me*.

"It's the best, too, though. But it's also the worst."

I scooch over to her and put my arm around her shoulders,

and we sit for a minute while she weeps. This feels so familiar. I miss sharing everything with her. And it's my own fault,
really.

"Hey, Em?" I say carefully.

"What?"

"I'm sorry for being such a shit about you and Brynn."

Em sniffs. "I'm sorry, too."

"I . . . I used to feel like it was you and me against the world,
you know? Like, 'CJ the Underachiever and Emily the, um,
Middle Achiever.'" Emily grimaces. "Okay, High Achiever."

"Whatever. Just go on," says Em.

So I do. "So when you started hanging with Brynn and her
friends, it felt different. Like you were changing and I wasn't.
And I freaked out. I didn't know what we were anymore." In
fact, it occurs to me, I'm still not sure.

Emily frowns at her knees. "We were friends."

Were.

Oh. Okay, then. I nod; I don't trust myself to speak.

"I mean, we *are* friends," she says. "Still. If you want to be."

"Well, yeah, I mean, I guess. If you insist." Cue smiles and
big sappy hug.

Em gives me a blow-by-blow of her version of the promposal. "It may have been the most embarrassing moment of my
life," she says of the moment when Brynn knelt and promposed.
"I thought I was gonna die."

"You looked pretty wretched."

"It was the literal worst."

Here's my chance. Instead of agreeing with Em, I say, "Don't you think it would be cool to be part of history, though? Like other people's history. For the sake of other people."

Em shakes her head. "No. You can't make me get back together with Brynn. And you definitely can't make me go to prom with her. I told you I don't want to be part of that show."

"The 'Brynn Is a Lesbian Superstar, So Fuck You, Dad, Just Accept It' Show?"

"Okay, that's a *bit* harsh. But yeah. The Brynn Show, basically."

"But what if it's not just The Brynn Show? What if she has to make herself visible at school so she won't feel invisible at home? Maybe she's making the world she wants to live in as a human being. Maybe she feels like being proud and like, joyful and unashamed of who you are helps spread positivity."

"Maybe."

"Or maybe she's also really ambitious. There's nothing wrong with that."

"Well that's new, coming from you." I can see Emily biting back a smile.

"You don't have to be the Lesbian Date of Our First Lesbian Prom Queen. Just be a girl who goes to prom with another girl who's totally in love with you."

"I'm not going to prom with her."

"Okay, fine. Be a girl who talks to another girl who's totally in love with you."

"She did say she's in love with me, huh?"

I smile. "In front of the whole school."

"Hm." Em is wavering.

"She just wants a chance to grovel, really. And maybe win you back."

"I am not a prize to be won."

"Right. It's totally up to you what happens after the groveling."

Em looks away and sighs. "Okay. I'll talk to her. But no promises."

50

"OKAY, FINE, I ADMIT IT. I'M GLAD WE CAME. This is cool."

Owen and I are standing inside the burned-out trunk of a giant redwood tree in Muir Woods, north of San Francisco. There's enough space inside for Owen and me both to stand comfortably and look up at the rest of the tree through a hole in the ceiling of this little chamber. It's so tall I get dizzy looking up to the top. This tree has a room-sized hole burned into the base of its trunk, and it's still growing. That's grit.

"I had a feeling you'd like it," I say. I duck out and scramble back up to the path with Owen close behind me.

On my way, I pat the burned-out tree and whisper, "Thank you."

I probably owe Hannah a thank-you, too. She may be the

world's biggest flake, but she's the one who suggested this place, and I'm glad I took her advice. Muir Woods National Monument is the only old-growth redwood forest in the Bay Area, and I've pretty much dragged Owen here with me today. I showed up at his house early this morning with a nosegay of star-of-Bethlehem and fresh-baked muffins from Sweet Emily's, and Owen's mom, who Hannah told me has also been rooting for the two of us for weeks—she's the one who told Hannah that Owen and Sabrina are no longer a thing—pushed him out the door.

It's ninety minutes from San Jose to Mill Valley. It was a long, quiet drive, and I was beginning to worry that bringing Owen here was a huge miscalculation. But the trees have won, as I hoped they would.

Redwoods are some of the coolest trees around. They're practically impossible to kill. They're protected by a chemical that makes them bug-resistant, fire-resistant and rot-resistant. If you cut one down, or if it falls, a ring of baby redwoods springs up around the stump, and little branches grow from the fallen trunk and eventually become real trees.

Also, they're majestic and beautiful and totally awe-inspiring to look at. You can't stay angry for long when you're walking through a forest like Muir Woods. The trees pretty much enchant you into a better mood.

Owen takes a few running steps ahead of me on the trail and calls over his shoulder, "Fun fact: Muir Woods is where they filmed the Ewok forest scenes in *Return of the Jedi*."

We come upon a clearing just off the main trail. A ring of ancient trees surrounds an even more ancient boulder splotched with pale green and rusty orange lichen. "Come on," he says. He jogs down the narrow path through the ferns and beckons me to follow.

The space is magical. Rays of sunlight pour onto the boulder and sparkle through the filter of the trees. The forest around us seems to fade away. Owen is standing next to the boulder, his face turned to the sky as he looks up at the canopy.

"Whoa, this is so trippy, Ceej! You gotta try it." He starts turning in a slow circle, still facing upward. Then he loses his balance and stumbles, and for a second I'm terrified that he's going to bash his head into the boulder, but he recovers. "Come on, try it Ceej."

I look up and am immediately overcome with vertigo. Is it the trees swaying, or is it me? "No."

"Dizzy?"

I nod.

"Come here, then. Come lean on the rock with me."

I walk over and lean against the boulder, and Owen moves next to me so that we're standing shoulder to shoulder with our arms touching. I look up and see the trees like spires, reaching for the white-blue sky, impossibly tall. I hear the rustle and creak of the branches and needles. And as the dizziness starts to lap at the edges of my brain, I feel the rock, sun-soaked and solid against my back, and the heat of Owen's arm against mine, and the ground firm beneath my feet. I close my eyes.

"I overreacted about voting Brynn off the committee," says Owen quietly. "I should have trusted us all to be okay without her. Talk about getting sucked into the white narrative. I'm sorry about that. That was fucked up."

"Mm." I wasn't expecting an apology. But I'll take it. "But you were right about me. I mean. Brynn messed up, and I'm not sorry we called her out. She needed to fix things. But I don't know. I started it for the wrong reasons. I was just trying to hurt her, and I ended up hurting all of us. And I am sorry about that."

Owen nods. He leans into me a little and I lean back.

He says, "So, about that. Nikki and Tulasi and Lili said you got Brynn to go and apologize to each of them and promise to do better."

"Huh." Good for her.

"And Brynn told me that Emily wanted to break up with her, but you convinced her not to."

I shrug and suppress a smile. "Possibly."

"That was really cool of you."

"Thanks."

"Aaaand I might have underestimated Shane."

This time, I can't help grinning. "Nah."

"No, really. He got his team to do a bake sale at their last tournament and they're donating the money to STORM."

"Shut up."

"No, for real."

"Well, he is a good guy," I say. Shane. Who would have guessed?

"Yeah."

I take a breath. "He's not the guy for me, though."

Owen doesn't say anything.

This is terrifying. What if I'm about to make a huge mistake? What if he doesn't feel the same as I do, after all? Or worse, what if he does, and I still screw up and ruin it somehow? But the trees whisper to me that life is bigger than my fears, and I clasp Owen's hand and lace our fingers together. He doesn't speak, but his fingers close over mine. I literally sigh with relief. We stand together for a while, holding hands, not saying a word. This is good.

"Look at these trees," Owen marvels, oblivious to the runaway what-ifs inside my head. "Look how big they are. Think about how old they are. They were here before the Gold Rush, before the Spaniards. . . . They were here when it just the Miwok and Ohlone."

"Yeah, I heard they were even here when the Jedi returned."

Owen smiles down at me and squeezes my hand. "Nice." What he says next convinces me that he was, in fact, reading my mind earlier. "I don't know what's going to happen to us in the future, Ceej. But I like you enough to want to know, and enough to risk screwing up. I'm not even asking you to fall in love or anything. I'm just asking you to be open to . . . to . . ."

"Happy endings?" I suggest. "Or happy beginnings,

anyway." I turn toward him and slide my hands over his chest and shoulders and clasp them around the back of his neck.

The corners of his mouth edge up as he pulls me close. "Happy beginnings is good. I like beginnings."

"For now, anyway."

"For now," he agrees.

In this moment, when all I see are his clear brown eyes and his lips just a breath away from mine, it feels as though we really are poised on the edge of something entirely new. I feel his lips graze my forehead, and he leaves the lightest trace of a kiss on my eyelids before moving down, brushing across my cheeks, to my mouth. And then I feel his lips on mine like a whisper, a soft, cross-the-bridge-with-me kind of kiss. The kind of kiss that's both question and answer, invitation and acceptance, that leads to another kiss, and another, and another.

He pauses, and I open my eyes and see his eyes dark under a fringe of short, thick lashes. Why did I never notice them before?

"Hi," he says, as if we've just met.

"Hi," I say back, because in a sense, we have. This is a new me, and a new Owen, with soft lips and those eyelashes, and straight, feathery eyebrows. He smiles at me and kisses me again, and this time I feel his arms around me, his hands on my waist and my back, and I'm surprised at how readily my body responds, and how much I enjoy his response, the quickening of his breath as I stroke the back of his neck, and at the energy and hunger of this blue-green wave of desire that's rising in me urging me toward him, toward something new and different and exciting.

And no matter what happens in the future, this kiss, this moment of connection right now, will exist forever.

I feel myself taking a tiny step toward the edge of the precipice off of which Hannah is forever flinging herself. I think I might understand how she can do it. I feel like by the time I am ready to step off the edge, instead of plunging to disaster, I might float away like a dandelion seed, away from the broken stems of my old mistakes and into something big and scary and wonderful and new.

51

SAND HILL ROAD IS HOME TO THE VENTURE capital firms that provided the initial funding for pretty much every major tech start-up, ever: Amazon, Microsoft, Google, Skype, and Facebook all got seed money here. Hundreds of millions of dollars' worth of transactions take place on this road every day as Sand Hill companies decide which start-ups they think will make it big. And McAllister Venture Capital is one of the OGs of Sand Hill Road. It owns pieces of a lot of very expensive, very successful pies.

So it's kind of preposterous to think you can just march right into Trey McAllister's office and ask him to hand over a million dollars to fund an initiative to change the name of a school that bears his grandfather's name.

But that's what we're doing.

Our proposal is still "under consideration" with the school board; whether it's true or whether it's just a cover for anti-change sentiments, the main obstacle they've cited is lack of funds. So when you think about it, it actually makes perfect sense to ask for help from someone who has millions of dollars pretty much going spare.

The first thing we did was start delivering flowers to Trey's office. One hundred and twenty roses, one for every thousand Japanese Americans that his grandfather helped send to the internment camps. And two thousand carnations, one for every million of the total of the estimated two billion dollars in income and property they lost—not even adjusted for inflation—during their three years in the camps. In bunches of two dozen. Owen, Zach, Emily, Nikki, Lili, Mizhir, Tulasi, Aviana, and I took turns making the deliveries. I would have loved to use black-eyed Susans for justice or purple lilacs for memory, but we couldn't afford to buy enough to make the statement we wanted with the cash we'd raised, so we settled for what was cheapest and most abundant.

The lobby is a riot of color; I guess Trey either ran out of room in his own office or got tired of being interrupted with deliveries pretty early on. Red roses cover the coffee table in the waiting area. Purple and pink roses are stacked on an armchair, and the floor is literally carpeted with a rainbow of carnations. There's just enough room for a path through the lobby that stops at the receptionist's desk and continues through the double doors into the inner recesses of the building. Alice, the receptionist, glowers at us from behind her desk as we walk up to it.

"Hi, Alice. Could we please talk to Trey?"

"I'm sorry, CJ, but I'm pretty sure he's in a meeting right now."

"Could you please check?"

"I have checked, hon. See? I have everybody's meetings on this schedule right here." She tilts her monitor at me to prove it.

"Okay. I guess I'll just call him, myself." Thank goodness for Mom. I snuck into her phone last night and sent myself Trey's number.

At the same time, Emily calls Mom, who, according to her calendar, is in the same meeting.

Five minutes later, Trey and Mom are in the lobby with us. Trey's features are arranged in a mask of composure. Mom smiles at us, but the set of her jaw tells me that she is not happy to see us.

"Hi, there, CJ. How can I help you and your friends today?" Trey asks, though I'm pretty sure he has no intention of helping any of us. Nikki starts the camera on her phone.

I introduce everyone, and hand him a bouquet with the things we couldn't afford to buy a ton of: black-eyed Susans, lilacs, plus a sprig of allspice for compassion and an almond branch for hope. It's a bit odd-looking, I'll admit. But I don't care. I explain its significance to him, and make our proposal:

Most of the objections to changing the school name are purely ideological, and pretty racist. The only logical objection we've encountered is that the process of changing the name would cost the school district a lot of money that could be used for other things.

I ask Trey to offer to pay for whatever it costs to change the school name from McAllister to Motohara. After digging around a little, we figure it should cost around a million dollars. Which is a ton of money, no doubt. But for a family whose net worth is ten thousand times that, it's not a big deal.

"You've done your research," says Trey evenly.

I nod. "We all have."

"And what can you offer in exchange?" he asks.

"You would know that you're putting your family back on the right side of history," I say.

Trey's eyebrow twitches when he hears this, but he says nothing.

"Plus it'll be great PR," says Aviana.

I focus directly on Trey's face so I won't see Mom out of the corner of my eye, and say, "Refusing to do anything sends a message to students like us—all of us—that your family isn't concerned about the racist implications of your grandfather's name on our school building. It tells us that you value tradition and personal glory over integrity. It shows us that you want us to honor a man who trampled all over what these flowers represent—families, hard work, and their hopes for the future—for his own personal gain."

Trey looks around the room at the sea of flowers we've brought in. All the lives, all the dreams deferred and crushed and stolen away. He looks at us. We look back: *We hold you responsible.*

Then I take a line straight from Mom's Advice on How to Live Your Life: "You have to have a mission statement for your life. I saw on the McAllister Foundation's homepage that its guiding principles are a commitment to acting honestly and with integrity."

Trey's eyebrow twitches again, and—maybe?—so does the corner of his mouth. Though I don't know if that's a good thing or a bad thing.

So I push onward. "People talk about protecting kids' feelings, but that's not the real issue. The real issue is whether you're going to take a principled public stand against the idea that it's okay to treat ethnic minorities as dangerous criminals and foreign invaders," I say. "You can't erase your grandfather's mistakes and their consequences. But you can do the right thing and acknowledge them. You can write a new paragraph. With Ryōhei Motohara's name on our school."

At the school board meetings, everyone wrapped up their speeches by saying thank you and walking away from the podium to huge cheers from our audience. But it feels silly to say thank you here; and no one's cheering for me now, that's for sure. So I just stand there, slowly suffocating from the tension in the room.

Mom's arms remain crossed, and her mouth is set in a hard line. Alice, at her desk, looks uncertain about what she should do. Trey just nods slowly.

It's kind of horrible.

Just when I think I'm going to pass out from anxiety, Trey says, "Well. That was very impressive. What do you think, Michelle?"

Mom nods but doesn't smile.

I don't know what do with that. I glance nervously at the others, but they seem as lost as me.

Nikki comes to her senses first. "So," she says, "will you consider funding the name change? With a statement about why, maybe?"

"I would love to give you a definitive answer," Trey replies. "But I'm going to have to table this issue for now and get back to you another time. I have a pretty important deal to negotiate upstairs, and I had to leave it to come down and listen to you all—not that I didn't enjoy the break."

Trey reaches out and shakes our hands, one by one, and says briskly, "It's been great to meet you all, but Ms. Katsuyama and I do have to get back to our meeting. Thanks for dropping in."

"All right, guys," says Mom in the tone she uses when she's kicking me off my phone. "You're done." She barely looks at me, and she doesn't even say goodbye before she turns her back and follows Trey through the double doors at the end of the path.

"Um, thank you for your time," Owen calls after them, and the rest of us barely have time to add our hurried thanks before two security guards appear and shepherd us out the door.

52

ONCE WE GET OUTSIDE, I'M SHAKING SO HARD I feel like I might collapse in on myself.

Emily gives me a long hug. "You did great."

"I don't know," I say. I'm afraid to let go of her. I feel like she's holding me together. "That was supposed to be our moment of triumph, and Trey just, like, dismissed us like we didn't even matter."

She releases me, and it's Owen's turn. "It *was* our moment of triumph," he says. "Right?"

The others murmur their assent.

"You have the video?" Mizhir asks Nikki.

"Right here," says Nikki. "And I sent the email with our statement. He can pretend this was all his idea and look good, or we can tell everyone that we gave him the opportunity and he turned it down."

It all feels like false hope to me. But I don't want to be a downer, so I smile and say they're probably right.

On the way home with Owen, though, I can't hold back. "This was a huge mistake. We never should have tried it. Did you see my mom? She's never going to forgive me."

"She saw you standing up for what you believe, Ceej. She saw you being proactive and going after your vision. All the stuff you said she loves. She can't be mad about that."

"She saw me sabotage her goals and she saw me fail, is what she saw."

Owen sighs and doesn't try to argue with me anymore. But he stops at Heart's Desire and makes me come inside with him.

Hannah gives me a hug and a cup of coltsfoot tea (for justice, she says). After a whispered consultation with her, Owen disappears into the storeroom and brings back three irises and a Monterey pine cone left over from our golf course caper, all tied together with a ribbon. "There weren't any green pine branches," he says apologetically. The irises are for a noble heart and the pine cone substitute means "hope in adversity."

His impromptu arrangement is clumsy, hopeful, heartfelt—a lot like what we just did at McAllister VC. It's enough to win me over, but I have my doubts about anyone else.

53

I SPEND THE REST OF THE EVENING AT OWEN'S house; I can't bear to face Mom after the way I flamed out this afternoon. To be honest, I don't know if I'd be able to face her if I'd totally crushed it, either.

When Owen finally drives me home at ten, all the lights in the house are off. We kiss for a while in the truck; finally, he says, "Time for you to go."

"Do I have to?" I kiss his square jaw, his ears. "Can't I go back home with you?"

"Believe me, I wish you could." He gives me one more long, sweet kiss, and pushes me gently away from him. "Good night, Ceej. I'll see you tomorrow."

Reluctantly, I say good night and go inside to my room. I'm finishing up the last of some history reading when I hear a knock on my door, and Mom appears, wearing a *PRINCETON LACROSSE* T-shirt and pajama pants.

"You got a moment?" she asks.

I nod, and she leans on my dresser and waits while I shut my laptop and put my history textbook away. Inside my skull, my mind is racing: *Is she mad at me? Is she hurt? Is she going to tell me about Trey's decision?*

"That was quite a stunt you pulled at MVC today," she says, at last.

That doesn't give me much to go on. "I know," I say. "I'm sorry. Do you hate me?"

"Of course not, don't be ridiculous," she retorts, and I relax a little.

"Okay. I thought you might be mad at me."

She crosses her arms and says drily, "Oh, I was mad. What you did was rude to Trey and Alice, embarrassing to me, and inconsiderate to the building staff who had to deal with the flowers. I spent a lot of time apologizing to a lot of people on your behalf. Not to mention it went directly against what I asked you to do."

I knew it. I knew it was a bad idea.

"I'm not mad anymore, though." She smiles. "In fact, I'm proud of you, kiddo. I just wanted to let you know."

Oh my god. This can only mean one thing. "Did Trey agree to pay for the name change?"

"Oh. Um." Mom hesitates before saying, "He didn't tell me, but to be honest, your chances aren't great that he'll personally bankroll the whole thing."

My heart sinks, and I realize that I'd been building up hope despite myself. Another crushing defeat for CJ. "Then why—?"

"Because you saw a creative solution to your problem and used what you had and went after it, even though it was risky. You were audacious and you were smart and you were resourceful, and I'm proud of you for that."

I want so much to enjoy this weird pocket in time where Mom is actually telling me in actual words that she's proud of me—*proud*. Of *me*. I try to take the compliment in. I try to bask in it like sunshine. But I can't, because I'm stuck on the fact that I failed, and her praise feels like a consolation prize: Nice try. Better luck next time.

"What's wrong?" she says. "I thought you'd be happy to hear that I was proud of you."

"But I totally blew it. It was—I don't know. I don't know why I ever thought it was going to work." I don't know what it is that does it: disappointment, self-pity, the cumulative exhaustion of years of trying and failing to be as great as she wishes I were. But tears well up from the bottomless pit of neediness that I've tried so hard to grow out of, and I choke on my next words. "Hannah says you've never been proud of anything I've done, and I believe her. All I ever do—I can't do anything right. Nothing you care about, anyway."

I realize that I sound like I blame her and I'm trying to start a fight, even though I'm not. She came in here to bond with me and make me feel better, and I'm ruining it. Why can't I stop screwing things up? She must hate it so much, how predictably I fall short. It must be torture to be so brilliant, so blazingly talented, so successful, and have to drag me shuffling and stumbling along behind her, unwilling and unable to keep up.

"Be honest, Mom. Did I ruin your life? Do you ever regret having me?" Even as I say this, I don't want to hear her answer. I'm so afraid, I can barely even look at her. And when I see her anguished expression, something around my heart squeezes so tightly that I wonder how it's still beating.

"Oh, Ceej. You know I chose to have you."

"But that's—" My voice cracks, and I have to fight to get the rest of the sentence out. "That's not the same thing as being happy about it. You told me last year that having a baby was like breaking a vase you couldn't fix. You said it would ruin my life. How would you know? It's because you think I ruined yours!"

"You didn't ruin my life, CJ. You have to believe that." Mom leans toward me, the intensity of her plea radiating off her like heat.

I want to. "But?"

She gathers herself back in, looks up at the ceiling. Closes her eyes. Takes a breath. "CJ, the tech world, the work world—it punishes women for being mothers. People think that if you're not willing to prioritize work over family time, you shouldn't have the job. They think that women won't work as hard when we have families. Having a baby when I was young and couldn't call the shots . . ."

"Got in the way of your career."

Mom looks pained, but she doesn't back down. "No one wants to promote a single mom, because no one believes she can work hard enough to do her job well. I worked harder than anyone at that office—including men with families—and everyone still assumed I wouldn't be able to handle as much responsibility as the men. I felt like a shitty mom *and* I didn't get promoted as fast as other people. It sucked."

"And that's why you regret having me." The unfairness of it all—to Mom and to me—leaves me feeling burned and blistered.

"No, CJ. I'm saying it wasn't easy. I didn't want you to go through the same thing. Babies slow you down. It's just a fact." She stands up and starts pacing. "The regret—sometimes I think I'm just not cut out for parenthood. And you're suffering because of it." She turns to me, pleading. "It has nothing to do with who you are, or anything you've done. It's me. Sometimes I'm afraid I'll never be able to be the mother you need."

"I'm not asking you to be the world's greatest mom."

"No. But *I* am."

"But that's not fair. It makes me feel like I have to be the world's greatest daughter. And I'm not. I'll never be." My voice breaks, and I look away and breathe, breathe, breathe, but the tears still come.

"Oh, Ceej." Her own eyes fill with tears, and she sits down and wraps her arms around me and I cry and cry, for all the times I've failed her, for the times that she's failed me, for how unfair it all is, and for the vast and barren emptiness that separates me from any idea of how I can fix things.

"It's so hard," she says, when I've calmed down a little. "I'm really good at what I do for work. I put in more effort, more time, and it pays off. But with you and me, I can never tell. Like now, I tried to make you feel good about yourself and ended up making you cry. I feel like a failure all the time."

"You're not."

"Neither are you."

"But what if I never become what you hoped for?"

"The important thing is that you become what *you* hope for."

"What if it's something you don't want?"

Mom grimaces. "I'm terrified of that, frankly. It's not up to me what you end up doing with your life, and I don't like it when things aren't up to me. But I'm working on it. And I'm fairly certain that you'll be okay."

I make a face because I'm not so certain.

"CJ." Mom puts her hands on my cheeks and gazes into my eyes. "You marched into the office of one of the wealthiest, most powerful men in Silicon Valley and demanded that he pay a million dollars to take his own family's name off a public building. Trust me. With a nerve like that, you'll be okay."

When I get home from school the next day, there's an unusual arrangement on my desk. It's a bunch of hawthorn branches: hope. Stems of fennel and a cluster of oak moss: worthiness and healing. It's all wound around and held together with strands of lace lichen: the bond between mother and child.

I turn it around in my hands. The bright green oak moss contrasts with the pink buds of the hawthorn blossoms. The textures, too, are varied: tickly soft fennel fronds, sharp prickles on the hawthorn branch, tender, tangled lichen. I can tell that Mom made it herself; it's messy and amateurish and unstable, and there's no easy way to hold it without getting pricked, or accidentally knocking some of the moss off. But I can feel her whole heart in it, and that's enough for me.

The History of the Katsuyama Family, Part III

April 2019

McAllister Venture Capital purchases Heart's Desire from Mimi and Hannah Katsuyama. They name it the Frank Katsuyama Building, after Mimi and Hannah's father, and make a commitment to use the space exclusively for, and I quote, "companies with members of underrepresented minorities in significant leadership positions, whose products materially improve the lives of others."

Mimi leaves MVC to start Katsuyama MicroVentures, Hannah locks the doors of Heart's Desire for the last time, and both of them spend the rest of April at home, driving each other up the wall.

54

BRYNN'S IN THE *MERCURY NEWS* AGAIN THIS
morning, looking stunning in a midnight-blue halter-top gown
sparkling with rhinestones. McAllister High School's first lesbian prom queen didn't bring a date, but she looks happy anyway, surrounded by a flock of #winners, including a girl with
a shy smile and a long chestnut braid woven with wildflowers.

"Looks like you had fun, anyway," I say to Emily through a
bite of chocolate croissant. There weren't any left in the bakery
display case when we got here, but Tim came through with
our secret stash from the kitchen.

"I did have fun. You and Owen should have gone."

"We had our own fun."

Last night was Hannah's last event ever for Heart's Desire.
It was a fifteenth-anniversary party for Tom and Delia Ohara,

parents of dimpled Blake and Aubrey-slash-Scarlett. Owen and I stuck around and drank champagne and ate fancy hors d'oeuvres off silver trays, and even danced a little bit. When Tom and Delia each stood up and made little speeches about how much they still loved each other after twenty years together and fifteen years of marriage, I may have gotten a little misty-eyed. (Owen for sure did because he's such a sappy puffball.) It was the way they smiled at each other that did it. It was definitely real.

Em smiles and says, "Maybe that'll be you and Owen in twenty years."

"Maybe not," I say. "I may have adjusted my opinion, but that doesn't make me a whole new person."

"Okay, well, maybe that'll be you and Owen at prom next year."

"Maybe don't even talk about next year."

"We'll all probably have plans for college by then," she muses.

"Okay, really. Stop now, please. I've already got my mom breathing down my neck about SATs and college counselors. I have a meeting with one this week, in fact." I shudder. I am not looking forward to it.

"But now you can put STORM on your like, list of accomplishments."

"You mean my list of accomplishment? Because it's just the one."

Em rolls her eyes.

"Plus, the school board doesn't even vote until after I meet with this counselor guy, so it's not like I can say we succeeded."

"CJ!"

She's so easy to fool. "I kid, I kid. I'm proud of us no matter how they vote. I bet I could even get Trey to write me a letter of . . ." I'm not sure he'd recommend me for anything, to be honest. I don't even know what he's decided yet. "A letter of something, anyway. He could talk about how I disrupted the nonprofit fund-raising model. That would be cool, right?"

"And there's your flower-magic business."

"Yeah. Though I prefer to call it a youth-oriented independent floral design enterprise." It's defunct now that Heart's Desire has closed, but I'm hopeful I'll get work somewhere, somehow.

I've seen the architect's plans for the transformation of Heart's Desire into McAllister Venture Capital Startup Incubator. Our comfortable little painted brick store is going to become a sleek modern space with lots of stainless steel and glass. It will be completely unrecognizable. But, as Hannah pointed out, it will still be a place to increase the odds of people finding happiness. Or as Mom put it once before I told her to speak English, a place to actuate the future and improve quality of life. I like to think of it as a place where people focus on possibility.

"I'm gonna miss Heart's Desire," says Em.

"Yeah, same."

"How do you feel, now that it belongs to the McAllisters again?"

"Sad, I guess? Hannah says it's fate." Flax, I think automatically.

"Do you think it's fate?"

I've thought about this one. "No," I say. "Calling it fate makes it seem like there's nothing you can do to change a bad situation, before or after it happens. But you can."

"You can't change a bad thing after it happens."

"But you can try to make things better now. You can make sure it doesn't happen again."

People talk about starting over after they've made a big mistake or a bad choice in life. But you can never really start over. You can't fully reset. And I don't think you should. There's no point in dwelling on the past, but you can acknowledge it and try to make things better. Or try a new way, and know that this time will be different.

A Note from the Author

Sometimes a new discovery can transform a story you thought you understood and make it come alive in ways you don't anticipate.

A few years ago, I learned that my late Japanese Canadian uncle was named after Mackenzie King, the prime minister who would eventually order all Japanese Canadians to be sent to internment camps during World War II. How had my uncle felt, I wondered, as he entered the gates of Tashme Internment Camp at twelve years old, bearing the name of the man who had sent him there? How had he felt decades later?

Because I couldn't stop wondering, I wrote this book.

This Time Will Be Different has changed quite a lot since its early drafts, but the questions driving it have always been the same.

How are we affected—as victims and as perpetrators—by the failures of the past? How do we measure the harm done to us as individuals, and as families, and as communities? How do we decide what to let go? What to forgive? What to carry into the future?

I hope this book has made you laugh and cry and fall in

love. I hope that it will spark conversations about taking a closer look at our personal and collective histories, how to take responsibility for those histories, and what it takes to move forward. And as our public discourse sounds increasingly, disturbingly familiar, I hope that CJ's story will inspire us all to make sure that this time really will be different.

Misa Sugi

Index of Flowers and their Meanings

Years ago, a family friend created a beautiful ikebana arrangement for my wedding and explained to me the symbolism of each different component: long life, good luck, high aspirations. That symbolism stuck with me, and I was excited to use it in *This Time Will Be Different*. But as I wrote, I realized that I wanted to show that the Katsuyamas—an American family— had broader cultural influences than just Japan. Because of this, CJ's system of flower magic, like her family and like our country, is influenced by traditions and interpretations from around the world. No two books or websites list the same meanings for all the plants, and there's lots of room for interpretation, so if you don't like the meaning listed here for your favorite flower, don't despair. Just find a meaning that you do like!

allspice (pg. 369)   compassion
almond branch (pg. 369).....................hope
aloe (pg. 62, 63)   grief, solace
aster (pg. 6) ....reciprocity

bay leaves (pg. 46, 47)...........................victory
black-eyed Susan (pg. 368, 369). ....justice

carnation, yellow (pg. 4, 5).................denial, disdain
cedar (pg. 235)..strength
chamomile (pg. 47)..............................patience, humility
chrysanthemum, red (pg. 82, 170) .....vitality, longevity

eucalyptus (pg. 1, 117, 170)..................purity, health

fennel (pg. 47, 380, 381)........................worthiness
flax (pg. 2, 171, 386) ....fate

hawthorn (pg. 380, 381).......................hope
heather, white (pg. 46, 168, 171, 298)..good luck
holly (pg. 82) ....purity, enchantment, magic
hydrangea (pg. 110, 114, 308)...............pride, frigidity

iris (pg. 298, 331, 374) ....noble heart, eloquence
ivy (pg. 1, 82, 84)...................................friendship, fidelity

pine, pine cone (pg. 117, 118, 374) .... long life, hope in adversity

rose leaf (pg. 112) .... hope
rose, pink (pg. 130, 302, 368) .... friendship
rose, purple (pg. 130, 168, 302, 368) ... enchantment
rose, red (pg. 1, 331, 368) .... love
rose, white (pg. 2, 302) .... self-worth
rosebud, pink (pg. 6, 130) .... new love, friendship

sage (pg. 82, 84) .... health, long life
southernwood (pg. 130, 168, 188) .... wit, charm
star-of-Bethlehem (pg. 2, 361) .... reconciliation
stonecrop (pg. 235) .... perseverance
sunflower (pg. 46, 47, 272) .... false pride

violet, blue (pg. 331) .... love, fidelity
violet, white (pg. 6, 112, 349, 351) .... take a chance on love

water lily (pg. 170) .... purity

Acknowledgments

This book was a monster to write. Second-book syndrome hit me hard, and I had to fight my way through writer's block almost every time I sat down to write. I would never have made it through without a host of wonderful people. A thousand thanks go out to the following:

My incredible agent, Leigh Feldman, gently steered me away from a couple of initial not-so-great ideas, assured me that the most important thing was to write a book that I loved (thus freeing me from the pressure of producing a manuscript RIGHT NOW), shepherded me through a maze of publishing industry detours, and generally had my back throughout the entire process.

The literal translation of the Japanese word for editor (編集者 henshūsha) is "one who knits and gathers," and that is exactly what Stephanie Stein did with the pile of loosely related scenes and characters that I (metaphorically) threw at her inbox before running away and hiding. Stephanie sorted through the chaos and showed me how I could pull the best parts together and connect them into an actual story around the heart that I knew was in there but couldn't find.

I owe so much to everyone at HarperTeen. The eagle eyes of Alexandra Rakaczki and Erica Ferguson saved this book from being littered with errors, echoes, and inconsistencies. If you love the cover as much as I do, it's due to designers Alison Klapthor and Alice Wang, and artist Mercedes deBellard (check out her Instagram!). *This Time Will Be Different* would not be in your hands without the efforts of the fantastic production, marketing, publicity, and school and library teams: Erin Wallace, Kristen Eckhardt, Aubrey Churchward, Bess Braswell, Patty Rosati, Rebecca McGuire, Stephanie Macy, Katie Dutton, Lindsey Karl, and so many others.

Robin Reul, Renée Ahdieh, Nancy Slavin, and Caroline Leech generously read an early-early-early partial draft of this book when I was ready to give up and move on to something else. I could hardly believe it when they encouraged me to finish, but I figured if four such talented writers thought I should keep going, then maybe I could.

My local writing group members Sandra Feder, Louise Henriksen, Angie Chan, Alicia Grunow, Rebecca Isaacson, and Viji Chary read key scenes, laughed in all the right places, and helped me talk through some of the tougher choices that CJ makes.

Michael Sera, president of the board of the Japanese American Museum of San Jose, graciously answered my questions, showed me around the museum, and pointed me to www.densho.org, a fantastic website dedicated to recording and preserving Japanese American history. If you want to know anything about Japanese American history, this is the first place you should look.

Stella Shen from Fleur de Lis in Mountain View, CA, graciously took time out of her busy schedule to answer a lot of questions and provide me with her perspective on being a florist.

Race, ethnicity, sexuality, religion, and teen pregnancy are tricky, sticky topics, and I owe a deep debt of gratitude to Ava Mortier, Neera Sivarajah, JC Welker, Dr. Mariama Gray, Lisa Nishimoto Kunze, Leah Henderson, and other early readers who offered their insights on the characters in this book and the complex issues they face. Any inaccurate or insensitive representations and assumptions that remain are on me.

My husband, Tad Hofmeister, stepped in during a weeks-long deadline crunch when I disappeared into a black hole, and cheerfully did double duty on the parenting and housework fronts despite the demands of his own career. I could never, ever do this author thing without him, that's for sure.

My sons are as different from each other as Mimi and Hannah, and they fight just as intensely. But they also share a deep bond of friendship that I hope will last forever. Boys, you bring me immeasurable joy, each in your own way, and I am grateful every day that you are who you are.

Also by Misa Sugiura

Keep reading for a preview!

1

"SANA, CHOTTO . . . HANASHI GA ARUN-YA-KEDO."

Uh-oh.

Something big is about to go down.

It's Sunday afternoon and we're almost ready to leave the beach at Lake Michigan, where I've begged Mom to take me for my birthday. It's just the two of us because Dad is away on business—he's always away on business—and I'm crouched at the edge of the water, collecting sea glass. I've decided I'm not leaving the beach until I've found sixteen pieces, one for each year. Sweet sixteen and never been kissed, but at least I'll have a handful of magic in my pocket. Sixteen surprises. Sixteen secret treasures I've found in the sand.

And now this: *hanashi ga arun'*.

Mom never asks if I want to "chat" unless she's actually

gearing up for a Serious Discussion. She walks over and stands next to me, but I'm too anxious to look up, so I continue picking through the sand as possible Serious Discussion Topics scroll through my head:

She's pregnant.

She has cancer.

She's making me go to Japan for the summer.

"It's about Dad," she says.

Dad's leaving us.

He's dying.

He—

"Dad got a new job with start-up company in California."

—what?

"It's the company called GoBotX," she says. "They make the robots for hospital surgery."

I don't care what the company makes.

"Did you say *California*?"

When I say Serious Discussion, I suppose I should really say Big Announcement Followed by Brief and Unhelpful Q&A Before Mom Closes Topic:

"How long have you known?"

"Dad applied last month. He signed contract today."

"Why didn't you tell me earlier?"

"No need."

"What do you mean, no need?"

She shrugs. "No need. Not your decision."

"But that's not fair!"

"'Fair' doesn't matter."

"But—"

"Complaining doesn't do any good."

"Are we all moving? When?"

"Dad will go in two weeks, at end of May. He will find a house to live, and we will go at end of June."

She doesn't know the answers to the rest of my questions: Where will we live, where will I go to school, what am I supposed to do all summer all by myself. Then she says, "No more questions. It is decided, so nothing we can do. Clean the sand off your feet before we get in the car."

We don't talk on the way home. Mom's not the type to apologize or ask questions like, "How does that make you feel?" My own unanswered questions swim in circles around the silence like giant schools of fish, chased by the most important question of all—the only one I can't ask.

When we get home, I go to my room to finish some homework. But before I start, I take out a lacquer box that Mom and Dad bought for me when we visited Japan seven years ago. It's a deep, rich orange red, and it has three cherry blossoms painted on it in real gold. Inside, I keep my pearl earrings, a picture of me with my best friend, Trish Campbell, when we were six, all the sea glass I've collected from trips to Lake Michigan, and a slip of paper with a phone number on it.

I pour in my new sea glass, take out the piece of paper, and stare at the numbers. They start with a San Francisco area code. Could this be the real reason we're moving?

The paper is small and narrow, almost like something I might pull out of a fortune cookie. Like if I turn it over, I'll find my fortune—my family's fortune—on the other side: Yes, these numbers are important. No, these numbers are meaningless. But of course the back of the paper is as blank as ever. I bury the phone number under the other things, put the box away, and lie down on my bed to think.

A few minutes later, Mom comes in and frowns when she sees me lying on my bed, staring at the ceiling. Mom is the most practical person I know. She doesn't sugarcoat things, and she doesn't look for a bright side. Which is okay right now, because a fake spiel about exciting new experiences, great weather, and new friends would just piss me off.

"I am sorry that you have to leave your friends," she says, not looking one bit sorry, "but the pouting doesn't make your life better. It just prevents you from doing your homeworks."

Then again, it probably wouldn't kill her to show a *little* sympathy. Also, she's totally off base about what's upsetting me. But since correcting her is out of the question, I just turn and face the wall.

"Jibun no koto bakkari kangaen'no yame-nasai. Chanto henji shina-sai."

I don't think I'm being selfish. But since "AAAGGGGH-HHH! I'M NOT BEING SELFISH!" is probably not the "proper reply" she's looking for, I just say, "I'm not pouting. I'm thinking."

"There is nothing to think about. If you want to think, you

- 4 -

can think of being grateful for a father who works so hard to get the good job."

"It's not that I'm not grateful—"

"Ever since he was teenager," she continues, "Dad dreamed of working for the Silicon Valley start-up. That's why he came to United States."

"But what about me? Don't *my* dreams count?" Okay, maybe now I'm being a little selfish. Especially since the truth is that I don't actually have what might be called dreams. What I have are more like hopes: Straight As. A love life. A crowd of real friends to hang out with. But it's also true that if I did have dreams, they wouldn't count anyway. Not to Mom.

"You are too young for the dream," she says. (See?)

I want to remind her that she just said Dad's start-up job was a teenage dream. But she has a conveniently short memory about things she's just said that contradict other things she's just said, so instead, I switch tracks. "What about *your* dreams?"

"My dream is not important."

"Ugh. Come on, Mom."

She crosses her arms. "My dream is to make the good family. I can do that in Wisconsin or California."

"Mom, why do you say stuff like that? Like, 'Oh, our lives are just going to change forever, no big deal.' It *is* a big deal! It's a *huge* deal!" I can hear myself getting screechy, but I can't help it. Dad changes our lives around without consulting anyone— well, without consulting me—and Mom just . . . lets it happen.

It would make anyone screechy.

"Shikkari shinasai," she snaps.

But I don't know if I'll ever be able to do that: gather myself into a tight little bundle with everything in its place—shikkari—like she wants. I put my head under my pillow.

She's quiet for so long that I begin to wonder if she's left the room. When I peek out from under the pillow, she's waiting for me, her face softer, even a little sad. "Gaman shinasai," she says, and walks away. *Gaman*. Endure. Bear it without complaining.

Her life's motto and my life's bane.

2

I'M UNDER ORDERS TO PACK ALL OF MY belongings into boxes labeled KEEP and THROW AWAY by the end of the week. Which is harder than you'd think, because who knew I had so much stuff? I'm drowning in a sea of books, old papers, and odds and ends that I've spent over a decade smushing into the corners of my closet, cramming into the back of my desk drawers, and piling on the edges of my bookshelf.

It started off easily enough:

My lacquer box: KEEP

Four Super Balls from who knows where or when: THROW AWAY

Collection of poems by Emily Dickinson, my favorite poet: KEEP

Assorted elementary school certificates: Perfect Attendance, Fourth Grade Math Olympiad Participant, etc.: THROW AWAY

But now it's getting tricky, because some of the things I've dug out have some messy feelings attached to them, and I'd rather not go there right now.

Don't think. Just sort. The wedding picture that I found in the attic last year and that Mom refuses to display because it's "showing off." KEEP. The Hogwarts robe that I loved so much, I wore it two Halloweens in a row. I'd meant to be Hermione but everyone said I was (who else?) Cho Chang. THROW AWAY. A cheap plastic vase left over from my thirteenth birthday party, which three girls skipped to go to the movies instead. THROW AWAY.

Don't think.

As I toss the vase into the THROW AWAY box, a scrap of fabric flutters out: a swim team ribbon that I found in the Glen Lake Country Club parking lot when I was seven. Hmm. Now *that's* a feeling I can do something about.

All the best families in Glen Lake belong to the Glen Lake Country Club, which has a historic redbrick clubhouse, a lush green golf course, and a lily-white membership. Back in grade school, when Trish and I spent more time together, she used to bring me with her to the club all the time during summer vacation for barbecues and lazy afternoons at the pool. But in high school, she became suddenly, dazzlingly popular. The boys and queen bees started swarming, her Instagram filled up with likes and pictures of people who barely acknowledged me in the halls, and our country club days became a thing of the past.

Don't get me wrong. It's not like she's been mean, or anything. Days might go by without her texting me, but she always answers my texts right away. She's usually too busy to hang out with me, but she's always apologetic. And even though it's painful to sit on the edges of her crowd at lunch, listening to stories about parties I haven't been invited to, it's not like anyone's ever asked me to leave the table.

When we used to see more of each other, Trish was always after me to "open up" and "spill everything." Which, whatever, she's an oversharer. For example, she texted me seconds after Toby Benton, her first boyfriend, put his hand up her shirt in eighth grade. **(OMG I just let Toby touch my boob!! Under my shirt!! 😵 🔥 🔥 🔥)**

But whenever I thought about telling her anything important, I froze. Even now, when people talk at lunch about who wants to hook up with who, or who hopes their dad gets custody on the weekends because he's totally cool about drinking at the house—I feel relieved that no one's especially interested in me or my life. I don't want anyone poking around and freaking out about what's wrong with my family, what's wrong with me. Like what if I'd answered honestly the first time Trish asked me at the beginning of freshman year, "Sana, who do *you* like?"

"Well actually, Trish, I think I might have a crush on *you*."

Nope. Forget it. Not happening. I'm not even a hundred percent sure it's true, and life is already complicated enough.

But now . . . things have changed. I mean, we leave in three weeks, and I might never see her again. So I'm going to ask her to bring me to the first Glen Lake Country Club barbecue of the summer, for old times' sake. I've got nothing to lose, right? We'll get drunk together for the first and probably last time—I've never been drunk before—and maybe . . . maybe if all goes well, she'll get nostalgic, we'll bond again, and . . . and . . . something good will happen. I don't want to think too hard about what, exactly. But something good.

On Friday, I find Trish in the parking lot after school, sitting with her boyfriend, Daniel, on the hood of his car. Daniel is a big-shot football player, with a face like your favorite love song and a body like fireworks on the Fourth of July; sadly, though, he doesn't have the brains or a personality to match. His biggest claim to fame is that he got a Mustang for his sixteenth birthday—and one week and a six-pack of Milwaukee's Best later, he drove it into a tree and his dad gave him *another Mustang*.

When I ask Trish about the barbecue, it turns out she's already going with Daniel, but she seems excited to have me come, too.

"Oooooh!" she says. "We. Are going. To get. So. Wasted. Together. It'll be so much fun! And Daniel can drive us back to my house afterward." She snuggles up to him. "Right, honey?"

"Sorry, babe, but Drew and Brad are back from college and they're bringing a bottle of Jägermeister tomorrow night." As he says this, a couple of football bros walk by. "Did you hear that?" he shouts at them. "Jäger shots!" The three of them high-five each other and howl together like a pack of teenage werewolves, and for the millionth time, I wonder what Trish sees in him. Beyond the obvious, I mean.

When Daniel sees that Trish—thank goodness—is unmoved, he whines, "Come on, make someone else drive."

Trish rolls her eyes at me. Then she wraps herself around Daniel and says, "I'll make it worth your while," and whispers something to him. She starts nibbling his ear and kissing his neck, and pretty soon they're making out right in front of me, and I have to look away or I'll vomit. If she's using her womanly wiles to get her way, he seems to be falling for it—though from the sound of it she's having as much fun as he is.

But at least he seems to have agreed to drive.

Don't miss these books from critically acclaimed, award-winning author MISA SUGIURA

JOIN THE

Epic Reads

COMMUNITY

THE ULTIMATE YA DESTINATION

◀ **DISCOVER** ▶
your next favorite read

◀ **MEET** ▶
new authors to love

◀ **WIN** ▶
free books

◀ **SHARE** ▶
infographics, playlists, quizzes, and more

◀ **WATCH** ▶
the latest videos